In memory of two women I love very much

Cynthia Lopez Quimpo
My fierce, beloved Mom who could light up any room
18 December 1936–4 April 2021

And

Susan Quimpo
Wondrous truth-teller, cousin, forever friend
6 February 1961–14 July 2020

Praise for *Wild Song*

'A shocking, refreshingly different coming-of-age story'
The Times Children's Book of the Week

'This YA companion to the acclaimed *Bone Talk*
confirms Gourlay as a brilliantly accomplished
and original historical novelist'
The Guardian Books of the Month

'A powerhouse of a novel'
The Observer YA Books of the Month

'[Gourlay's] sparse and feathery prose has an
almost mesmeric quality – and succeeds in building
a beautiful story out of harrowing events'
The Telegraph, ★★★★★

'*Wild Song* is a stunning achievement . . . Gourlay's
brilliant storytelling will have the reader turning
every page eagerly, willing Luki on at every step'
The Bookseller Book of the Month

'A potent and powerful novel that is as unforgettable
as it is beautifully and accessibly written'
LoveReading Book of the Month

'From the first page, this book transports you to the
mountainous regions of the Philippines . . . vivid
and convincing . . . very thought-provoking'

'Candy Gourlay writes in prose that is both accessible and profound, the compassion she feels for the people whose stories she is telling shining out'
Andrea Reece *Books for Keeps*

'A vividly told, very thought-provoking book as well as a thrilling adventure'
BookTrust

'An involving story . . . Luki's optimism and agency shine through'
Historical Novel Society

'Vividly imagined'
Global Media Arts Network

'A powerful story of courage and bravery . . . impossible to put down . . . vivid, compassionate and heartfelt'
Jasbinder Bilan

'Vital storytelling, poignant and powerful'
Sophie Anderson

'My book of the year'
Marie Basting

'This is a potent and powerful novel that is as unforgettable as it is beautifully and accessibly written'
Joy Court *Love Reading for Kids*

Also by Candy Gourlay

Tall Story
Shine
Bone Talk

For younger readers
Mike Falls Up
Is it a Mermaid?

Non-fiction
First Names: Ferdinand (Magellan)

WILD SONG

CANDY GOURLAY

David Fickling Books

31 Beaumont Street
Oxford OX1 2NP, UK

Wild Song
is a
DAVID FICKLING BOOK

First published in Great Britain by
David Fickling Books,
31 Beaumont Street,
Oxford, OX1 2NP

www.davidficklingbooks.com

Hardback edition published 2023
This edition published 2024

Text © Candy Gourlay, 2023

Cover by Leo Nickolls

978-1-78845-208-3

1 3 5 7 9 10 8 6 4 2

Papers used by David Fickling Books are from well-
managed forests and other responsible sources.

DAVID FICKLING BOOKS Reg. No. 8340307

A CIP catalogue record for this book is available from the British Library.

Typeset in Baskerville by Falcon Oast Graphic Art Ltd
Printed and bound in Great Britain by Clays, Ltd., Elcograf, S.p.A.

In 1904, more than a thousand people from the Philippines travelled to the United States to take part in the World's Fair in the Louisiana Purchase Exposition, also known as the Saint Louis World's Fair. Among them were indigenous people called Igorots.

Part One

1

Hunting

The tree was singing.

No it's not, Samkad would have said. But he wasn't here yet and anyway, what did he know about anything?

I pressed my cheek against the bark to feel the tree's voice rumble in my blood, rough and low and shapeless, unlike American music with its pom pom pom. *I like your song,* I whispered to the tree. *It calls my spirit.*

Which was a good thing, Mother, because I'd been sitting on that branch for hours, and I could barely keep my eyes open. The boar I'd been hunting for days was nowhere to be seen.

My right leg had gone to sleep and, when I straightened it, my knee made a cracking noise, sudden and deafening as an American gunshot. Which was unnerving in the moss-muffled silence of the forest.

Eheh, you've been dead a whole year, Mother, but I still glanced down nervously, half-expecting to see you in the clearing below, fists planted in your waist, ordering me down from the tree like you'd done countless times before, bombarding me with questions. How had I acquired that breechcloth I was wearing? What had I done to my skirt? What if the Americans had caught me? Didn't they forbid hunting in the dark?

The stillness was suddenly split by a violent screeching of monkeys in the next tree. What had set them off? I searched the gloom carefully. But there was nothing there.

During the war, a lowland soldier had tried to hide in the mossy forest, but the Americans were not far behind and he was soon captured. When the war was over, American patrols trawled through the forest, making a mess, hacking trees and shooting everything in sight. But now the patrols were gone and the forest was quiet again. The Americans had finished their warring and turned their attention to ruling us. So many new laws! *Ancients must listen. Women must wear blouses. Children must go to American school.*

But no, Mother, as far as I was aware, hunting in the dark was still allowed. And nobody, not the Americans, nor the ancients, needed to know whether I did so wearing a skirt or a breechcloth.

Up the sun rose. The sky bloomed pink. The tops of the trees turned gold. A thick, white mist boiled up on the forest floor. And the boar came.

It was a great black lump, gliding through the mist. Squealing softly, it began to root between the tree's toes, tail flicking its great, meaty flanks. Mother, it was even bigger than the last one I killed.

Crunch.

The boar's head jerked up, ears pricked.

Was that a human-shaped shadow, Mother? There, by that bush? The boar turned and stared.

Then, from the opposite direction, running feet. And barking.

'Little Luki?' Samkad, the idiot, burst into the clearing. His dog, Chuka, yapped from somewhere behind him.

The boar spun to face Samkad. It lowered its head to attack.

I leaped, landing between the boar and my friend so hard my teeth rattled in my skull.

The boar launched itself, and I found myself on my back, its weight pinning me down, its head turning right and left, its tusks within gouging distance of my eyes, the hot, stinky breath washing over my face, its hairy hide coarse and wiry against my skin, the hooves scrabbling painfully on my waist.

My spear was buried deep in its throat. The boar glared at me, its eyes sparking with anger and fear. I pushed the spear deeper. It grunted. The eyes began to glaze, and the hot, hairy body slumped against me. I wrenched myself from under it, backing away as the creature fell onto its side. Its feet began to run, as if it was racing from its own death. I watched the hooves kick and kick and kick, and then stop as its spirit drained from its body. The boar's soul was running in the invisible world of the dead now. And its flesh had become meat.

I turned to check on Samkad, and Chuka the dog promptly stopped her yapping to throw herself in front of him, in case I tried to kiss him or something. Mother, I swear it's embarrassing to have a dog for a love rival.

Samkad was fine, of course, gazing at me with wide-eyed admiration as Chuka danced about as if to say, 'Me! Me! It's me you should look at!'

'Do you need me to finish it off?' Samkad asked.

But I hushed him. That rustling again. 'Who's there?' I yelled, scooping up a rock and throwing it into the bushes.

'What is it?' I could feel the heat of Samkad at my back.

'Shh! Just before I jumped down, I saw someone.' If it was someone from the village, they would be rushing to report me to the ancients, I thought.

'Where?'

'Over there,' I said. But there was nothing there; no footsteps, no trampled grass, no broken twigs. Had I imagined it?

'Maybe it was not a someone, but a some*thing*?' Samkad said.

Yes. Maybe it was just a monkey, casting a large shadow.

Mother, don't you dead people see everything? Was it a person? Shake a tree branch for yes, toss a pebble for no!

Samkad turned to the boar. He'd already forgotten about it. Kneeling, he laid a hand on its head. 'Thank you, beast,' he whispered. 'May you live contentedly in the invisible world.'

Then he got back to his feet and wrapped his arms around me. He smelled of damp soil and wet fern. His mouth, pressed against my forehead, was soft, like fruit. 'It looks like I got here just in time.'

I snorted. 'Just in time. You were lucky it didn't gore you!'

'It was not luck, it was you! You were magnificent.' Samkad nuzzled my hair. 'That boar – it's twice the size of the other two. You did well.'

'That's not what *they're* going to say.'

'No,' Sam said. 'There will be no thanks from all the hungry folk who are going to share this boar.'

He pressed his lips against mine and all the ungrateful people of Bontok melted away in a rush of sudden heat, as if we'd both tumbled from the cold outdoors into a warm, dry hut.

Mother, it must amuse you to see us like this when just five years ago, we were scrawny best friends with scabbed knees, brawling in the dirt when we weren't traipsing up and down the hills, pushing each other into rice paddies. But now we were both sixteen and everything had changed.

Later, when I had washed in a nearby stream and swapped my hunting breechcloth for a fresh skirt and blouse, Samkad tied the boar to a strong bamboo pole. We each shouldered one end, Samkad in front, me at the back. The boar swung easily between us as we walked out of the forest and up the steep, green slope towards the village.

Samkad grinned over his shoulder. 'What shall we tell the ancients this time?'

'All the excruciating details.' I laughed. 'How you waited in the tree. How you leaped in front of the boar. How you speared the boar, just so.'

Sam hooted with laughter.

And when we got there, that was exactly what we told them. How Samkad had waited in the tree. How he leaped in front of the boar. How he speared the boar, just so. And the ancients – gazing up at Sam's amiable smile, those honest brown eyes, those broad shoulders, that deep chest etched with tattoos that marked him out as a brave man – believed everything he said.

2

Deception

Sometimes, I think about all the times you had to face the wrath of the ancients over me, Mother. Luki's been wearing a breechcloth again, Chochon! Chochon, your daughter was fighting with a boy! Chochon, the girl was playing with a spear when she should have been pounding rice with the other girls!

You stood there, listening calmly, and when we went home, it was your turn to do the scolding. You talked about duty, you talked about manners, you talked about modesty. But after a time, I saw that you were only scolding because that was what the ancients expected of you. You put your fury on like a hat and then, just as quickly, took it off.

Even so, the ancients filled me with rage. Look at these tattoos on my face, Mother, look at these tattoos on my shoulders! All those years ago, the ancients rewarded me with tattoos and called me brave when I raised the alert that our blood enemy

9

the Mangili was about to attack. But in the same breath they forbade my carrying a spear and prohibited my hunting.

'Luki,' you told me patiently. 'The ancients esteem women. We bear children. We plant the rice, we cultivate the soil. We nourish the village. We are the future.'

'So why can't I hunt?' I complained.

'Because women don't hunt,' you said. 'We never have. Not since before we began to remember.'

That's what you said, Mother. But you didn't sound convinced.

I tried to be good. I tried to be like all the other women. I followed the new American rules. I wore a blouse. I did my chores. I learned how to speak American at Mister William's little school. I kept out of trouble. Apart from hunting.

Now the Americans are emptying the forests so quickly with their guns, we need all the meat we can get. And, Mother, you have to admit, my arrangement with Samkad is perfect.

Samkad was playing his part well. The ancients couldn't look away from those flexing biceps and that boyish smile. As Samkad began to talk, you could see them relax, settling down on their haunches in front of the Council House fire, the wrinkles hanging looser from their foreheads, their faces spreading wide in toothless smiles. They began to thank the spirits of our ancestors for the boar – *my* boar. A crowd began to gather and I pushed my way to the back, my empty belly growling mercilessly to the chanting of the ancients.

I felt an elbow in my side. A spiteful voice hissed into my ear.

'*Pssst!* What are you so pleased about, Luki?'

My belly clenched with annoyance. It was Tilin, Bontok's meanest girl, who slept on the pallet next to mine in the House for Women. You'd think the ten of us unmarried girls would be friends, sleeping side by side on our narrow pallets, heads to the wall, feet pointing towards the warm fire in the cooking room next door. Well, I guess they tolerated me when you were still alive, Mother. They liked *you. You* were easy, *you* made people smile. But I am not like you, am I, Mother?

Tilin glared at me. Looking at her, it baffled me that young men were constantly hanging around the House for Women, waiting for a glimpse of those dark butterfly eyebrows and that too-wide mouth that made her look like she was smiling even when she was smirking. Which was what she was doing now.

'Well?'

I sighed. Obviously, in my rush to go hunting I must have forgotten some important chore.

Tilin snorted. 'Guess who had to trample manure this morning because you weren't there?'

'Oh!' I clapped a hand over my mouth. I'd completely forgotten that it was my turn. I turned to face her and the sun struck my eyes like a blow. 'I . . . I was helping Samkad!'

'Samkad, Samkad, SAMKAD!' Tilin was practically spitting in my ear. 'Why does he always need YOU to help him? What does Samkad see in you?'

Samkad loves me, I thought. And it was not Samkad who needed me. *I* needed him. I could not hunt without Samkad.

11

I scowled at Tilin. There was a flower in her hair, and a neat string of seashells from far away held her long hair away from her face. Her blouse looked crisp and white and her small feet were not blackened with forest mud like mine. Even so, she didn't look very strong. *I could fight you*, I thought. *I could rub your pretty face in the dirt*.

But then a small voice murmured at my knee. 'Tilin, I'm bored.' It was Sidong, Tilin's little sister. 'Where is my book? I want to draw.'

Instantly, Tilin was on her knees with her arms around Sidong. 'You can't draw now, little chick,' Tilin murmured. 'The ancients are not finished.'

Looking at the two of them, I felt rotten for thinking horrible thoughts. Maybe *I* was the meanest girl in Bontok.

While Tilin busied herself with Sidong, Kakot, who slept on the pallet on my other side, took over. 'And where were you last night, when the rice needed to be put on the boil?'

'Probably with Samkad,' someone murmured behind me. 'She's never there when there are chores to be done.'

The others joined in.

'Never there when babies need to be carried.'

'Never there when rice needs husking.'

'Luki's no help!'

'Luki's no use!'

They hawked my name like gobs of spit. *Luki! Luki! Luki!*

'Luki.' We all turned. 'Let's go.' Samkad was standing right next to us. When did the chanting end? And did he hear

12

them chastising me? His face was smooth, it gave nothing away.

'Come on, Luki, help me carry the boar to Father's house so that I can butcher it,' he said.

Mother, the other girls were smiling at him. Smiling! Right in the middle of their nastiness! I rolled my eyes at Samkad, but he was too busy showing the girls his straight white teeth to notice.

'Congratulations,' Tilin simpered, stretching her chin out, clearly trying to make her neck look longer. 'Another boar! What a skilful hunter you are, Samkad!'

If it hadn't been for Sidong, I would have scooped up a handful of mud and smeared it on her silly neck.

Samkad led me to the boar and we lifted it up on his signal. The boar was heavier now that it was weighed down with the ancients' good wishes. We carried it out of the court-yard, Chuka leading the way to the hut that once belonged to Samkad's dead father. Although he lived in the House for Men with the other unmarried men, Samkad had continued to tend his father's house. After you died, Mother, was where Samkad and I had cooked and shared many meals, and it was where we always butchered the meat from our hunts. Someday, in the far away future, when we're ready to marry, we can make our home in it.

We had barely left the Council House when Samkad signalled me to stop and lower the boar to the ground.

'What?' I said.

He folded his arms across his chest. 'You've got to try harder, Luki.' His voice was gentle but chiding.

I flattened my face and hid all my feelings. 'Don't know what you mean.'

'They are your friends.'

I scowled. 'HAH! They were never my friends.'

'Give them a chance.'

'A chance to annoy me?'

'No, a chance to know you.'

'They have known me since we were children. They can't stand me.'

'They like you really, Luki.'

'They liked my mother. Me? They don't want to know.'

'That's not true,' Sam said quietly. 'It is you who reject them.'

Didn't he get it? The more time I spent with the other girls, the less they liked me. And what if they found out about my hunting expeditions? They would probably rather I became an expert manure trampler than a hunter.

Mother, that was when it occurred to me that this was all *your* fault. It was you who thought it amusing to dress me in a breechcloth because I liked playing with boys. It had pleased you when I learned to throw Father's spear and you had shown me how to practise with a target. It was you who made me different. And now you've gone to the invisible world, Mother, and left me to face the consequences.

Sam continued to give me advice. 'Make light of things!

14

Have a laugh with them! Then they won't be so hard on you. Smile!'

Smile! It made me scowl so hard I could feel the strain on my ears. He was a man, he was allowed to fight, to choose his wife, to hunt. He had no idea what it was like to want something you couldn't have.

Just then, I heard a voice murmuring by my right hip. I didn't catch it all, just *Luki-something-something-Samkad*. All this time, some idiot had been listening.

I spun around.

'I DARE YOU TO SAY THAT TO MY FACE!'

Oh, Mother. Why didn't you teach me more self-control? It was Sidong, chasing after us with a ledger from the American school under one arm.

She stared up at me, her mouth open, tears trembling on her brown cheeks.

Samkad was suddenly beside her, smiling. 'Of course you can, Sidong. We don't mind, do we, Little Luki?'

'Mind what?' I muttered.

'She asked if she could come along. She wants to watch us prepare the boar.'

Guilt swelled into a lump in my throat. 'Sure,' I mumbled. 'Come along, Sidong.'

My voice must have sounded normal and maybe I even managed a smile, because the little girl's face brightened immediately. She gathered up her ledger and followed us as if I hadn't just screamed tears into her eyes.

3

Brothers

Samkad and I hoisted the carcass up on the bamboo scaffold outside his father's hut and then I watched as he began to cut into the beast with a thin blade. Soon he was tugging the pelt off to reveal glistening pink meat. He took up a larger knife and began to carve out neat slices of meat, slowly filling the large basket at his feet. Chuka sat next to it, never taking her eyes off his face.

Sidong sat on a nearby log with her ledger on her lap, drawing with a stubby pencil. I saw her pick up a lump of charcoal from the charred pile where Samkad lit his fire. Mister William, the American schoolteacher, told everyone that Sidong had a talent for drawing. He actually hiked across the valley to the new Episcopalian Mission in Sagada to beg for pencils and ledgers for Sidong to draw with.

As Samkad worked, he spoke softly to the boar's spirit,

promising that its gift would not be wasted, naming each piece and who would benefit from it. 'This the ancients may keep, because their teeth can cope with it,' he told the boar. 'This the ancients will give away. And this –' he glanced at me – 'Luki and I will keep. We will remember you as we become strong with your meat.'

Mother, back when we were still attending American School, Mister William showed us a magnet and how some objects were drawn to it helplessly. That was how we have always been, I thought. Since we were little, Samkad has been like a magnet, drawing me to him.

Now the basket was towering with cuts of meat, and all that was left hanging on the bamboo pole was a vaguely boar-shaped thing made of gristle and bone, ready to be boiled into soup. Samkad tossed a large bone in the air and Chuka caught it gratefully.

I felt a tug on my skirt. Sidong held up her ledger for me to see.

At first glance, it was just a dirty page, streaked with charcoal. But the more I looked, the more I began to see. The black resolved into Samkad's hut, the scaffold, the carcass dangling from it. She had left places unshaded so that everything looked dappled by sun. One wavy scrawl was unmistakably Chuka, alert for a treat. And then there was Samkad. And there was me.

How did she do this? In the picture, Samkad's back was turned as he hacked at the meat, but in those black smudges, I could feel the weight of his body, the power in his arms.

Looking at myself, the tilt of my head, the way I leaned towards him, I could see all my feelings.

'Is that how we look?' Samkad whispered over my shoulder.

He smiled at me and I smiled at him, and for a moment, I pictured a warm fire, a cauldron bubbling, and children sitting around it, laughing . . . and they all had Samkad's eyes.

Suddenly, Tilin's voice began to call: 'Sidong! Sidong!'

'Ay!' Sidong clapped her hands. 'He's here!'

'Who's here?' I asked.

She leaped to her feet, putting her pencil stub away in a pouch and hugging the drawing ledger to her chest. 'Truman Hunt!'

'Is that today?' Samkad said.

'Yes, don't you remember? The ancients reminded everyone about it the other day.' Sidong peeked up at Samkad. 'How could you forget? Kinyo is going to be there to speak American for the ancients!'

Samkad turned his face away. When his adopted brother, Kinyo, had decided to move down to the river to work for Americans, they had quarrelled bitterly.

'Sidong!' Tilin sounded impatient. 'Don't keep me waiting!'

'Go, little one.' I smiled.

Sidong waved and disappeared round the corner.

I felt the clap of a hand on my shoulder.

'Where is this giant boar?' someone boomed in my ear. 'I've been told that everyone will be eating meat tonight.'

'Kinyo,' Samkad said softly. 'Hello, brother.'

18

Kinyo's mother and Samkad's mother had been best friends. When Kinyo was orphaned, he had been cared for by an aunt who had married a lowlander. They lived in a lowland village, even after his aunt was widowed. Growing up in the lowlands, Kinyo had filled his throat with lowland words, and then Mister William came to live there and taught Kinyo English as well. When the war rolled through the lowlands, Samkad's father had risked his life to fetch Kinyo and his aunt to the safety of the mountains. They brought Mister William with them.

Before Samkad's father had died, he declared Kinyo his son and brother to Samkad.

I stared at Kinyo. He was wearing trousers and a shirt, buttoned up to his chin. His hair was cut in the American style, close to his head and around his ears so that they stuck out like the handles of a cauldron.

The trousers made him stand in a different way, hand in pocket. And what a difference the haircut made! He looked sleeker somehow. I liked it!

But I didn't dare say it out loud. Not when Samkad looked like he wanted to smash boulders with his bare fists.

'You look like an idiot,' he said. 'You think you look American, but people only have to look at those bare feet to know you're a fake.'

Kinyo stared sadly at his toes. 'Don't worry, I intend to buy a pair of shoes and socks when I've saved up enough money.'

He smirked at Samkad. 'Brother, aren't you tired of looking like a wild man?'

There was a pulsing in Samkad's temple. He shook out his hair, long in the back and long over his eyes. 'So you think I look like a wild man?'

Kinyo sighed, offering his hand to Chuka, who'd been sniffing, as if trying to decide what was different about him. She licked it enthusiastically.

'Eheh, thank you, Chuka. It's nice to feel welcome.'

I tugged at his elbow. '*I'm* glad to see you, Kinyo, even if Samkad is not. How are you? What's it like, working for those Americans?'

'It's great!' He grinned. 'My boss, Mister Jenks, is writing a book about us. He is collecting objects from here to show off when he returns to America. He'll buy anything – baskets, bowls, spears, shields. They are kind, and they pay me well. It's fun. Mrs Jenks gave me this suit.'

'And it was she who made you cut your hair, I'll bet!' Samkad snarled.

Honestly, Mother, Samkad was determined to make a quarrel of everything. I frowned at him but he ignored me.

Samkad continued. 'Americans think our hair is dirty. Did she tell you your hair smelled bad? Was she afraid you had lice?'

'Samkad,' I hissed. 'Leave him alone.'

'Shut up, Samkad,' Kinyo groaned. 'I can grow my hair if I want to.'

Samkad tapped his head. 'It's not your hair that's the

20

problem, it's what's inside your head. Look at you. Do you even know who you are any more?'

'So you would rather I stayed here and helped you dig your paddies,' Kinyo snapped.

'They are not just mine. The paddies belong to both of us. Father left them to *OUR* care. Why am I tending them on my own?'

'It is not my fault you want to tend the paddy fields,' Kinyo said. 'Is that your plan, brother? To stay in this village forever – hunting boar, planting rice, trampling manure?'

Samkad pushed his face into Kinyo's. 'It's our way of life. I am proud of it.'

'It's a *TINY* life!'

They looked like goats about to ram each other. Chuka yapped nervously, ears flat.

I shoved myself between them. 'Enough!'

They glared at each other over my head.

'Brother, do you know why Truman Hunt is here?'

'Of course I do.'

'Do you?'

'He's signing people up for a trip to America.'

'But it isn't going to happen,' I interrupted. 'The ancients have forbidden it.'

Kinyo raised his chin. 'I've signed up. My name is the first on his list.'

Samkad grabbed Kinyo by the shoulders. 'As your brother, I order you to take your name off that list.'

Kinyo shrugged him off. 'You are *not* my brother.'

Samkad hands dropped from his shoulders. He stared at Kinyo.

'You know as well as I do that I'm adopted.' Kinyo said. 'We are not really brothers. You cannot forbid me to do anything.'

Samkad's eyes turned red.

'My father called you his son,' he whispered. 'He gave you his own axe. He gave you shelter. He fed you.'

'He was a good man, and I loved him and called him Father,' Kinyo said. 'But I don't have to call you my brother. Do you want the axe? I have no use for it. You can have it.'

'Kinyo, you don't mean any of that,' I stammered.

But he'd already turned to leave, the pale fabric of his trouser legs swishing against each other as he sauntered to the Council House.

4

The Invitation

'Come, Samkad,' I said. 'Everyone is required to be there.'

Reluctantly, Samkad put his knives away and stowed the meat safely in the hut. He followed me into the alley, now choked with people. Chuka skittered past us, wriggling quickly through the forest of legs and out of sight.

There had been a sizeable throng when we had presented the boar to the ancients. Now there were many times that number, come to listen to Truman Hunt.

He and Mister William were perched on wooden chairs made of pinewood. The ancients squatted alongside, close to the ground, while Kinyo stood next to them, ready to translate American into Bontok and Bontok into American.

Five years ago, we had all been aghast when the Americans conquered the lowlands and announced that the highlands belonged to them as well. At first the ancients had resisted.

'We are not lowlanders! We govern ourselves.' But we had no choice but to accept the new state of affairs. As you explained to me, Mother: 'How can we make war with men who tower over us like giants? Whose guns can kill twenty of our men before they had managed to take aim with their spears?'

They took control of the mountains, flying their striped flag everywhere, carving roads up and down the valleys, felling forests and floating the trees down the Chico River to build jails, missions, chapels and schools. We obeyed when they commanded women to cover their shoulders under clumsy blouses. And we obeyed when they ordered warring villages to cease their fighting.

But, Mother, it hasn't been all bad has it? We all love Mister William and the American School – those tall stacks of magazines filled with photographs of American towns and trains and buildings taller than trees and women in outlandish hats and great big skirts. And what child wouldn't rather go to Mister William's school and learn English than toil in the rice paddies with their parents?

The courtyard was packed. Samkad and I slowly pushed our way through.

Hunt sat, there, waiting beside Mister William with a slight smile on his pale face, his forehead beaded with sweat despite the cool mountain air. His hat, one of those American ones shaped like an inverted bowl, was pushed to the back of his head. He kept reaching into his waistcoat and looking at his watch as if he was nervous, even though he shouldn't have been.

24

Hunt was one of many American soldiers who downed their guns at the end of the war and hurried to the mountains, thinking to get rich on our gold. But unlike the other Americans, who traded with us in trinkets, matchsticks and bolts of cotton, Truman Hunt traded in cures – syrups that could cool fevers, stinging solutions that washed the fester out of a wound, sweet pellets that relieved headache, diarrhoea, and all manner of ailments. We all liked Truman Hunt. His cures worked better than the chants of the ancients and when the American powers realized how popular he'd become, they made Truman Hunt governor of a bracelet of mountains.

I could feel the crowd leaning towards him in anticipation. We were just like that last time when Hunt announced that Theodore Roosevelt, the President of the United States, would like to invite us to visit America. After he delivered the President's invitation, we were all talking too fast, and laughing too loudly, like we'd been chewing too much betel nut. I remember you were so enthusiastic, Mother! But right after you died, the ancients told us, no, it was impossible. They forbade anybody from accepting the invitation. Truman Hunt was about to discover that he'd been wasting his time.

Now here was Truman Hunt repeating the invitation. After so many years in Bontok, he had learned quite a few Bontok words and seemed to enjoy the laughter when he got it wrong. But he still needed Kinyo to make himself understood.

I wondered how accurate Kinyo's translation was. Did Hunt really mean it when he said President Roosevelt would send a boat the size of a mountain – a whole mountain! – to ferry us across the ocean? Did he really mean thirty days when he told us how long it would take to sail to America? And then there would be a train – Mister William told us they were like houses on wheels – to take us to a city called Saint Louis, where we would live in a village built specially for us.

'Unfortunately,' Hunt said, looking nervously at the ancients, 'it is not a journey to be taken by those who are elderly or infirm.'

It was called a 'World's Fair', Kinyo translated. In a place called Saint Louis, they had built a magnificent city of white buildings, great gardens and waterfalls. At night, the city was strung with stars from the sky so that it was lit up as bright as day. Tens of thousands of Americans were coming to Saint Louis just to see us. And people from all over the world too.

We hung onto every translated word, glancing at each other with wide eyes.

But, as Hunt spoke, we could see the ancients' faces growing longer and longer. The corners of their mouths drooped right down so that I was afraid their lower jaws might fall off completely.

'We will arrive in America in March and leave in December. There will be a payment of thirty-five American cents for every day you are in Saint Louis,' Kinyo was saying.

American cents! Mister William had taught us about money, twenty-five cents was a quarter, ten cents a nickel and five cents a dime, but none of us had ever seen such coins –

apart from Kinyo, who earned them from his American employers.

'President Roosevelt has appointed Truman Hunt manager of all Igorot guests,' Kinyo said. 'He will look after you. He leaves for America next week; those who wish to go must give him their names before he leaves today.'

Around me, faces were shining with hope. But then it was the ancients' turn to speak, and one by one, they told Truman Hunt why nobody would be going to America.

First of all, there were the paddy fields, carved into these mountains by our forefathers. They could not be left untended. There were stone walls to be repaired and weeded, seedlings to be planted, ground to be tilled, rice to be harvested, granaries to be filled, before the winds turned and the monsoon rains began to thrash the valleys.

Second, the journey was deemed unsuitable for ancients. How were young people to cope? What would we do without the guidance of our elders? Who would read the portents? Who would make all the vital decisions?

Third, how could we leave behind the invisible world of the spirits? Our ancestors watched over us, kept us safe from harm. Without them, we would be utterly defenceless!

After Kinyo finished translating, Mister William stood up and said something about how he had hoped we would be able to see for ourselves all America's wonders. Then Truman Hunt rose to speak, his eyes red-rimmed, as if he wanted to cry. His voice was petulant, like a small child. 'How can you not want to go? It's the chance of a lifetime! You are invited to the World's Fair and you would rather stay here and plant rice? You have no idea what you're turning down!'

Kinyo had hardly translated everything when I decided it was time to leave.

'I've had enough,' I whispered to Samkad. As I picked my way through the crowd I heard Tilin say, in a loud whisper: 'There she goes. She just can't help calling attention to herself.' I blushed angrily and tried to move more quickly, but only succeeded in stepping on a man's instep. A very loud man, it turned out, because he gave out a yell that sent a flock of rice birds fluttering out of the Council House's thatched roof.

'Miss! Excuse me, miss!' I was startled. Truman Hunt was calling *me*?

I felt all the blood rush to my face. I was really hurrying now, practically leaping over the heads of people sitting on their heels.

I felt a large hand close around my shoulder.

'Miss, I'm talking to you!'

I looked up, aghast. Truman Hunt had actually waded in to get to me.

'Oh my,' he said. 'You're the girl in the tree!'

My mouth dropped open.

I had thought I'd heard someone in the bushes this morning. It was Truman Hunt!

I began to splutter, 'No! Let go of me! I don't know what you're talking about!'

'But I saw you!' Hunt said. He took my arm and began to tug me towards the ancients. I wanted to pull away. I wanted to run. But my feet stumbled after him obediently.

'She dropped out of a tree and killed the boar with one thrust of her spear.' My English was good enough so I didn't need Kinyo to translate Truman Hunt's words. 'At first I thought it was a boy, but I soon realized that it was a girl.' He grinned at the ancients. 'You should have seen her! The boar attacked, but she was ready with her spear. It died right on top of her. It was the most extraordinary thing I've seen in my life!'

The ancients were all glaring at me, Mother. I could see them listing all my past misdemeanours in their heads. I glanced at the crowd and saw Samkad's face, jaw slack with shock.

'Don't believe him!' I cried desperately. 'The American is lying!'

Mister William had risen to his feet. He lived in the village, he knew exactly how serious this was. 'Hunt,' he said urgently. 'Shut up.'

'But you were magnificent!' Hunt turned to me. 'Magnificent – do you know the word?' He turned to the old ones. 'Kinyo, translate! Tell them she must come to America. Tell them, I am begging them to let her come! Tell them I had no idea your women were hunters too.'

Then he made a tiny squeaking noise as I grabbed him by the shoulders and pushed him into the fire.

5
A Betrayal

Mother, you should have seen the look on everyone's faces. The crowd was agog. The ancients were boiling mad. Kinyo was in a panic, his usual smugness wiped from his face.

And Truman Hunt? He continued to beam at me as Kinyo extracted him from the sputtering fire, smoking and sooty, like a pork chop carelessly tumbled from a pan. He was laughing, Mother, as he brushed himself off and patted the smoke from his hair, as if the whole thing was a joke. 'Ha ha! You were extraordinary. Better than a man! So strong! I've never seen anything like it!'

Everyone was agitated now, the courtyard hummed with disapproval. *The girl killed the boar? Impossible! But didn't Samkad say he had done it?*

Samkad was suddenly behind me, he put an arm around my shoulders as if that would shield me from all the gawking eyes.

The ancients were barking angrily at Truman Hunt. 'Mister Truman, Mister William.' Kinyo looked from one American to the other as he translated. 'The ancients are saying this meeting is over. You both have to leave now.'

Mister William was shaking his head, looking sympathetically at me. He tapped Truman Hunt on the shoulder. 'Let's go, Hunt.'

The other American looked bewildered. He tipped his hat at the crowd, saying in a bright voice. 'I will be at the school, just in case anybody decides to sign up.'

'NOBODY IS GOING TO AMERICA!' snapped Salluyud, the oldest of the ancients, not even bothering to wait for Kinyo's stuttering interpretation. Now everyone was gawking at him, astonished that he had spoken so much English. 'LEAVE NOW.'

They left.

The ancients tottered to their feet and ordered everyone to clear the courtyard. Everyone except Samkad and me.

'Shall I stay?' Kinyo said.

Salluyud just glared at him until he shuffled away, rubbing the back of his neck.

The ancients gathered around us. Salluyud, Pito, Dugas, Maklan. These snaggle-toothed and wizened old men had been ancients since we were children. They had watched us grow up, performed the rituals that eased us from age to age, taught us the names of our ancestors, punished us for misdeeds, rewarded us when we did well.

Right now they were glowering at me, their crumpled faces more deeply cut than usual, like the bark on ancient trees.

'YOU killed the boar?' Salluyud croaked.

'No!' I said.

'Yes!' Samkad said. I noticed that his arm tightened over my shoulders. He wasn't holding me to comfort me. He was trying to stop me running away. I shook his arm off.

'No!' I told the ancients. 'I didn't kill the boar.'

'Yes!' Samkad said. 'She did.'

He tried to put his arm round me again, but I slapped it off. 'Stop it!' I hissed. 'What do you think you're doing?' Then I looked at the ancients and fear curdled in my belly. They knew! I could see it!

I glanced at Samkad fearfully. As the man, Samkad would bear the brunt of any punishment the ancients had in store for us. Samkad's face was smooth. He looked serious. But he did not look worried.

'Samkad,' Old Dugas spoke heavily. 'We discussed this yesterday, did we not?'

'Yes, old one.' Samkad bowed his head.

Discussed this yesterday? *Yesterday?*

There was a buzzing in my head, as if a swarm of bees had suddenly taken up residence behind my eyes.

Dugas shook his head. 'You confessed, and yet still you were lying.'

Confessed what? Lied about what? Samkad, what did you discuss with them?

Samkad hung his head and suddenly we were both small children again, lined up in front of the ancients, accused of some prank. *Which one of you put the dead snake on the path? Speak, or face a harsher punishment!*

'So, Little Luki.' Now it was Maklan speaking, pointing a crooked finger at me. 'It was you who killed the boar today, yes? Speak the truth. Samkad has already admitted that he takes you on secret hunting expeditions.'

'YOU IDIOT!' I shoved him hard in the chest. He staggered, stopping himself in time from tumbling into the fire, like Truman Hunt. 'WHAT WERE YOU THINKING?'

'Old one,' Samkad croaked. 'I was sincere in telling you that I had been hunting with Luki. That was all true. The only thing I lied about were the boars. I didn't think you were ready to know that they were not mine. Luki killed all three.' Sam stepped in front of me, as if his broad chest could shield me from their sharp glances. 'Weh. Three boars. Surely Luki deserves praise for bringing so much meat home.'

But the old faces were gurning with anger.

'PRAISE?' Pito cried. 'We indulged you when you said you took her hunting even though hunting is not a woman's job. We have all known Luki since she was born. We have always known about her deviant impulses. But you, Samkad. You *allowed* her to make the kill.'

'But we brought you food!' Samkad insisted, his voice desperate.

'You brought us SHAME!' Dugas snapped.

A voice piped up over my right shoulder, shrill and mean. 'She wears a breechcloth as well! I've seen her!' It was Tilin, hovering by the entrance to the courtyard.

There was an intense buzzing in my ears. I wanted to grab her by the hair, I wanted to scratch her hateful eyes out. I threw myself at her, but Samkad dragged me back and held me still. The hard stares of the ancients poked into me like pointing fingers.

Mother, now that they knew, they could see the evidence all over me. The dried mud on my knees, the deep scratches on my arm, the dark circles under my eyes.

Old Pito flicked his long hair away from a bony shoulder. 'Samkad, when you came to speak to us, we thought highly of you. Yes, we thought you were soft to indulge this girl's silly desire to hunt . . . but we also thought you were brave to come to us and speak about it so openly.'

'We thought you made up for it because you were such a great hunter,' Salluyud said. 'But now we know: not only are you weak, you are a liar.'

They were all gazing at Sam now like he was dog dirt plopped on the stone paving before them. Panic churned in my belly. Now I was afraid they could banish him, send him far away.

'It's not Samkad's fault,' I cried. 'I *forced* him to take me hunting!'

'Silence!' Dugas smacked his hands together. 'Young man, we have agreed a solution, have we not?'

34

A solution? Mother, I looked at Sam but he was looking everywhere except at me.

'The truth about these hunting trips has not changed the outcome we have decided.' Pito said. 'The girl must be taken in hand.'

'Taken in hand!' I snarled. 'What do you mean?'

But still they ignored me.

'I was hoping to find the right moment,' Samkad mumbled.

Right moment for what?

'Samkad,' Salluyud said evenly. 'Now everyone knows what you have done, if things continue as they are, we will look like fools. You know what you have to do.'

'Yes, you will fix this as we agreed,' Maklan said.

'You must do your duty,' Dugas said.

It was as if the ancients were holding me under the churning waters of the Chico River. I was floundering, desperate to breathe.

I grabbed Samkad's hand, searching his eyes.

'Luki,' he whispered. 'We need to talk. Not here. Come with me.'

Mother, as I followed Samkad out of the courtyard, I glanced back at the ancients. They were all smiling.

Not once did Samkad look at me as we made our way to his father's house. And even when we got there, his eyes still avoided mine, gazing at the carcass still hanging on the scaffold. He shook his head.

'Luki, I had to tell them. They kept praising me, saying I was a great hunter, like my father. I felt awful because I knew that it wasn't true.'

'But you are a great hunter!' I cried. *It's just that I'm better than you*, a small voice whispered in my head.

'They wouldn't stop saying it. "You are a hero, Samkad", they said. "You will save the village, Samkad", "Because of Samkad, nobody will go hungry".' He shook his head. 'It felt so wrong. It wasn't fair. They had to be told the truth. My plan was to tell them bit by bit. So I started by telling them I took you along when I went hunting . . . and then, maybe a few weeks later, I thought I could tell them who really killed the boars.'

I was speechless. How could he? I didn't want praise. I wanted to hunt. And now . . .

'They were so grateful for the meat, I thought they would understand,' Samkad continued. 'But instead they were furious that I had taken you with me.'

I shook my head. How could he sound so astonished! Did he expect them to say, well done, Samkad, for indulging that headache of a girl?

He swallowed.

'They said I didn't deserve to live in the village. They said they would make me leave.' He looked stricken. 'I was devastated. I begged them to reconsider.'

He paused.

'Then Maklan said there was a solution . . . He said I might

36

even like the solution because it means you and I can hunt as much as we like. He said . . .' Samkad paused, and for the first time, he looked directly at me. 'He said we should marry.'

I stared at him. I felt like all the warmth had suddenly drained out of my body. Mother, wasn't this what the ancients had always wanted? A way to tether down this wayward girl who would never do what she was told. And they'd convinced Samkad to do it for them.

Samkad's face slowly turned a dull red. 'Stop looking at me like that.' He held up his hand as if to shield his eyes, even though we were standing in the shadows and there was no sun to guard against.

'Luki, I thought you would be pleased,' he whispered.

Mother, I said nothing.

Samkad took a big gulp of air. 'But can't you see, they're right! We should marry. Our parents are dead. You hate living in the House for Women and I can't wait to leave the House for Men. We can make our home in Father's house. We have your mother's and my father's paddy fields to till. And once you're mine, you can do anything you like! You can hunt as much as you want! I won't be like the other men. I will allow you to do it!'

I will allow you to do it.

'You will be my wife. We will live together. And we will have a family. The ancients are eager to announce it. They will give us a good celebration.'

I didn't resist when Sam gathered me against him. He

37

would repair the roof of his father's house, he whispered. The yield of the rice paddies he'd inherited from his father would easily feed up to six children. He would build a small chicken house to one side of the house.

And as he mused, all I could think was: I am not a wife. I am not. Mother, now you were dead, I was no longer a daughter. So who was I? An annoyance, according to the ancients. A sluggard, according to the other women. A nothing, according to me. I squeezed my eyes shut and I saw them again, those children with his eyes, reaching as if they wanted me to take them in my arms.

'*NO!*' I cried, pushing him away.

Samkad staggered backwards, his face a picture of surprise and hurt. 'What?'

'I do not want to be your wife.' I glared at him.

'But . . .' Samkad's eyes glistened with unshed tears. 'Luki, don't you love me?'

I turned on my heel and began to walk away.

'Luki! Where are you going?'

I glanced briefly over my shoulder. 'I'm going to the school to give my name to Truman Hunt. I'm going to America.'

6

It Will be Grand

Mother, I was not afraid to leave, but I was afraid of what would happen if I stayed.

So I made my way through the village and out the other end to Mister William's school where the ground began to drop down to the mossy forest. Samkad did not chase after me. No doubt he had returned to the Council House, asking the ancients what else he could allow me to do.

I remember how we all turned out to help Mister William build the school, with a room where Mister William could sleep and a large veranda that would soon become our classroom. It was so exciting when a blackboard arrived from Manila, balanced on the back of a small pony. We helped Mister William nail it the wall of the veranda. How we loved writing on it with those sticks of white, crumbling rock called 'chalk'. We pinned Mister William's stripy flag above the door to his bedroom. It's mildewed and stained by the weather now. Remember how Mister William made us sing to it? I can still sing the first lines: *My country 'tis of thee, sweet land of liberty* . . .

On the other side of the door, that portrait of President Roosevelt you like so much still hangs. I am sorry to say that a speckled brown patch has spread over Roosevelt's forehead. But it only adds to the ruggedness of his pose, in his deerskin suit and fur hat with a knife in his belt and a rifle on his knees.

They saw me approaching from a distance. Even from afar, I could see Kinyo's shocked, wide open mouth, his eyes black dots leaping out of his head and the pleased white grin spreading over Truman Hunt's face.

Mister William stared over the pot he'd been stirring on his fire. 'Miss Luki, what are you doing here?' he asked.

'She's here to sign up for the trip!' Truman Hunt said, pulling the hat from his head and pressing it against his heart. 'Aren't you, miss?'

'You're coming too?' There, just behind Hunt, dismay on her face, stood Tilin.

She had signed up? Mother, it had not occurred to me that Tilin might want to go to America. I could have screamed.

'But who's going to look after Sidong?' I exclaimed.

'Sidong is coming too,' Tilin said. 'We have no parents to hold us back. We are free to go where we like.'

I glared at her even though in the back of my mind I was thinking, *I too have nobody to hold me back now.*

'Everyone is talking about how you are going to marry Samkad,' she said. 'When I left the Council House, the ancients were waiting for the two of you to come to them and ask for their blessing. What are you doing here? Where is Samkad?'

'It's not going to happen,' I said bitterly. Then I squared my shoulders. 'I'm going to America instead.'

Tilin's eyes widened. 'You have refused Samkad?' For a second she looked at me and then her nose and mouth began to twitch. And then, Mother, she burst out laughing.

We all watched, bewildered, until at last she swallowed a final giggle. She smiled at me.

'They wanted me to marry too. But like you, I said no. That's why I'm here. They can't make me get married if I'm in America!'

I felt something spark inside me, like a firefly had suddenly lit up in my belly. I wanted to smile at her, to throw my arms around her and laugh about our shared predicament. But I had not forgotten her mean little jibes: *Luki's no help. Luki's no use.*

Abruptly, I turned my back on her and nodded at Kinyo. 'Tell the American to put my name on his list.'

Truman Hunt listened carefully to Kinyo's translation, then turned to me. 'Are you sure? I realize now that I put you in a spot back there. I wouldn't want you to do anything you were uncomfortable with. Do you really want to go?'

I nodded firmly. Yes, I was sure.

Truman Hunt wrote my name down with a flourish, talking some more, too fast for me to follow. I looked at Kinyo.

'He's still talking about how impressed he was when he saw you kill that boar,' Kinyo said. 'And that he had been certain Samkad would not allow you to go.'

My face glowed hot, as if someone had passed a torch in front of it. Even Truman Hunt thought Samkad ruled over me.

'Let me see that list!' I demanded.

Hunt handed me the piece of paper and I peered at it, wishing I'd paid more attention when Mister William was teaching us how to read and write. I knew enough to recognize the **L U K I** of my name. But that was not what caught my attention.

There was hardly anything written on the sheet.

There were four scribbles. One would be for Kinyo's name. The other two would be for Tilin and Sidong. And then the fourth one would be me. Mother, it was going to be so embarrassing, the four of us lining up before the President. 'Well now,' he would say. 'Is that all?' And then he would shrug his mighty shoulders, tug his moustache and wish he had not bothered to invite us.

Truman Hunt though, looked unworried. He grinned, thanked me, thanked Kinyo, thanked Tilin, then began to enumerate a list of items we should pack for the journey – mats to sleep on, blankets for the cold, something to carry water, rice to cook, cured pork, sweet potatoes. And for America we should bring our finest adornments, necklaces, headdresses, gangsas, shields, weapons, anything the American public might appreciate, any musical instruments we played. All of which had to fit in the packs we would be carrying on our backs or on our heads. He would be back for us in a week's time.

'It will be grand, it will be an adventure!' he assured us. 'Saint Louis is one of the most glorious cities in the United States. You will love it.'

And that was what I told myself, Mother. Over and over again – *It will be grand. It will be an adventure!* – as I spent the loneliest week of my life, preparing to leave. Samkad kept himself away, and I was glad. I had nothing to say to him. The ancients turned away whenever I so much as walked past the Council House. The other girls in the House for Women pretended that they were not at all curious about Tilin and our impending trip. Tilin herself went about her daily chores as if nothing was unusual. We stored our packs in the back of the House for Women, out of sight. Sidong, unaware of all the tension, chattered incessantly about the trip, asking us an endless stream of questions. What did the lowlands look like? Where were we going to sleep on the way? How would we eat? How long would it take? What was Manila like? How would we eat on the boat? She followed me into the forest and watched as I offered a chicken to the spirits and asked for their protection and forgiveness. I poured tapuy over your spirit figure, Mother, and I begged the invisible world to understand why I had to go.

But the day before our departure, a wind gusted down from the mountain top with a great howling and took the roof off one of the granaries. It blew down a tall post adorned with the skulls of ten carabaos and one of the skulls came crashing to earth. Were you trying to send me a message, Mother? Was this a portent of things to come?

It will be grand. It will be an adventure! I told myself. Anything to stop myself thinking about how I was never going to become Samkad's wife. Anything to stop myself changing my mind.

7

Lowlanders

I was worried that we would be President Roosevelt's only guests, Mother. But I was wrong.

We left the village, and on the first day we followed the meandering trail along the Chico River, bright blue from the recent rains, shifting and winding as it followed the shape of the mountain. At every turn, we found people waiting for us. Two men from distant Tanudan, five from Sadanga, eight from Sagada, four from Barlig. And on and on they came, more groups from other parts of Bontok: Sabangan, Bauko, Natonin, Besao . . . until there were seventy of us in all. All Bontok. All strangers to each other.

On the second day, we plunged down, down, down, on a trail that went beyond Bontok, rice paddies climbing in tiers above us. We walked small forests, past thick plumes of bamboo. Until eventually we reached a busy town called Cervantes, populated by migrants from the lowlands.

There, on the banks of a river called the Abra, another group was waiting for us – a huge one. Twenty-five were a people called the Suyoc, most of them members of a family of miners from Mankayan. Seventeen were a people called the Tinguian, who had come down from the far northern mountains.

After all that, there were now more than a hundred of us in all, Mother, walking down the mountain.

Theodore Roosevelt should be flattered.

We walked up and down hills, in and out of small valleys, until the third day, when we made our final descent and put the highlands behind us. Mother, the few men in our village who had made that journey to the lowlands had described magnificent flat lands rising to meet them as they walked down the mountain. But the sun tugged great dark clouds over its head and sent rain smacking down on us in such heavy gobs we could barely raise our eyes – and then we found ourselves walking through a deep jungle. There was no view to see, and anyway, it was unsafe to look up because the ground under our feet was steep and slippery with moss.

All of a sudden the cool fog that had been our constant companion, swilling around our feet throughout the journey, vanished. We were on level ground.

When had the air thickened into this *warm* soup? And the trees! They seemed taller somehow, stretching their arms up high, their leaves bigger and broader. Insects were everywhere, biting, vicious. I could feel my armpits prickling, and I had an urgent need to bathe.

We wiped mosquitoes from our faces and walked out of the trees into a wall of heat, into a world so flat it pushed the sky away, shrinking the sun to a tiny thumbnail. Weh, I had never trodden on such flatness. I felt light-headed, rolling around on the balls of my feet. On either side of the road, rice paddies spread all the way to the horizon. Mother, I had not imagined fields like this, bigger, broader, greener than our mountain terraces. These paddies had no mountain shadows to stunt the grain. They had an uninterrupted landscape on which to flourish. Kinyo had told us about his childhood in the lowlands. But he had not told us about this.

Growing up, our elders had taught us to think badly of lowlanders. Lowlanders were cruel, they said. They were violent, uncivilized people. They were not to be trusted. They were incapable of carving mountains and coaxing life out of barren soil as we did. But all this time the lowlanders had this and we had no idea.

'Luki, are you all right?' Kinyo was suddenly there, a sympathetic hand on my shoulder. Did I look so dismayed that he had left Truman Hunt's side?

'Yes,' I lied, as I lowered myself to my heels, folded my arms on my knees and buried my face in them. 'Just having a quick rest.'

But now Kinyo was lowering himself next to me.

'I know how you feel,' he said softly.

'You don't know how I feel.' I didn't raise my head.

'I really wanted to go to America,' he said. 'I was determined to go, never mind what anybody said. But that moment, when we turned our backs on Bontok, I felt a terrible wrench. I was missing home so much and I had barely left. I was missing Samkad, even though he's decided to call me the enemy.'

'I don't miss Samkad,' I lied.

'Weh, that may be so. But he will definitely be missing you,' Kinyo said softly. 'And he will be sorry he drove you away.'

'He didn't drive me away,' I snapped. 'I decided to leave.'

He touched my elbow. 'You have me, Luki. I will look out for you.' Then he quickly got to his feet, walking away as if he was embarrassed to be caught feeling sorry for me.

I had never experienced such heat. In Bontok, there were warm days, but not like this. It weighed heavily on us, making sweat run down our backs, so that our packs slipped. We tied cloths over our heads to keep the sun off, but the cloths were quickly soaked through with sweat. Sidong struggled and soon Kinyo had to carry Tilin's pack as well so that she could put Sidong on her back.

Our pace slowed and the long line wavered and broke whenever people stopped to rest. Truman Hunt became impatient, galloping his horse into the distance and back again and ordering Kinyo to make us walk faster. But Kinyo just told everyone to ignore him. 'This is how we must walk in the lowlands,' he explained. 'It is hot. Save your energy.'

The long road unfurling before us had its own cruel magic.

Several times we saw shiny, silvery streams crossing the road up ahead. We all raced to fill our bamboo containers, but the streams vanished at our approach only to reappear further down the road.

'It's a trick of the heat,' Truman Hunt explained, wiping his red face on his sleeve. 'It's called a mirage.'

As the sun was beginning to lower, we spotted thatched roofs and a grove of banana trees in the distance.

'Look, a village!' I heard Tilin cry. A murmur of anticipation ran down the cordon behind us. We had been walking for two hours and had yet to glimpse a single human being. I began to run, overtaking Truman Hunt's plodding horse in my haste to get there first.

But what I saw made my stomach churn.

The village might have been alive once, but not any more. There were small squares of scruffy, overgrown shrubbery that must have once been vegetable gardens. The bamboo huts were burnt ruins and trees were blackened by fire. A larger building, made of stone, had been smashed in.

Mother, seeing all this destruction brought back that terrible night when our blood enemy, the Mangili, attacked and burned down the village. Even now that we've rebuilt everything, the thought of it still makes my skin crawl.

Draped on a fence was a flag. It was not the stripy American flag that fluttered everywhere in Bontok. This one was different. It was riddled with holes and faded by sun and rain, its edges singed and tattered. One half was blue, and the other red. There was a white triangle on one side, with a golden star in each corner. In the middle of the triangle was a yellow sun, with stern eyes, nose and mouth.

I heard a snort. 'The impudence of these people!' Truman Hunt exclaimed as he jumped off his horse, handing the reins to Kinyo. Behind him, the others were gathering in a clump, murmuring to each other, eyes wide with curiosity. Hunt marched across the debris and grabbed the strange flag. 'The war is over. This flag is forbidden,' he exclaimed.

'Is it the Filipino flag, sir?' Kinyo said.

'It is nobody's flag,' Hunt replied, rolling it up into a ball and tossing it into a pile of rubble. 'The stars and stripes is the only flag allowed to fly over these islands now.'

'Mister Hunt!' Kinyo suddenly said. 'Look!'

Behind the wreckage of a hut, stood a lowlander, clad in a pair of tattered trousers, clutching a long knife.

Truman Hunt looked suddenly pale.

The man was shouting, his face ugly with hatred.

'Sir, he is angry that you threw his flag away,' Kinyo said.

The only word I could understand was 'Amerikano', which the lowlander spat out as if he couldn't bear for it to be on his tongue.

The man suddenly ran up to Truman Hunt, pointing his knife just a hair short of Truman Hunt's neck. The American jumped back, his eyes round with horror.

'No!' I cried. I had never seen anyone treat an American with such disrespect. I found myself diving for the man's legs, knocking him off his feet. His knife flew from his fist, striking a stone with a ringing noise.

Truman Hunt was already clambering onto his horse. 'Get everyone out of here,' he shouted at Kinyo. And then he kicked his horse and galloped down the road.

'He's abandoned us!' I heard Tilin cry.

Couldn't Tilin see that Truman Hunt needed to get away from that man? As I got back onto my feet, I turned to argue with her. But the words died in my throat. She was looking past me one hand covering her mouth.

I whirled around. There were one, two, three . . . more than twenty people watching us from the rubble of the ruined village. Hollow-eyed men and women, ragged and gaunt, muttering to each other. I heard the word 'Amerikano' and then 'Igorot'.

'Let's get out of here,' Kinyo cried. 'Everyone, get moving!' Tilin put Sidong on her back and began to run in the direction Truman Hunt had taken. Everyone followed suit, shouting and stumbling.

But there were still some people just arriving at the village with no idea of the danger. I stumbled, my muscles slow to unfreeze.

A lowlander woman bent down to pick up a brick. The low-landers without knives were picking up planks of wood and pieces of rubble. They wanted to fight.

As Kinyo turned, shouting warnings at the stragglers down the road, the woman flung her brick. It landed at my feet. I felt someone else grab me by the hair.

My new assailant was jabbering. '*Igorot!*' Her lips worked and she spat into my face. Kinyo managed to drag her off me. 'What is wrong with you?' I screamed, wiping the spit off my cheek.

Lowlanders fanned out around us, cutting us off from the others. I could see the glint of their knives. How were we going to fight our way through?

Suddenly the air convulsed with the sharp peals of a bell.

Knives clattered to the ground. The lowlanders dropped to their knees, their hands flying across their chests in some kind of mystical gesture. They bowed their heads and clasped their hands to their breasts.

Kinyo and I ran. It was properly dusk now and we could barely see the others on the road ahead. We all ran until the ruined village was out of sight. And then we ran some more.

And then suddenly there was Truman Hunt. On his horse, he made a tall shadow in the middle of the road. He waved us into a copse of trees along a thin creek. We collapsed under the trees, bewildered and frightened in the dark. As we began to set up camp, Truman Hunt wandered amongst us, asking if we were all right.

When he got to me, I couldn't see his expression properly, but the hand he laid on my shoulder was warm. 'Thank you, Luki,' he said softly. 'You are a life saver.'

'Well, that was nice of him,' Tilin said grumpily as she unrolled a mat for Sidong under a tree. 'But I won't forget he left us to face the knives.'

'He was in danger,' I replied. 'I didn't see *you* lingering when the lowlanders began to attack.'

'I guess the war isn't over for those lowlanders, even though the Americans say it is,' Tilin said.

'But then they stopped. Why did they do that?' I asked Kinyo.

'It's called the Angelus,' Kinyo said. He explained that a bell tolled three times a day – and everyone had to kneel and pray to their spirits.

He shrugged. 'I did it too when I was growing up in the lowlands. It may not seem normal to you, but it is normal down here in the lowlands.'

I had no reason to disbelieve him, Mother. Though I wondered how much longer the Angelus could remain a normal part of their daily life. In Bontok, we'd become used to Americans changing what was normal.

8

Manila

Truman Hunt decided it would be safer for us to travel at night and sleep during the day, camping out of sight. We did this for five more nights, walking under dark skies, villages and towns looking identical in the dim glow of the moon.

One night we felt a faint current, a freshening that made us all stop and spread our arms wide to feel the breeze. There was a whispering in the distance. Truman Hunt pulled his horse to a stop and grinned.

'Mister Hunt says it is the ocean,' Kinyo translated. *The ocean. The ocean. The ocean.* The low rushing did not seem so far away. But the road to Manila never did take us near enough to see it. We could hear the ocean, sighing and groaning and thundering. But it stayed out of sight.

And then the sighing stopped, the breeze warmed, the starry clumps of fireflies in the trees blinked off and we heard roosters, hundreds of them, crowing as the sun began to breach the horizon.

Truman Hunt turned in his saddle and held up his hand. The early morning light cast long yellow rays. His hat looked like it was on fire.

'We have arrived,' he announced. 'Welcome to Manila. I know you are tired, but if we keep moving, we should reach the harbour by the afternoon.'

Everyone's mouths were agape with astonishment. It had happened without warning. None of us had noticed the dwindling of the rice paddies, the road hardening to paving, the houses turning from bamboo into stone, their rooftops changing from thatch to iron sheets and pottery.

We had dream-walked our way into Manila.

Manila is the capital city of the Philippine Islands. Mister William had made us recite this in school. But no matter how many times we repeated it, the words meant nothing. Manila had seemed a long way away.

But now here it was. We marched slowly, staring at the houses by the side of the road, the windows had shutters glazed with oyster shells. The bigger windows had elaborate bulging ironwork hung with ferns. The deeper into the city we walked, the closer together the houses seemed to huddle.

Then as the morning grew later, people began to appear. Small children darted around us like fish. One white-haired woman with a large cigar dangling from her lips marched into our midst and dragged two children away, hiding them behind her skirt, as if she needed to protect them from us. Men put down the yokes across their shoulders to stare.

Entering the city, I had been so excited it had felt like there was a swarm of bees buzzing in my belly. But my excitement quickly dulled before the lowlanders' relentless ogling. Their eyes wandered over our bodies as if they were staring at animals they had never seen before. I could feel them looking at the tattoos on my face, the fall of my blouse and the hem of my skirt – it made me feel ashamed somehow.

I found myself looking away, pretending not to notice.

Soon the road began to fill with carts of all sorts, pulled by horses and carabaos. Truman Hunt ordered us to walk on the side of the road.

Soon the rough paving became more evenly cut. The houses became bigger, their rooftops made of tile instead of thatch.

We found ourselves walking onto a large, grassy field. The road skirting around it was lined with even taller buildings, decorated with carved screens, stone urns, glass globes, windows, columns, arches, and doors three times the height of a man.

'We will rest under these trees,' Kinyo announced, but everyone was already surging towards two huge stone bowls filled with water, with sprays of water spouting out of the middle. Some children had already leaped right in, splashing about as if they were playing in the Chico River.

'Hey!' Truman Hunt yelled. 'Hey, come back here!'

I wasn't thirsty. I lay myself down in the cool shade and watched the frenzied rush.

I heard a man shouting, 'Not allowed! Not allowed!' and then sharp screams. Men in blue uniforms were moving through the crowd, swinging wooden canes – the children, who moments before had been laughing and splashing, were now howling with fear and pain. It was pandemonium, people and belongings scattered across the grass like seed.

Truman Hunt ran right into the chaos. 'Enough!' he bellowed, grabbing a cane from one of the blue uniforms. 'Leave them alone!'

Our attackers paused as one, staring at the American. Mother, Truman Hunt was not as tall as other Americans I'd seen, but at that moment, he pulled himself up so that he seemed to stand a full head and shoulders above everybody else. His voice, deep and powerful, rose over the field. The blue men looked at each other in dismay and dropped their canes.

'Sir!' one sputtered. 'We are security, sir. For the hotel over there.'

'What do you think you're doing?' Hunt cried. 'These people are under my care.'

'Sir, sorry, sir! Igorot. They bad for hotel.'

'Well, these people are wards of the United States government, and I am their manager,' Truman Hunt bellowed. 'How dare you beat them! I brought them here to rest and you have treated them like dogs.'

Several of our men had snatched up their spears, and were advancing on the blue uniforms. Without taking his eyes off the blue men, Hunt called, 'Kinyo! Tell them to stand down! I can handle this.'

And he did, Mother. The blue men cowered as he cursed at them. Our people resumed collecting water at the stone bowls. The children returned to their splashing.

But somewhere in the distance, I heard a child scream.

It was Sidong, Mother, on the far edge of the field. She must have gone off to draw. Two men were bent over her and I could see her feet flailing.

Tilin was already racing across the field. She lunged at one of the men, but he pushed her away easily, with a smirk.

I dropped my pack and set off after her. 'Help!' I yelled, over my shoulder. 'Kinyo! Truman Hunt!'

One of the men began to drag Tilin across the street by the arm. The other man tossed Sidong over his shoulder and followed his friend into an alley between two buildings.

'Kinyo! Truman Hunt! Help!' I panted as I ran to the alley.

But nobody came.

9

Lost

The gloom of the alley blinded me. But I could hear them jabbering away in lowlander, laughing and grunting as Tilin screamed. The alley had a sweetish smell, like there was some-thing dead in there. I clenched my fists.

Tilin screamed again, but the sound was abruptly cut short. I gagged to think of their dirty hands over her mouth. No time to wait, I launched myself into the darkness, crashing into one of them.

He whirled round, swatting to get me off him, but I already had my legs wrapped tightly around his waist. I sank my teeth into his stinking neck and dug my fingers into his face. He screamed, thumping my leg with his fist. But I didn't let go. You can't, once you've got a grip on your prey.

The other man screeched. Tilin was doing her own good work. A loud thump and I felt the jolt of a body slamming into us. I jumped clear as the two men collapsed against the alley's dirty brick wall. Fingers closed around mine. 'Quickly, quickly,' Tilin hissed, but the groaning lump of men blocked the route back. 'This way,' Tilin grunted, tugging me in the opposite direction. Sidong was whimpering somewhere on the left. 'I've got you, Sidong. This way!' Tilin murmured.

The other end of the lane was blocked by a tower of stuff – baskets? Rubbish? We couldn't really see, but it disintegrated after a few kicks. Light, hot and dazzling, tumbled into the alley. We ran out. All at once, we were surrounded by women, baskets of goods, children, men and horse carts. A market.

People looked up. The children stopped playing. There was a sharp smell, as if everyone had suddenly broken into sweat at the same time. They began to murmur. *Igorot. Igorot. Igorot.* Oh, that hateful word. It rippled around the market as if carried by the wind.

What did Mister William always say? 'That is what the rest of the world calls you. Don't expect them to know that you are Bontok.' It wasn't just the word though. It was the way people said it as if they were biting into maggoty fruit.

'Watch out!' Tilin cried.

Something tiny and sharp hit me on the cheek. A stone, thrown by a small boy wearing trousers too large for him. He pawed the gravelly paving for another.

A man wearing a straw hat left his horse, and stepped right up to me, so close I had to throw my head back to look up at his face.

'What do you want?' I was amazed the American words came so quickly to my lips.

But he didn't speak American.

The man's mouth was working and chewing. Then with a great throaty noise, he spat a great gob of saliva onto the front of my blouse. You might have expected me, the best boar hunter of my village, to strike back promptly, stamp on his instep, punch his stupid face. But no. The corners of my mouth began wobbling uncontrollably. Tears sprang in my eyes. To my shame, I began to cry.

But Tilin was not having any of it. She rushed at the man with a terrifying roar. '*RAAAAAAH!*' He backed away, terror on his face.

'You coward!' Tilin shouted, not caring that the man would not understand a word of Bontok. 'Spitting is what cowards do!' She pulled Sidong onto her back and yanked my elbow. 'Move, Luki. Let's get out of here.'

Tilin marched us out of there, pointing. 'If we walk around that building,' she said, 'we will get back to the others.'

But the two men we had just escaped appeared at the corner, faces bruised and bloody where we'd scratched them, caked in the grit of the alleyway. They wanted revenge.

We turned and ran back into the market, the paving jarring under our bare feet. We pushed through bodies and knocked baskets of fruits into their path, but they managed to keep up, leaping over the obstacles we threw in their way.

'This way,' Tilin called, slipping into another alley.

But they were right behind us. So close. Until we ran into a street.

A sharp neighing and a screech of iron wheels. It was a busy one, and we were right in the middle. Horses, a carabao, even oxen clattered back and forth pulling their carts and carriages. Our tormentors hesitated by the side of the road.

'This is dangerous,' Tilin cried. 'We need to get out of here!'

'No!' I said, throwing my arms around Tilin and Sidong, holding them in place. 'They can't get to us here.'

Horses shrieked, carriages swerved around us, drivers bellowed with rage. The two men shook their fists at us, but, spitting on the ground, they turned back towards the market.

'Over there. That must lead back to the field,' Tilin murmured, as we slowly made our way to the other side. I couldn't tell anymore which way was where, so I followed.

But it was the wrong way. The road turned into an arching bridge spanning a broad river, choked with small boats. We walked up the bridge, thinking we would be able to see our way back from a height. But Manila just looked like a confusion of alleyways and carts and people.

'Look! What is that?' Tilin pointed.

On the other side of the bridge stood great blackened ramparts. We could just make out a small city within the walls, with church towers and red tiled roofs. A great big American flag fluttered from a pole at the top. The ramparts plunged right into the river on one side. Inland, the other walls were guarded by a stagnant pool, green with water muck. We could smell its reek from the bridge. The shore fronting the pool looked pleasant and grassy, with several stands of trees. It was surprisingly empty of people.

Tilin looked at me. 'We need to rest, Luki. I can't go on. Aren't you tired?'

She was right, Mother. We'd been walking all night. We hadn't eaten. My muscles felt like brittle firewood. I was utterly exhausted.

Tilin pointed at the trees on the other side of the bridge. 'We can rest there. Out of sight.'

We made our way down the bridge, turned our backs on the traffic and walked to one cluster of trees. Sidong slid off Tilin's back with a loud sigh and we all sank down onto the grass.

Sidong nestled in Tilin's arms. 'Tilin, do you think Mister Hunt has our packs? I want my drawing book.'

Tilin put her arms around Sidong. 'I'm sure he has,' she whispered. Then we must have fallen asleep because the next thing I knew, something was prodding my cheek. I opened my eyes. Standing over me was a grinning boy with a twig in his hand. Two girls peered over his shoulder.

'GET AWAY FROM ME!' I bellowed. The three children squealed and ran back towards the road.

'That was easy,' Tilin said softly.

'I'm fed up with being chased, spat at and poked.'

'They're just afraid,' she murmured. 'We look different, I guess.'

'Pah!' I grunted.

Tilin sat up, stroking Sidong's hair. Her face was smudged with dirt and drooping with tiredness, but when she spoke, she sounded determined. 'We'd better go back over the bridge and look for the others.'

I nodded. I wondered how long we'd been asleep. Whatever, it didn't feel long enough. I got to my feet and stretched. The sky was pinking up, the walled city had turned into a looming shadow. Distant roosters were crowing. It would be dark soon.

Then I felt it. A breeze. Cool and fresh, washing the heavy heat of Manila from my limbs.

I turned towards it, willing it to blow harder.

And then I saw it.

There, under the pink sky.

The sea.

And where the sky met land, there was a bright glow, like someone had built a hundred fires on the shore. I could hear a soft rumble of voices. And music.

'Luki, where are you going?' Tilin called.

I was walking towards the lights, the sea, the music. I couldn't help it, Mother. I reached the end of the grassy field and I could see now that the lights came from the tops of hundreds of tall posts, glowing like giant candles. They lit up an open space filled with people, more people than I'd ever seen in one place. Horse-drawn carriages pranced slowly, round and round. At the centre, on a raised platform with an elaborate tiled roof, sat about thirty men playing music.

A band! I'd seen pictures of bands and musical instruments in Mister William's magazines, and we'd listened to band music on his wind-up music box. But this was the first time I'd heard it being played in real life. Mother, it was strange and enchanting.

'What is going on?' Tilin had caught up, Sidong following reluctantly, rubbing her eyes.

And then my blood cooled. A figure had appeared in the shadows. A man, striding towards us. Not again, Mother. I couldn't bear another chase . . . but he was upon us before I could tell Tilin to run.

It was a young man, hair cut close around his head and dressed in the uniform of a soldier. '*Buenas noches*,' he cried. He was smiling and he held his arms out, as if to show that he would do us no harm. '*¿Hablas Kastila?*'

Tilin and I looked at each other. He was speaking in yet another tongue.

When we didn't respond, he tried again. 'Speak English?'

'Yes,' I said reluctantly. 'A little.'

He nodded and pointed to himself. 'My name is Johnny. I am Philippine Constabulary.'

We nodded. We knew the Philippine Constabulary. They were a kind of police . . . The Americans had recruited many mountain men to join it, arming them with guns and dressing them in uniforms.

'You are Igorot?'

I flinched at that word, but I nodded.

'And you are looking for Truman Hunt?'

This time I was so surprised I couldn't nod.

Johnny laughed. '*Os está buscando*. He is looking for you.' He clapped his hands, 'And here you are!'

10

All Aboard

Someone had found our belongings scattered in a corner of the field. That had led to a frantic search. Someone had seen me dart into the alley. Someone else had seen two men chasing us in the market. Truman Hunt had jumped on his horse and galloped to the police station to ask for help.

And that – Johnny explained – was how he happened to be out looking for three lost Igorot girls. He pointed at the musicians playing on the bandstand. 'That is where I should have been. *¡Toco la trompeta!*' he said. 'I play the trumpet.'

He walked us across the circling track and through the crowd, arms out wide so that people had to make way. I have to admit, Mother, after the day we'd had, I was nervous to be in the midst of so many people. But it was practically night-time, the crowd was a confusing jumble of shadows and people couldn't really see us properly even if they tried to. Besides, they were too busy concentrating on the music.

Johnny took us to the back of the stage, where he sat us down in a walled-off little space, with chairs and a flickering lamp. Then from out of nowhere he presented us with bottles of water and a paper bag full of small round loaves of bread.

Mother, we fell on the food like dogs. We had not had a single bite to eat since sunrise.

When I finally sat back, belly full and head clear, the music had gone silent and there, standing in the opening of the enclosure stood another man in a Constabulary uniform. He was a whole head and shoulders taller than Johnny, and broad where Johnny was slight. I could see that a thick moustache draped over his top lip. Because of his height, I would have guessed he was an American, but he didn't look like any American I'd ever met, because his skin was as black as the boulders in the mossy forest back home.

'Sorry to disturb,' Johnny was saying.

Tilin straightened and Sidong buried her head in my lap.

'This is my boss, Lieutenant Walter Loving.'

I had not heard that word, 'boss', before. But it was obvious it was someone to defer to, the way Johnny bent his head and lowered his eyes.

I was trying to work out how to greet him, but the man wasn't even looking at us. He just turned to Johnny and in a low voice began to speak rapidly in Kastila.

Johnny nodded, muttering, '*Sí, sí*. Yes, sir.'

Then Lieutenant Walter Loving clapped a hand on Johnny's back and, without another glance at us, walked out into the darkness. We could see that the other musicians followed in his wake, carrying their instruments.

Johnny turned to us and explained, in slow English, that the ship that was going to carry us across the ocean to the United States was moored out in the bay and that the other Igorots and Truman Hunt had already boarded it. We would have to spend the night in the Constabulary barracks, where Johnny and the other men lived. He would take us to the ship early the next morning.

I felt Tilin's hand searching for mine.

'What?' I said. 'What is it?'

'They're already on the boat,' she whispered. 'And tomorrow, we will be too!'

Her fingers were trembling.

Mother, I could not possibly tell you the route we took to the barracks, though it was lit by more of those tall candle poles. We made our way there, the paving hard under our feet, and we were so tired that if we had stopped to stand still for even a moment, I'm sure we would have fallen asleep. The barracks turned out to be a long building with many rooms. Johnny put us in an empty room with beds raised high off the floor on iron legs. We had never slept on American beds before, so when Johnny wished us good night and left us alone, we pulled the blankets off the beds and laid them out on the floor to sleep on.

It seemed I'd barely closed my eyes before Johnny was knocking on the door again. We followed him back to the river, where he bought some rice cakes from a street vendor for our breakfast.

I had not paid much notice to the river yesterday. But this morning it had my full attention. The water was yellow with the morning sun. It smelled of fish and mud and rotting vegetables. And bumping up and down on the waves were dozens of boats – some were dugouts like the ones we had back home on the Chico River, but there were also rafts that sat low in the water, boats topped by what looked like little huts, boats with smokestacks and towering ships with tall masts.

'¡Aquí! Over here!' Johnny was waving from a long boat with a huge funnel blowing a column of smoke into the air. Inside were rows of benches. A faded American flag drooped from a pole on its tip and a man stood on each end pushing long poles into the riverbed to keep the bobbing vessel pressed against the shore.

Johnny hopped into the boat and help us across the watery gap. We tottered across the tilting wooden floor to a bench, where we sat down, with Sidong safely wedged between us.

'Your ship's name is the *Shawmut*,' Johnny said. 'This launch will take us out to where it's anchored.'

There was a shout and the pole men began to push us away

from the embankment. The boat made an awful grating noise. We looked at Johnny, horrified.

'*No hay problema*,' Johnny cried over the noise. 'It's a motor! It is what moves the boat!'

The men tucked their poles away and the boat swung out into the middle of the river, just missing two small boys paddling by in a hollowed tree trunk. A man raised his hat as he floated past on what looked like a raft made of coconuts. We sailed down the river.

Tilin nudged me with her shoulder. 'I can't wait to see the ship!'

I looked at her. Her hair was whipping around her face, her cheeks were tinged with pink. Her excitement was infectious.

'No more rice paddies to plant!' I cried.

'No more grain to thresh!' Tilin giggled.

'No more . . .' I looked at her. 'No more marrying people we don't want to marry.'

We both shrieked with laughter. But Sidong tugged on my sleeve.

'Don't you love Samkad anymore, Luki?' she said.

I threw my arms around her and gave her a squeeze. But I had no answer for her. Right now, all I wanted was to get on board the *Shawmut*.

'America is going to be amazing, Luki,' Tilin said dreamily, holding her arm out over the water to feel the cool sea breeze. 'I know it!'

A huge wave. The boat rose up and then splashed down, and

I realized that we had left the river behind. Gusts of wind dampened our faces with light sprays of sea water. We were in the ocean.

'*¡Allá! Ahí está vuestro barco,*' Johnny cried. 'There it is!'

In the distance, almost where the sky touched the sea, stood the *Shawmut*, tall in the water, with steep black sides and a huge funnel. The swirling waves that had our little boat bouncing up and down had no effect on the great boat. It stood there, still as a rock.

We could see the steps suspended at a diagonal along the ship's steep side. Ropes were thrown and tied, and soon our boat was fastened to the stairway.

Johnny held out his hand.

'This is goodbye?' Tilin said.

'No, no!' Johnny said. 'The Constabulary Band is going to America too. But we are taking another ship. We will soon join you in Saint Louis!'

It pleased me to hear that, Mother – it was good to know that we would have at least one friend in America.

I gazed up the ship's enormous black side. At the top I could see beams and ropes, strings of tiny flags, an enormous smokestack, and heads looking down at us over the rail.

'We'll have to step over the ocean to get to the stairs!' Tilin looked a little panicky.

I felt my stomach lurching, but I grabbed Johnny's hand and quickly stepped across.

I held my hand out to Tilin and soon she was standing next to me on the little platform.

Johnny lifted Sidong into our arms. 'Go on,' he said. 'We will wait until you are safely on board.'

'Shall we go to America, Luki?' Tilin said.

'Let's go!' I replied gaily.

Step by step we climbed, with Sidong between us. Looking up at the ship, it had seemed immoveable, but now I realized it was moving on top of the waves. The stairway banged against its side, keeping time to the pounding of my heart. Soon we had reached the top and stepped over a metal lintel. A burly man slammed a gate shut behind us. The floor was crammed with wooden crates, trunks, bags and people of all sorts – highlanders, lowlanders and some who looked like they were neither. High above it all was a balcony crowded with Americans watching the scene below.

'Luki.'

My heart leaped. I stared at the smiling face, the lean planes slightly shadowed by stubble, the dark hair hanging long over his forehead.

'Samkad! What are you doing here?' Tilin cried.

But I couldn't speak. I could feel a pulse in the soles of my feet. I wanted to run away. But where could I run? We were in the middle of an ocean.

Samkad scratched the back of his head, the way he always did when he'd done something he knew would upset me. He reached out to touch me but I drew back. 'Luki, let me explain.'

'I don't think Luki wants to talk to you,' Tilin said.

But Samkad stepped between us, turning his back on Tilin. He spoke quickly, his voice heavy with emotion. 'I'm sorry I avoided you before you left. I was just so . . . disappointed. I thought it was over between us. But when you'd gone, I realized I couldn't bear to be away from you. I needed to be with you, Luki. So I followed you. But when I caught up with the group, you and Tilin had gone missing. I'm so relieved they found you. I can't believe I'm here! I can't believe we're together again.'

He raised a hand and took a step towards me.

I didn't think, Mother. I just grabbed his arm and swung him into the ship's rail. Then I bent down, scooped up his legs, and heaved him over the side, into the sea.

Part Two

11

Leaving

I watched him vanish in a white puff of sea foam. After a moment, his head bobbed up to the surface, hair now slicked back, eyes shocked, mouth open, gasping and shouting. But I couldn't hear him for the explosion of noise around me as people rushed to the rail to have a look. The ocean began to swell. Bigger and bigger and bigger until it swallowed Samkad's little head. What had I done? But Mother, I couldn't help it. How dare he push himself into my life, as if what I wanted had meant nothing.

Hands pushed me aside. Voices boomed. *Man overboard, man overboard!*

Then the giant wave began to roll away and there was Samkad, coughing up sea water and shaking the hair from his eyes.

Johnny's boat was still tethered to the stairway and the

boatmen soon pulled Samkad out of the water, glistening like a freshly born baby. Cheers erupted from the balcony above us. The Americans were enjoying the spectacle enormously.

I willed Samkad to stay in Johnny's boat, Mother. Stay on that boat and let Johnny take you back to the shore! But no. Samkad quickly hopped onto the stairway and began to make his way back up.

An iron hand closed around my arm. It was the man who'd been opening and shutting the gate. He grabbed Samkad with his other hand.

Truman Hunt came running. 'Wait! What are you doing?'

'Taking them to the captain,' the man said. 'Him over there.'

He pointed at the balcony. A tall man with long white whiskers and a visored hat was waving him on impatiently. 'Captain don't tolerate this kind of behaviour. The savages will have to leave the ship.'

Truman Hunt hurried alongside as the man steered us both through a door, up some stairs, and into a little room where the captain was now waiting.

The captain opened his mouth to speak, but Truman Hunt was already chattering away.

'Captain, sir, I am so sorry this happened. The Igorot are a simple people, sir, they are like children.'

The captain sighed. 'Hunt, you assured me it would be safe to allow these savages on board – and then this happens! I should have the whole lot of them sent back to shore.'

'It will not happen again, Captain, sir.' Hunt clutched his bowl hat to his chest and sighed. 'I promise!'

The captain turned to stare at Samkad. His eyes seemed to trace the swirl of tattoos on Samkad's chest.

'I chose these Igorots myself,' Truman Hunt said. 'I assure you, sir, these are the sweetest people in the world. Do not believe what the newspapers say about them being violent people. They are harmless. What happened was the result of a love quarrel. I will make sure the young man and young lady are kept apart throughout the journey. There will be no repeat of this incident.'

The captain kept shaking his head, but in the end he let us go.

When the door closed behind us, Hunt stopped and glared. 'I don't want any more trouble from the two of you. If you don't stay away from each other you'll be confined to quarters with no fresh air for the rest of the journey! Are we agreed?'

As I nodded, I glanced at Samkad. There was a smugness to his smile. As if he'd gotten away with something.

It was a good thing we weren't standing by the ship's rail, Mother. I would have thrown him back into the sea.

We could watch the changing shore from the small round windows of the women's room. On our first day of sailing, Tilin, Sidong and I sat on the bed for hours, staring. It was quite beautiful, rice fields turning into green jungle turning into sandy beach. And then, Mother, quite suddenly, mountains!

Tilin and I looked at each other. Somewhere in the melting blue of those distant mountains was the invisible world of our ancestors. Somewhere up there were our friends and neighbours working on their rice paddies, and the ancients sitting around the fires. Everyone that we had left behind.

And then the mountains vanished and soon the land was gone too, and there was only ocean and sky left for us to watch.

Back home, I was used to sleeping in the House for Women, to the heat of so many bodies in the same space, the noises of many women dreaming. But in the *Shawmut*'s room for women, there must have been two hundred beds crammed together under a low ceiling. I had never been so close to so many strangers.

Most of the other women in the room for women were lowlanders called 'Visayans'. They rolled their hair high on their heads, wrapped skirts on top of skirts, wore several blouses all at once . . . and then stared at us as if we were the ones who looked odd.

Tilin said to not mind them, but many times I caught her watching the Visayan women with a wondering look, as if she was trying to imagine what *she* would look like if she twirled her hair and wore double skirts too.

There were also people called Mangyans, who dressed simply but covered themselves in beads, and there were people in breechcloths and simple clothing who told us they were called Aetas, but whom everyone insisted on calling Negritos, the way everybody called us Igorots.

They were all going to Saint Louis. I felt foolish, thinking that President Roosevelt had only invited Bontoks.

Later, the ship stopped at a port called Yokohama, and a large family got on board. The men were heavily bearded and the women had tattoos around their mouths. I wasn't surprised to hear that President Roosevelt had invited them too.

I wondered if Theodore Roosevelt would be pleased by this turnout. What would it be like when Truman Hunt finally presented us to him? Would his English be easy to understand? Would I manage to find words in my throat so that he could understand *me*? Surely he would be delighted to meet us. I imagined pouring him a cup of tapuy, how he would be amazed at its rich flavour and grateful for the gift of our friendship.

The part of the ship we lived in was called 'steerage'. Americans lived on the ship's upper floors. Whenever we came out to the open deck, we could hear them talking, laughing, even singing on the balcony. But the only Americans we saw in steerage were Truman Hunt and the other managers, or the crew.

We got used to life on the ship very quickly. Got used to sleeping with so many women in the same room. Got used to the beds built one on top of the other. Got used to water coming out of tubes in the toilet. Got used to sitting on a bowl to make water and move our bowels. Got used to pulling a chain to make it all disappear. Got used to eating on a long table, with food and drink served in tin pails.

At first Samkad kept trying to speak to me. He seemed to be everywhere, waiting outside doors, standing in dark corners, hovering in the long, narrow corridors. 'We have to talk,' he whispered whenever I walked past. 'Come, we can talk outside.'

Mother, I was sorely tempted! I kept my lips firmly pressed together and refused to look at him. I wasn't going to allow him to talk me into marrying him. After a while, he gave up. And when everyone was out on deck, enjoying the sunshine and fresh air, he no longer crossed to our side of the *Shawmut*.

That was how it was, Mother. Even when I saw him with Kinyo and I burned with curiosity to know whether the brothers had called a truce, I stayed away. Sidong liked to play with him, but I stayed away. And I stayed away even though I wanted to tell him about every new thing. For days and days and days. I told myself that was how it should be.

The weeks passed. The sky darkened and an icy wind began to blow. People ceased to venture on deck, preferring the warmth of the stuffy indoors. Even Tilin stopped going outside. She busied herself with finding ways to entertain Sidong, watching over the little girl as she drew incessantly in her ledger.

But no matter the weather, I made my way outside. Often I was the only person on the slippery deck, leaning on the rail and watching the clouds thickening then dissolving then thickening again, watching the great grey ocean swilling about beneath the *Shawmut*.

One early evening, when the moon was already casting a yellow ripple in the ocean swell, I heard a low wail. It wasn't human, I was sure of it. Then there it was again. Deeper this time. Then I felt it, a humming. It was in the ocean. It was in the air. It travelled through the cold metal of the rail and into my fingers. And then I could feel it coursing in my blood. The ocean was singing.

And then, slowly, beneath the waves, something moved. I leaned out, out, across the rail, not caring that the icy spray was needling me.

A shadow pressed up against the surface. The water began to cascade around it like a waterfall.

A great eye opened, the iris glistening and grey around a massive black pupil.

The ocean looked at me.

It was an eye that had seen many things, that knew the answer to many mysteries. If the ancients had been here, they would have known what to say.

I swallowed. 'Ocean, what do you know?' I whispered. 'What awaits me in America?' My knuckles shone white on the rail.

For a moment, I thought I saw a spark, a tiny flash of light in that massive eye.

But then the lid pulled down. The waters swirled inwards. The ocean looked away and though I listened hard, I could no longer hear its song.

12

America

At first America was just a shadow on the horizon, just a suggestion. And then it became longer and darker. And soon we could see green swathes that could be trees, and the shapes of rocks. And then we weren't in open sea any more, because we were sailing between islands, we could just see their shorelines in the distance. And then the water became narrower, great white birds flocked around us, and we could see branch and leaf and bark of the trees massing on the shore. The water became narrower still. And the land began to close in.

All day, passengers had crowded the deck, watching America approach. There was a sociable atmosphere, the air humming with eagerness and conversation. But at mid-afternoon, when it became obvious that the *Shawmut* would soon be touching land, the hum turned into silence. Forty-nine days we had been at sea, Mother. It felt momentous. It was hard to believe our time on water was coming to an end.

Tilin had hoisted Sidong up in her arms to see. They leaned against me as we watched the thin line of the shore turn into a small city.

The city was called Tacoma and, Mother, in the lowering sun, the sweep of brick buildings gleamed like gold. Hundreds of columns of smoke spiralled from every rooftop. It was a hilly place, the buildings seeming to stack one on top of the other. From the boat, the horse-drawn carts moving up and down steep streets looked tiny. Behind the city loomed a great white mountain. A *white* mountain! How could that be?

On the waterfront, a huddle of boats made a twiggy forest with their masts. A wooden platform jutted right out into the ocean. We could see another ship already tethered to it, and hundreds of tiny figures swarming on it like ants. Soon the *Shawmut* would be taking its place there too.

Unexpectedly, I found myself searching the crowd around us for Samkad. I felt myself blush. Having avoided him for forty-nine days, why was I seeking him out now? Habit? Had I forgotten my rage? I had walked away from marriage and he'd followed, thinking himself irresistible.

Samkad was standing with a group of Bontok men on the rail across the deck from us. The breeze riffled through his dark hair. Like everyone else, his gaze was distant and dreamy, watching the approaching shore. He was not looking for me like I was looking for him.

Mother, how could I be so foolish? How could I claim I didn't want him and yet feel this need to see him?

Slowly, slowly, the *Shawmut* turned its great bulk until it was parallel to the wooden platform, which Truman Hunt called a 'pier'. Men ran alongside, shouting as ropes were thrown. When the *Shawmut* finally came to a halt, we all erupted into cheers of joy and relief. On the balcony above us, the Americans whistled and clapped and threw their hats in the air.

We were in America at last.

Later, when the sun slipped behind a grey cloud, we began to feel the American cold. The pier's icy wooden boards stung the soles of our bare feet. It felt like the freezing air was rubbing our faces raw. We pressed our hands against our cheeks to warm them, only to find them numbed with cold. The Americans disembarked, pulling hats over their heads, wrapping their necks in warm cloths, and sheathing their fingers in thick mitts. And then everyone gasped to see that Kinyo, whom we had envied his warmer American clothes, had changed into his old breechcloth. Like us, he had to tug a blanket around his neck for warmth.

'He promised Truman Hunt that he would dress like an Igorot when we got to America,' Tilin whispered.

Truman Hunt was looking at us anxiously. His voice was apologetic as he began to speak. Kinyo translated: 'First of all, Tacoma is a cold place and it will be much warmer in Saint

Louis, which is further south. The Northern Pacific Railway has prepared warm clothing for you at the station, which is a very short walk from here. At the station, we will board the train to Saint Louis. Don't worry, it won't be cold on the train. They use steam to keep the train heated.'

Which was a relief to hear, because he'd told us that the train journey to Saint Louis was going to take five days. Five days! That is how big America is, Mother. Had we taken the train to Manila, it would have taken us one day instead of five days' walking. But the train to Manila didn't allow Igorots, according to Truman Hunt.

'What is that noise?' Sidong suddenly said.

It was a strange howling from the end of the pier, where passengers stepped onto the streets of Tacoma.

Truman Hunt leaped up on a wooden crate, talking so quickly Kinyo could barely keep up. 'Hear that? Those are people! Hundreds have come to Tacoma to see YOU!' He threw his arms wide. 'All the newspapers have been writing about your arrival for months. Igorots are famous. People are desperate to meet Igorots!'

Mother, I was nervous as we trudged down the long, icy platform. If I had learned anything from our hateful encounters in Manila, it was not to expect a warm welcome. It didn't help that my feet had become unused to solid ground. I found myself staggering as if the ocean was still rolling underfoot.

The pier ended in a cobbled road flanked by buildings. It was packed with people. As we approached, the howling sound rose to a deafening din. '*Igorot! Igorot! Igorot!*' There were people standing shoulder to shoulder on steps and in doorways, faces peered out every window, men perched on the branches of trees, and small boys sat on the crossbeams of every lamppost.

They stared at us with wide eyes and big grins on their faces, they reached out as if they were desperate to touch us. The only thing that held them back were rows of men in blue uniforms clutching wooden clubs.

Truman Hunt yelled, 'Igorots! Stay together!' For once, none of us protested that we should be called Suyoc or Bontok or Tinguian.

The men in blue made a narrow corridor for us to pass through but the sight of us emboldened the crowd. 'Hey! Hey!' they shouted. '*Igorot!*'

One man broke through the cordon, and the men in blue promptly struck him with their clubs, forcing him back.

'I can't tell if they want to embrace us or they want to eat us,' I whispered to Tilin.

We were relieved to follow Truman Hunt into the train station. We walked into a building, through a narrow room and out again onto a long platform, already crowded with the other groups going to Saint Louis. I wondered if the crowd had been just as wild for them.

Truman Hunt signalled us to stand around him. 'That wasn't so bad was it?' he beamed. 'Now we just have to wait for the train.'

A yellow-haired boy dragged a huge sack to Truman Hunt.

'Ah, this must be the warm clothing from the Northern Pacific people.'

The boy could not take his eyes off us, his eyes darting around in their sockets, as if he was trying to see every single one of us at the same time.

'Sir, is it safe, sir?' he squeaked.

Truman Hunt frowned. 'What do you mean, boy?'

'Sir, them's being wild people, sir. They're not going to chop my head off, are they?'

The boy was mumbling, but I understood everything he said. Why would we chop his head off?

'That's what they think we do here in America.'

I flinched to hear the familiar voice speaking in Bontok. Samkad was just behind me, easing his pack onto the floor. His face was flat, expressionless, as if nothing important had ever happened between us. 'They call us headhunters, you know.'

'Son,' Truman Hunt was saying to the boy, 'don't you worry, I'm their manager. They won't be chopping any heads off as long as I'm here.'

The boy pushed the sack towards Truman Hunt. 'Compliments of the Northern Pacific Railway, sir.'

'Are they donations?'

'Yes sir.' The boy looked nervously around him. 'There was a box, right there on the platform. But it weren't enough. So the boss, sir, the station master, he got a writing to all the undertakers for miles around. And the undertakers obliged by writing to their customers. And they were plenty obliging, sir. The kinfolk of the dead had plenty of coats to spare.

Kinyo frowned. 'How do I translate "undertakers"?'

'That's what you call people who get the dead ready for burial.' Truman Hunt reached into the sack and held up a thick blue coat.

Suddenly, Samkad was there, snatching the coat from him. 'These . . . belong to dead?' I could see that Samkad was searching for the right words in English.

Truman Hunt snatched the coat back and stuffed it into the sack. 'Well . . . I guess you could say that. But they don't need it any more, do they?' He pushed the sack towards Kinyo. 'Son, you'd better begin handing these out before people turn into icicles.'

But Samkad was pushing the sack towards the yellow-haired boy, who was staring at him with terrified eyes.

'You!' he said. 'You keep.'

The boy screamed. He ran down the platform and into the station door.

'What the hell!' Hunt cried.

Samkad turned to Kinyo. 'Tell Truman Hunt we cannot wear these. We cannot offend the dead in this country. Please, brother, translate this for me.'

'They are gifts! It would be rude to return a gift.' Kinyo shook his head. 'We're in America now. Things are different here.'

'What? Do you think the spirits of the dead are any different here in America than they are in Bontok? It will insult them for us to wear these! They will bring harm upon us!'

'What is he saying?' Truman Hunt demanded.

Kinyo translated with a resigned look on his face.

'Superstition!' Truman Hunt cried. 'You're being ridiculous, this is a freezing cold climate. I order you to put these coats on!'

Mother, hearing him say that, I realized I was shivering. He was right. We could not bear this cold any longer.

But Samkad was shaking his head angrily. 'They are not the gifts of the dead but of the living.'

I stared at Samkad. I knew that stubborn look. It was that look of certainty. It was the look on his face when he assumed I would say, *Yes, let us become husband and wife, I shall start planting camote and having babies*.

I stepped forward and reached into the sack.

'Tilin,' I said. 'Come and have a look.'

Mother, I was freezing. An American coat was just what I needed.

13

The Dead

Samkad was silent as Tilin and I chose coats for ourselves and for Sidong. Kinyo was right. We were in America now. The Americans gifted us the coats. Surely that must mean that they know the American dead would not take offence. Perhaps the dead in Bontok were more easily outraged. We should wear the coats and be grateful.

The other Igorots seemed to agree. Every single one took a coat from the sack.

See, Mother, how naturally I called us Igorots.

The Americans knew us as Igorots. We were in America now, why would we not also call ourselves Igorots?

'It is like a snake,' Sidong observed when the train arrived at last. It did look like a snake, its head a great black thing with a large chimney poking out of its nose, that exhaled thick clouds of smoke. Its long body was made up of joined up little houses called 'cars'.

Truman Hunt gathered us together to point at a tall, thin man who was shouting instructions at some men loading baggage into the cars. 'That's the conductor,' he said. 'He's like the captain of the *Shawmut*. You all mind him now. He's in charge.'

Truman Hunt and the other managers took forever to settle us in the cars and show us where the supplies of food were kept and the little stove to heat water on and the toilet stall with its little bowl and chain to dispose of our waste. They gave us each enough rations for the five-day journey, food in tins that had to be cut open with a sharp tool, and something called 'hard tack', squares of tasteless biscuit that would not spoil during the trip.

'Don't worry, I'll be looking out for you,' Truman Hunt said. But he went to sit in another car, with the other Americans.

More shouting. Then, as the train hissed and gasped, we began to move.

We were so hungry that we had managed to eat the tasteless food without complaint. Afterwards, Sidong sat between us, her head on Tilin's lap and her feet on mine, and everyone in the car fell into an exhausted sleep.

Everyone but me, Mother. I wanted to look out the window and watch America flowing by like a river. I wanted to examine Tacoma's great white mountain. I wanted to see all the forests and fields and small settlements. I saw men working in fields. I saw children playing. There were blue mountains, boulders, canyons, and streams white with rapids. And then I watched the sun set. Could it really be the very same sun that lit the skies over Bontok?

Everything amazed me, Mother. Seeing America was like eating an enormous meal. It filled my belly.

And then everything went dark. I could still feel the vastness of the country, sliding silently past. I could really feel my exhaustion now and I fell into a dream, like a stone.

I was standing at the ship's rail, staring at the boiling ocean. The ocean's eye opened in the white froth. It glared at me. And then, Mother, it turned into a great black mouth, opening wider and wider. I was falling into the ocean's throat.

But then I opened my eyes; I was back on the train. Sparks from the train engine were flying into the window. I tried to turn my head, but I couldn't. I tried to stand but I couldn't. I was made of rock and earth and I could not move.

Then a hand, gleaming white, thrust into my vision. It grabbed the lapels of my new coat.

'Mine.' I heard the voice, but it was so quiet, it might as well not have been there. 'Give it back.'

I could feel fingers moving down my front, unfastening the buttons. The coat fell open. It was dragged from my body, the sleeves peeling painfully off my arms like skin.

In the aisle, there was movement. A swarming. A darkness. It paused at each seat, swirling around each frozen person. One by one by one.

I heard more voices, rising over the steady thundering of the train.

'Mine.'

'Mine.'

'Mine.'

'Luki! Wake up!' I opened my eyes. Was that Truman Hunt? What was he doing in our carriage?

He was shaking Tilin awake. 'Tilin! Tilin!'

I tried to open my eyes but I couldn't. I tried to breathe but my lungs felt like they had shrunk to nothing.

'Luki!' Tilin's voice. She sounded frenzied. 'Luki!'

Strong fingers shook me violently. 'Luki!'

Samkad!

I opened my eyes.

Samkad and Tilin stood over me. Next to me, Sidong was watching with frightened eyes. Truman Hunt was somewhere up ahead, trying to wake someone else up.

I blinked and something crumbled from my face. Was that ice? Samkad still had his hands on my shoulders and I pushed him away. I realized that I wasn't breathing and opened my mouth, opened my throat and air filled my lungs. When I finally exhaled, my breath turned into cloud. But now my teeth were chattering so hard I clapped a hand over my mouth to make them stop.

'Are you all right?' Samkad whispered.

I nodded, but I couldn't make words leave my throat.

Tilin sat down and wrapped her arms around Sidong. I could hear the soft chatter of their teeth. I could hear the clatter of the wheels on the tracks. But the air was so cold it cut into me like a knife. It hurt to breathe.

My shivering became violent. I clapped my hands hard on my face and I felt the blood rush to my cheeks.

Samkad, clutching a blanket around his shoulders was racing up and down the carriage with Truman Hunt and Kinyo, shaking people awake.

The door at the end of the carriage opened. It was the conductor.

'What's going on in here?'

Truman Hunt spun round, glaring at him. 'You!' he bellowed. 'Turn the damned heating on!'

The conductor snorted dismissively. 'They'll be fine. Savages don't need heating.'

Truman Hunt lowered his head like a boar on the attack. 'Turn the heating on, dammit.'

'Oh, come on,' the other man scoffed. 'Look at them. They're used to it.'

Hunt marched towards him, speaking so fast, I couldn't understand what he was saying. He reached for the conductor and just about grabbed the man's lapels when we all heard a most peculiar sound. A strangled noise. And then weeping.

Hunt turned.

Kinyo's voice was high pitched and panicky. 'Mister Hunt! Mister Hunt!'

'What is it, boy?' Hunt clattered down the aisle.

Tilin and I stood up on our bench to see. Kinyo was trying to wake two men. Their faces were unnaturally pale. Their heads lolled around. Their eyes were shut tight.

'Are they dead?' Tilin whispered. People got to their feet and crowded the aisle.

'Wake up! Wake up!' someone implored. 'Tilt their heads back and open their mouths,' Samkad called from somewhere. 'Help them breathe!'

I glanced over my shoulder. The conductor was lighting a pipe. He made no effort to join the crowd around the two men.

'They're frozen!' I heard Kinyo say. Everyone rushed to fetch blankets, passing them overhead to Truman Hunt and Kinyo.

'Breathe. Breathe.' Truman Hunt was half sobbing.

But as everyone pressed around them, I collapsed heavily next to Sidong. She threw her arms around me and buried her face in my shoulder. The cold clamped down on us, like a heavy hand. The coach seemed to be filling with a white haze. I could still hear the voices in my dream.

'Mine.'

'Mine.'

'Mine.'

The carriage was warming slowly. We all sat, stunned by the heat. Going from cold to hot felt like being burned, Mother.

Like you were sitting too close to a fire. I could feel my blood moving sluggishly, and then faster, sending crackles of pain all over my body.

At the back of the carriage, I could hear Truman Hunt. 'Wrap them up with those blankets, there you go.' He said. 'Now, gently, gently, you take the feet, you the head.' Kinyo's voice was like an echo, translating in the background.

Truman Hunt edged past, followed by Kinyo and several of the men carrying the two blanket-shrouded bodies. They took them out of the carriage door to the freight car where baggage was stored.

Afterwards, Truman Hunt told us solemnly: 'They will be undisturbed until the end of this journey. We will bury them when we get to Saint Louis. I will make sure these men are accorded the respect and care they deserve.'

I glanced over my shoulder at the fearful faces behind me, I knew what everyone was wondering. In Bontok, the spirits of the newly dead would have joined the invisible world of our ancestors. But we were not in Bontok. Where would these souls go?

And Samkad had been right. By taking the coats, we had angered the spirits of their dead owners. They had come in my dream, these American ghosts, and plucked the coats from each of our backs. And then killed two of us for good measure. The two men were kin to no one. They only had us to mourn them, which was not the same as friends and family. Had they been in Bontok, their families would have built death chairs for them, and sat them down before a good fire. They would have conversed with them, to ease their way into the world of the dead. They would have sung the songs that would signal their arrival in the invisible world, to give them the best chance of a good life there.

The American spirits had doomed them and avenged themselves.

The train spat and snorted. The heat settled on us like guilt.

Then Samkad rose. 'We need to honour them,' he said, simply. 'They did not deserve a death like this.'

Samkad took his gangsa and began to play a funeral rhythm. One by one, the other men joined him in the narrow aisle of the train, beating their gangsas. He began to sing. He begged the dead to remain our allies and do us no harm. He begged the American dead to welcome these strangers into their invisible world. He begged their forgiveness. On each side of the aisle, we women raised our arms in dance and added our voices to their song.

We did our best, Mother.

But were we too late? Did the souls of Americans listen to strangers?

When we finished, what we had to do next was obvious. Samkad was right. There was no question that the coats were not ours to keep.

We took the coats off and threw them out of the windows into the darkness.

14

Saint Louis

Afterwards, the heating in our car rose to a fever.

'The conductor has decided to boil us to death,' Tilin said.

I smiled at her joke, but it was hard not to be affected by the fearful mood in the car. What if it happened to us? What if we died here, in America? What would happen to our souls? I turned away so that Tilin couldn't see the worry on my face. Suddenly we could all see what death would mean here in America. It meant cold and exile and being alone forever. If I died here, Mother, if I never returned to Bontok, my spirit would never be reunited with yours. You and I were going to be lonely forever.

'Tilin, this was a big mistake,' I whispered. 'Mother would never forgive me if I died here!'

Tilin looked at me as if I'd lost my mind. 'Luki, if you can hunt boar, you can stay alive until it's time for us to return home,' she scolded. 'Look at us, we are healthy right now . . . and we are going to stay that way!' And then she made me eat a dry cracker and half a tin of beans.

It was hard to shake the feeling though. It was hard not to listen to the mutterings of the others, regretting that they had ever thought it was a good idea to come. Nobody felt safe.

When Truman Hunt next visited us, he stared at our bare shoulders. 'What's this? Where are your coats? What happened?'

Kinyo explained, telling Truman Hunt we had no choice but to throw the coats away, otherwise the dead would punish us with even more horrible calamities.

I was gratified to see Truman Hunt listening with a thoughtful expression, arms folded across his chest. When Kinyo finished, all he did was raise his head to say, 'I am truly sorry for your loss.'

And that was all.

America continued to flow by at an incredible pace. But inside the train, the hours lumbered by at an achingly leisurely pace. We sat, ate, sat, ate, sat, ate, then slept. The next day we had to do it all over again.

The only highlight was Truman Hunt's daily visit. He would turn up, red-faced from the walk through so many carriages. Then he would stand at one end of our car, talking.

He must have sensed our doubts because, after asking about our wellbeing, and whether we had enough food, and if we were keeping the toilet clean, he would try to remind us of the delights that awaited us in Saint Louis.

'It is no ordinary celebration, it is a World's Fair!' he gushed. 'There will be sights and sounds you've never seen before. The best of America will be on display. You will see things you did not even know could be imagined.'

The first time he had told us it was called a World's Fair, we had looked at him blankly. We knew what 'World' meant, but Kinyo struggled to translate 'Fair' – 'A celebration,' he said, 'such as the feasts we have after the harvest.' But Truman Hunt seemed to be describing something bigger.

He said there would be grand buildings and statues and water fountains and people from faraway lands dressed in different costumes. He said there would be demonstrations of new technology such as machines that could send and receive messages through thin air, there would be cars that could fly, and there were even machines that could take pictures of the bones inside your body. There would be giant animals that we'd never seen before. He knew for a fact that there would be a horse that could talk and count.

It sounded incredible, Mother, hard to believe. 'He's exaggerating,' Tilin giggled.

'I'm not exaggerating,' Truman Hunt said. 'You will see for yourself, I promise I will take you around myself! I can't wait!'

Even so, the hours between Truman Hunt's visits dragged slowly by and after a while, even his cheerful talks became boring too.

The souls of the dead men were definitely bored too, Mother, because they began to have some fun with us. They tickled our throats with hacking coughs. They made us sneeze and caused our noses to stream. They made our bellies reject our food so that we all had to take turns throwing up into the carriage toilet. The Tinguian did some sort of dance in the narrow aisle to appease them. The Suyoc sang an appeal to the dead. And we Bontok tried pounding our gangsas to beg their forgiveness.

When we finally arrived in Saint Louis many of us were red-eyed and snivelling. Truman Hunt had promised that Saint Louis wouldn't be as cold as Tacoma, but it was still much chillier than our blankets were made for.

The dead continued to play their teasing games, unbalancing us as we struggled to heave our packs onto our backs, knocking spears and axes out of our hands, tripping us up as we climbed down from the carriage's high step to the platform.

I saw Truman Hunt talking to a man writing on a small pad.

Tilin and I trudged past with Sidong in tow, sneezing and coughing. The man raised an eyebrow. 'The Igorots look rather worse for wear. Are they struggling with the climate?'

'The Northern Pacific Railway kindly took up a collection to provide them with coats,' Hunt said. 'But on the way here, they threw all the coats out the window.' He raised his shoulders and held up his hands. 'You have to understand, these are *wild people*, sir. They would rather be naked than warm.'

'Fascinating,' the man murmured, scribbling on his pad.

'Mister Hunt!' I called. 'Why you say that?' My ears were better tuned to American words now. I had understood the whole exchange, Mother. Was Truman Hunt making a joke? Why would he tell the man we'd rather be naked?

But Truman Hunt was lunging to retrieve a small Suyoc boy who was toddling in the wrong direction. He didn't hear me.

It was such a long queue out of the Saint Louis train station that we couldn't even see the Visayans who were at the head of the line. There was a cordon of men in blue again, except their uniforms were fancier, with high red collars and bright gold buttons.

Truman Hunt gathered us together. 'Now listen, everyone,' Kinyo translated. 'These men are called the Jefferson Guard. They will be policing the World's Fair. They are here to protect you. If you are ever in trouble, just look for a Jefferson Guard and he will help you.'

Like Tacoma, there was an excited throng waiting for us. Once again, we found ourselves walking between lines of blue-clad men. After all of Truman Hunt's briefings, we were so excited to see the fair, I thought we would walk out of the station and instantly find ourselves gawking at all these amazing things.

But no. There were only people, jostling and shouting. 'There they are! The Igorots!' 'Hey, hey, hey!' 'Igorot! Igorot!'

Truman Hunt looked at us as if we should be pleased at

104

such an exuberant welcome. 'Wave!' Truman Hunt shouted over his shoulder. 'These people have been waiting for hours to catch a glimpse of you!'

But, Mother, the squirming, reaching mass made me feel exposed. I felt like running away.

The police line shook as the mob pushed against it. A small dog burst out of the crowd and hurried to us, wagging its tail. Sidong bent to pat it.

'Keep your hands off her!' someone screamed. A woman crawled under a policeman's arm and, snatching the dog up, raced back into the crowd as if we'd chased her away.

Sidong looked up at me puzzled. I shrugged. 'Don't mind her, everyone looks frantic,' I murmured, taking her hand.

A man suddenly appeared, reaching for the plug in my earlobe. I slapped his hand away, snapping, 'Don't touch me!' A guardsman grabbed him and dragged him away. 'Igorot!' the crowd shouted. 'Igorot!'

Up ahead, I heard a cry. 'Here they come!' Someone tossed something in the air that spattered down on the heads of a group of men, chanting: 'This is the water of everlasting life!'

'Ignore them!' Truman Hunt yelled. As we hurried past, icy droplets of water sprinkled down on us. From behind the police barrier, a woman screamed: *EVERLASTING LIFE! EVERLASTING LIFE!'*

Someone grabbed my elbow. 'Leave me alone!' I snapped.

But it was Sidong. 'Luki, something is wrong with Tilin!' she cried.

'Nothing's wrong!' Tilin grunted.

But I could see that Tilin was sweating, even though it was freezing, and we didn't have coats any more. Her hair was soaked, her blouse was sticking to her back. Her eyes were glazed and the way she put one foot in front of the other, she might as well have been dream-walking. Her upper lip was practically a wound from all her rubbing.

'You don't look good,' I said.

She glared at me with bleary eyes. 'Nobody could possibly look good after five days in a train.'

Samkad was suddenly next to us. 'Do you need to sit?' He put a hand on her forehead. 'You feel hot.'

'We can manage,' I told him. 'We don't need your help.'

Tilin shook her head. 'I can't sit with a million strangers watching.'

'Sit,' I said. 'Just sit on your heels. We will stand here and shield you from their eyes.'

She shook her head again.

I felt Sidong's hand tugging. 'Luki, look, up there!'

I raised my head nervously, fearful that another hand would make a grab for my ears, or somebody would try to throw more water at us.

I saw the sky, as big and blue as it had been over Bontok. And then I saw a wheel. It confused me. How could it be up there against the sky, as if someone had lifted it up and hung it on a hook? It was rotating slowly. And then I saw that there were train carriages, dangling from it at intervals, like fruit.

Tiny carriages, Mother, with windows and all. And inside them, figures in the windows, moving. People, Mother, so far away, they looked like insects. It reminded me of how, looking down at the cascade of valleys below Bontok, I had often thought about lowlanders with pity, crawling like ants on their flat lands, unable to see beyond their own noses.

But here, the Americans had simply built themselves a giant wheel. They had created their own advantage. 'Tilin!' I cried. 'Tilin, look!'

But then Sidong began to wail.

And there was Samkad, kneeling.

And there on the ground lay Tilin.

She had landed on her back. That is, she had landed on her pack, which was a great basket, filled with blankets and provisions. Her arms were spread wide, her face was flushed and her eyes were slightly open, as if she was watching us from under her lids.

Mother, for a terrible moment, I thought she was dead. 'We are healthy and we are going to stay that way,' she'd said, but now she was dead. Mother, I felt a sudden anguish in my chest, like a monstrous hand had wrapped around me and squeezed. Tears flew out of my eyes. I was shocked by how quickly I began mourning this girl who had unexpectedly become my friend.

Then I saw that her chest was rising and falling rapidly. My anguish gave way to relief.

Someone in the crowd had handed Samkad a bottle of

water. For once the crowd was silent, goggling at us with their mouths open. He splashed some on her face and she groaned. In seconds, she was pushing herself up and shaking herself. 'What happened?' she asked groggily.

'Drink, drink,' Samkad said, putting the bottle into her hands.

She drank.

We helped her to her feet. Tilin scowled at all the gawking faces around us, but it was me she snapped at. 'What are you staring at?'

And there was nothing to do but continue the journey. The mob on either side resumed their staring and chattering.

'I am all right, I am all right,' Tilin kept telling me.

But, though I let her be, I continued to watch her surreptitiously. She looked strange and dazed, her hairband slipping low over her eyes. She didn't look fine at all.

Samkad, who had been walking just behind us caught up. 'What about you, Luki? Are you feeling all right?'

'Leave me alone,' I said. 'Can't you see I'm busy?'

15

The Reservation

Samkad tied Tilin's pack to his own and took Sidong firmly by the hand.

Tilin feebly tried to push me off, but she couldn't manage on her own, and in the end we shuffled the rest of the way, with Tilin leaning heavily on my shoulder, and me whispering encouragements for her to put one foot in front of the other.

So, Mother, on that first day, we didn't see much of the glorious World's Fair Truman Hunt had been boasting about for weeks. And anyway, what was there to see, except guardsmen and crowds?

Soon, we arrived at a tall wooden fence. The crowd wailed as the guardsmen stopped them following us through the doorway. Oh, Mother, what a relief, to emerge on the other side to find trees and no crowds! The trees were young, standing in neat, evenly spaced rows, their branches arching over the path – nothing like our vine-tangled forest back home.

The mob's cries faded as we made our way down the path. Tilin seemed instantly better. Her eyes were brighter and though she walked unsteadily, she seemed much stronger.

A fresh breeze was blowing from a lake, just beyond the trees. Sidong let go of Samkad's hand and ran to the water. 'There's an island!' she called. 'Oh, look! I've seen that before!'

We joined Sidong on the lake's sandy bank.

'What do you see, little one?' Tilin was saying. And then she gasped.

I was staring at it in disbelief. There was a bridge crossing over to the island. It was a massive bridge, with stone columns rising out of the water supporting stone arches. Iron posts stood at intervals, curving delicately at the top to dangle lamps.

It was the very same bridge that we had fled across in Manila.

And on the other side were the same stone walls and inside it, the very city we had glimpsed from the bridge in Manila. Somehow, the Americans had plucked it from the other side of the ocean, and set it down here, in Saint Louis.

Truman Hunt waved at us to cross the bridge.

It was not the actual bridge, but a copy. And so was the walled city, with its looming black walls, complete with the American flag fluttering on top. A copy of the real one in Manila, without its stinky bog.

'This is the Philippine Reservation,' Truman Hunt announced.

I wouldn't have been surprised if someone had suddenly shaken me awake, because the Philippine Reservation felt like something in a dream. Hadn't we walked past these same buildings in Manila, bulging with fancy ironwork and sparkling with oyster shell shutters? And look, Mother, carabaos! Groves of bamboo! Banana trees. If it hadn't been so cold, I would have thought we'd somehow magicked ourselves back.

Then we heard the music – the same music we'd heard when we'd met Johnny. And there, in a field outside this other walled city, was the same round stage with its tiled roof. The men making music were the same Constabulary men. And standing there, waving a baton to the rhythm, was Lieutenant Walter Loving.

As Truman Hunt walked us past, Lieutenant Loving nodded.

'Can you see Johnny?' Tilin whispered. I tried to spot him, but we were moving too fast and soon we were in another part of the Reservation, and Truman Hunt was explaining that the different groups would be living in their own villages.

He pointed out a village of small, thatched huts by the lake for the Aeta called the Negrito Village. There was a cluster of large wood and stone houses for the Visayans called the Visayan Village. And behind a bamboo palisade was a village for us called the Igorot Village.

Looking around the Philippine Reservation, I couldn't

111

believe that President Roosevelt had created this for us. But how could I have imagined that he would deign to share a fire and sip tapuy with us? He was a big man, able to summon the world to his feet, able to order pieces of the Philippine Islands to be recreated in Saint Louis.

It made me feel very, very small.

16

The Igorot Village

The Igorot Village needed more building work before we could move there, Truman Hunt explained. He would take us to see it tomorrow.

For the meantime, we had to sleep in a building called a 'cuartel' which reminded me of the Constabulary barracks where Tilin, Sidong and I spent our last night in Manila. It was three storeys high, with large rooms filled with beds. There was a fire outside where we could cook and a building filled with lavatory stalls.

That first night, Tilin didn't look well at all, pale and squinting from a headache. She couldn't stop coughing. I was glad to lay her down on a bed and tuck a blanket around her.

'Is she going to die?' Sidong whispered as she lay down in bed beside me.

'Of course not!' I said cheerfully. 'Go to sleep now. I'm

113

sure she'll be fine in the morning.' But long into the night, I couldn't sleep, listening to Tilin's wracking coughs.

In the morning, there was a great cauldron of rice and some cured pork for breakfast. Tilin got up to eat but soon returned to bed, leaving her breakfast uneaten.

'Are you going to be all right?' Sidong asked, and Tilin laughed, pulling her little sister on top of her. 'I'm just tired!' But it didn't convince Sidong, who began to whisper into Tilin's shoulder.

'What are you doing?' I called. 'Truman Hunt is here. We are going to the Igorot Village now.'

'I'm telling Tilin's spirit to stay where she is because if she decides to wander, Tilin might die.'

Tilin laughed and kissed Sidong goodbye. When we left she was snoring.

It was not far to the Igorot Village behind its bamboo wall, so closely lashed together it was impossible to peek through to the other side.

Outside the tall entrance gates were little huts where, Truman Hunt said, people would buy tickets to enter the village. He unlatched the gates and pushed them open.

Eheh, Mother, it was not a village at all. It was a mess.

There were piles of lumber, bamboo and rubble everywhere. Several men, Constabulary by the looks of their uniforms, were labouring over the beginnings of huts, some just wooden posts. None of the huts had rooftops. The one building that looked finished was a little jail. It was a small box house with three walls, bars on one side and an iron roof. It was odd to see it. The Americans were always pressing the ancients to build a jail in our village, but the ancients saw no reason for it.

Truman Hunt looked happy though. 'The World's Fair does not open for a few weeks yet, and by then we should be done building the village. I had all these materials shipped from the islands,' he said. 'These men have made a start, but you will need to finish them. The thatch is arriving tomorrow, and you will have the chance to build the rooftops to your own satisfaction.'

Everyone began talking at once. The Suyoc pointed out that the buildings had the wrong supports and cross beams. The Tinguian complained that the houses should have been built higher above the ground on thicker posts. The Bontok from the lower valley protested that the walls should have been only shoulder high, while the Bontok from the upper valley complained that the walls should have been taller. And what about these carabao skulls tied to a post? At home, each skull would have represented a wedding, a death, or a moment of great import – but none of these could have happened in a place where no one had ever lived.

And then Samkad pointed out that there was no Council House where ancients could build their fire. No boulders arranged in a circle where ancients could sit. He looked scandalized.

Truman Hunt smirked at him. 'There is no Council House

because there are no ancients! No ancients to tell you what to do!'

Personally, I couldn't understand why everybody was complaining so much. Yes, the houses were not precisely like the ones we had at home, but we were not at home, we were in America! Anyway, we may have started out as different peoples – Bontoks, Tinguian and Suyocs – but we were Igorots now . . . and this was the Igorot Village. This thing President Roosevelt had created was incredible, we should just be glad to be part of it.

'Mister Hunt—' Samkad was trying to be heard above the clamour.

'There will be plenty of time to finish the houses before the World's Fair opens to the public,' Truman Hunt was saying. 'There is—'

'MISTER HUNT!'

Truman Hunt sighed, folded his arms across his chest and glared at Samkad. 'What?'

Samkad did not bother to ask Kinyo to translate. 'Where did you get?' he barked, pointing at a ledge above one of the doorways.

It was a row of human skulls.

Mother, remember when Samkad and I were little and we sneaked into the Council House on a dare and dragged out that basket packed with the skulls of our enemies? We got into so much trouble!

Old Pito found us and marched us before the other ancients

and made us beg for the forgiveness of the invisible world. 'These are not to be trifled with,' he had said. 'As long as we keep the skulls of our enemies, their spirits can do us no harm. These give us power and we must keep them hidden.'

When Americans came to Bontok, they were obsessed with seeing that basket. They wanted to make a photograph of it. But of course the ancients refused. Some Americans even offered money for them, but that made the ancients so angry, they ceased to be polite.

And now here they were. How did they get here?

'You steal!' Samkad cried. He lunged at Truman Hunt, swearing.

I threw myself between them. He may have been a full head shorter than Hunt, but Hunt was as soft as those small round loaves Johnny had fed us. Samkad would have squashed him, and then what?

Samkad glared at me.

'Samkad, you can't do that, we are visitors here,' I scolded. 'Give him a chance to explain.'

'Yes, Samkad, stop being so difficult,' Kinyo sighed.

But Samkad pointed a finger at Truman Hunt. 'Thief!' he roared, angry ligaments bulging in his neck.

I could feel Hunt quaking behind me.

'What are you going to do? Jump on a train? Go home?' I snapped. 'The Americans are our hosts. Show some respect!'

'Show respect when they show *us* no respect —'

'The skulls are NOT from Bontok,' Truman Hunt

interrupted. 'Kinyo, help me explain. We didn't steal them. We bought them. *Here*, in Saint Louis.'

They weren't Bontok skulls! See, Mother? No need to overreact.

Kinyo sounded breathless as he began to translate what Truman Hunt was saying. 'The skulls were very well guarded in Bontok, it would have been impossible to steal them, not that we would do something so disrespectful. But we felt that the village would look more authentic with skulls decorating the place.'

'Kinyo, tell him even so, the spirits of the dead to whom these skulls belong will not be happy to be used for decoration.'

Truman Hunt nodded solemnly. He put a hand on Samkad's shoulder. 'I salute you, Samkad, for advocating for your people. Thank you,' Kinyo translated. 'But we acquired these skulls from several scientific institutions where the dead donated their bones so that scientists could learn from them. I believe they would have considered it an honour to be part of the Igorot Village.'

Samkad shook Truman Hunt's hand off. 'Luki, can't you see how wrong it is? We would never display skulls back home.'

But I had already joined the others, who were examining a corner of the village that had been dug up to look like rice paddies.

17

Ashes

None of us were skilled thatchers. The ancients would have been in hysterics to see the rooftops we built on those huts.

'Well, if you narrowed your eyes and tilted your head to one side, they almost look right,' I reported to Tilin, who was still too ill to leave her bed. She laughed so hard, she ended up coughing for an hour.

Truman Hunt didn't need to squint. He thought our clumsy handiwork beautiful. He sighed with admiration. 'Lovely,' he murmured. 'Excellent work.'

When anyone pointed out to him that the huts didn't look like huts back home, Truman Hunt replied: '*You* are Igorot and *you* thatched them, therefore they *are* Igorot huts.'

I know what you're thinking, Mother. He called us Igorot! The truth was, we were weary of objecting to the word. The whole of America was calling us Igorot and we might as well be at ease with it.

We couldn't wait for the Igorot Village to be finished. The cuartel was next to the field where soldiers from the Philippine Scouts and Constabulary practised walking around carrying guns. This was called 'drilling' and they had to do it to the *ratatat* sound of a drum. And when the troops weren't drilling, the Constabulary Band was practising its tunes and making screeching noises with their instruments. Upstairs at the cuartel, the Visayans were also waiting for their village to be ready. They liked singing at all hours of the day and sometimes practised their dances, which involved pounding the floor with bamboo poles.

Mother, it was mayhem. We couldn't wait to move into a village that would be just for us.

The weather turned freezing, the bitter cold burning any exposed skin. All work had to stop until Truman Hunt came up with a sack of coats and rubber boots for us to wear. This time, he assured us, they definitely did not come from dead people.

'How do we know that is true?' Samkad said.

'If you don't think it's true, then don't wear a coat,' I snapped. It was hard to care when one's fingernails were regularly turning blue with the cold. Samkad refused a coat, but he wasn't too proud to borrow blankets from people who could spare them.

There weren't enough coats for everybody, so only a few people at a time could work at the Igorot Village. It didn't matter, people were happy not to work and Sidong wanted to be with Tilin anyway.

But I made sure I was one of the people who went to the village every day. I preferred the sky over my head and the open air, never mind the cold.

We had been working for a week the day two Philippine Scouts arrived and positioned themselves by the gate. The two lowlanders had smart blue uniforms and sour faces.

'They are here to keep you safe,' Truman Hunt explained. 'Fair officials have been rather alarmed by the mobs that have turned up. There is so much interest in you that officials have decided that the Igorot Village must be guarded at all times. The United States government has promised to return you safely to your homes when the fair is over. For your safety, it has been decided that you must not leave the Igorot Village without protection.'

Kinyo frowned. He turned to Truman Hunt. 'Sir, do you mean we are not allowed out of the Reservation at all? Not even to see the fair?'

'Sadly not, son,' Truman Hunt replied.

Samkad snorted. 'Eheh, they don't want us walking around freely because they're afraid nobody would *pay* to see us in the Igorot Village.'

'What did he say?' Truman Hunt looked at Kinyo.

As Kinyo translated, I peered over my shoulder at Samkad. I had not thought of what paying to see us might mean to Americans.

Truman Hunt turned to Samkad and Kinyo dutifully

translated his words. 'You are right, young Samkad. People will be paying to see you. The money will pay for all the expenses of transporting you from the Philippine Islands to America. And don't forget, the United States government pays you each thirty-five cents a day to be here.'

Mother, I had forgotten that we had been promised money. Thirty-five cents seemed an enormous amount when you'd never even held a coin in your hand. After five months, how much would thirty-five cents a day add up to? I couldn't get my sums right. I found my thoughts wandering to what I would buy with the money. Perhaps more ledgers for Sidong to draw on? Bowl hats like Truman Hunt's, to present to the ancients? Or perhaps a ride in the giant wheel?

But still . . . had we really come all this way to be stuck in the Igorot Village?

'Kinyo, he promised we would see the fair!' I said.

'Mister Hunt says not to worry, you will get your chance,' Kinyo said. 'He will arrange an escort.'

We let it go at that. It was too cold to stand around talking about it. Besides, Truman Hunt had always been good as his word. We had no reason to doubt him.

One day, we were finishing the last of the thatching when I felt something brush against my face. It was just a touch, like a cold fingertip tapping my nose. I ignored it. But then I felt it again. And again. Like many gentle fingertips brushing against my face.

Was it raining? I looked up to find tiny white flakes falling everywhere, each tuft swinging delicately one way and then the other.

Ashes.

There must be a fire. My heart began to pound.

Five years ago, during the war, soldiers came to the village – American soldiers – and forced the men to clear the dead from a mountain pass where a deadly battle had just been fought.

Our blood enemy, the Mangili, realized that the village had been left undefended. They attacked – but not before we had managed to flee: ancients, children, mothers, even pigs and chickens hiding in the caves in the next rice valley. Finding the village deserted, the Mangili set fire to it.

The sky had turned red, the fire made an awful rumbling, snapping noise. And then down they came. Ashes, like so many white feathers, drifting unhurriedly from the sky.

But these ashes were cold, not hot. And there was no red glow, no black column of smoke.

On the next rooftop, a Tinguian was holding both arms wide, as if he wanted to catch all the ashes.

'Where is the fire?' I called to him.

'It is not ash,' he replied. 'It is called "snow" and the low-landers call it—'

'*¡Nieve! ¡Nieve!*' I was startled to hear the guards shouting. It was the first time I'd seen smiles on their sour faces. They had their arms around each other, whirling round and round in delight. Then they stopped and stuck their tongues out, trying to *eat* the white stuff right out of the air. In the distance, I heard the trill of a musical instrument as the Visayans began to sing.

'Miss Luki!' Truman Hunt was standing below me, puffing on a pipe and grinning at the sky. 'Enjoying the snow?'

Snow. That was what it was called.

The snow began to fall faster. Not so gentle any more. It began to gather on the ground in white heaps. My coat, which was a dark grey, was soon dotted like a starry sky.

The Scouts were cavorting about like small children. They fell on their knees and began to gather it into balls and throw them at each other. The snowballs crumbled harmlessly on contact and the Scouts cried out, their throats full of joy.

Not everyone was happy. Several people were sheltering under the eaves of the finished houses, watching the white flurries with fearful eyes.

The snow covered everything swiftly. Soon every tree wore a white cap, and every tree branch was traced with white. The unfinished houses wore white rooftops instead of thatch.

Truman Hunt waved at the fearful people. 'Hey, come out from there. What are you afraid of? Look at me! Does it look like it's done me harm? Kinyo, boy, translate that. Tell them not to be afraid!'

Kinyo opened his mouth to speak, but Samkad, who was standing in the doorway of one of the houses, interrupted, rolling his eyes. 'Tell the American we are not afraid. We are cautious. Tell him that, Kinyo. Or do you need some words to flatter him as well?'

Kinyo glared. 'I am just doing my job.'

'Sure you are,' Samkad sneered.

'That's not fair, Samkad,' I cried.

'Oh, but you don't know anything, Luki. Guess what I just discovered. My dear brother – who only recently stopped dressing like a pretend American – brought with him his axe. The one that Father gave him. The one he said he had no use for. But now that we're in America, he's planning to strut around waving it like a Bontok warrior!'

Kinyo blushed red.

'What is he saying? What's going on?' cried Truman Hunt.

'Stop it now, you two,' I said. 'This is no time to quarrel.'

'You have no right to talk to me like that. It was my axe to bring!' Kinyo said.

'But weren't you just saying I could have it if I wanted it?' Samkad snapped. 'Do you know what we call people like you, brother? Pretending to be American then pretending to be Bontok? A FAKE. That's what you are!'

Kinyo lunged past Truman Hunt at Samkad, dragging him out of the doorway and pushing him down on the ground. I couldn't believe it. When I had seen them together on the boat, I had thought they had reconciled. But now here they were, rolling about in the snow with murder in their eyes.

'Guards!' Truman Hunt yelled.

The Scouts dropped their snowballs and made their way to us reluctantly.

'What are you waiting for?' Truman Hunt bellowed. 'Split them up!'

One Scout grabbed a stick from a pile of lumber.

'What the hell, put that away, you might hurt them!'

He dropped it, and together, the Scouts began to circle the struggling pair. They dived to grab them, but Kinyo and Samkad rolled out of reach. Someone behind me laughed. The Scouts got up and tried again . . . only to miss again. Now everyone was laughing. People left their shelters for a better view, as if it was a game.

I shook my head.

And then I saw.

The gates were wide open.

Wide open.

Mother, I couldn't help myself.

Everyone was concentrating on the two fighting boys.

It was my chance. I slid down the ladder, slipped past the crowd, and ran straight out.

18

Up a Tree

I ran out the gate, past the little huts where people would soon be buying tickets to see us, and into the open space between the pretend walled city and a pretend Manila building.

For a moment, I stood still, watching the snow swiftly coating everything in a smooth layer of white. *Where do you think you're going, Luki? Shouldn't you have stayed and played the peacemaker between those two?*

I shook my head. Kinyo had been drawn to the Americans since they'd arrived in Bontok. Why couldn't Samkad just let him be? But that wasn't Samkad's way, was it, Mother? I mean, he couldn't let me be when I walked away from him.

Since Tilin had fallen ill, I had allowed Samkad to talk to me just a little bit. Perhaps I shouldn't have, Mother. We could well end up in a never-ending quarrel like him and Kinyo.

The Reservation was transformed – cheerful white caps

topped the church tower, a statue, and the tops of the bamboo and banana trees. The tiled roofs of the Visayan buildings had vanished under plump white blankets. The dark stone walls of the fortress were dusted with white powder.

Suddenly, in the distance, a roar of laughter, then applause. The Visayans were singing again. I glanced back at the open gate. If anybody had noticed me missing, there should be people chasing after me already. I wondered if I should go back.

But, at that moment, a mischievous spirit took hold of me, Mother. I found the snow flying under my boots as I began to run. I turned my back on the Visayan Village and followed a faint line in the snow towards the lake. A bridge, caked with snow, crossed to the other side where we had walked in the forest of neatly spaced trees on that first day.

My feet had me over the bridge before my mind had even begun to debate whether to cross or not. My heart was beating fast, Mother. It couldn't be that far to the giant wheel, I thought. I could run there and back just to tell Tilin and Sidong that I had done it.

But then I heard a shuffling noise. Through the trees, a man was making his way carefully down the path. He wore a bright blue suit with gold buttons, a high red collar and a matching cap. A Jefferson Guard.

Eheh, Mother, the guardsman would be the end of this adventure. He would march me straight back to the Igorot Village!

Just then, I floundered; the snow was deeper than I had thought. The icy stuff was seeping into my rubber boots. Oh, Mother, it burned my bare skin. I pulled the boots off.

But now what was I going to do? I couldn't walk on the snow in my bare feet!

I grabbed a low hanging branch. Its tree trembled as I climbed, up and up and up, dislodging great clumps of snow. I climbed almost to the top, where the branches were mere twigs, before I squatted down in a bough's elbow, leaning against the young tree's slender trunk and pulling my knees up to my chest so that I could wrap my coat around my cold feet.

The guardsman kept walking. He disappeared in the trees.

I lifted the coat and peeked at my feet. My toes looked red. All this time the snow had not stopped falling and a fresh layer had already erased my footsteps. Down below my boots had vanished too.

And then I saw her. A woman, riding a tall white horse. I'd never seen anyone ride a horse like that before: she was not sitting astride, she had both her legs down one side, her long black skirt smoothed over her knees.

She rode right up to the tree and looked up at me.

'Hey, you!' she said.

A cloud must have moved overhead because suddenly her face was lit up by a ray of sunshine. She had large blue eyes and a sprinkling of light orange freckles across a face as pale as carabao milk. Tufts of hair the colour of dried grass escaped from her tall black hat.

'What are you doing up that tree?'

I couldn't think what to do so I hid behind the tree's trunk. She tilted her head to one side.

'If you can see me, I can see you!'

Mister William had taught us to say: 'How do you do?' . . . but my lips couldn't seem to remember the shape of the words. Before I knew it, the woman was speaking again.

'I saw you climb it.' She grinned. She had great white teeth that stretched her mouth across her face. 'You were up there quicker than a squirrel!' She moved her horse to right under the tree.

Were Americans like the ancients? Did they disapprove of women climbing trees? 'You want me . . . go down?' I said at last.

'She can speak!' The woman laughed. It was a hearty noise, like the laughter came from deep inside her belly. 'No, don't go down. I'll come up to you!'

To my amazement, she suddenly sprang to her feet, right there, on her saddle. The horse didn't seem at all surprised, as if this was something she did all the time. I could see now that she was wearing a short black jacket over a dress that tapered to the tiniest waist I'd ever seen, flaring out again into a thick billow of skirts.

'Hold still, Skyrocket,' she muttered to the horse as she grabbed a branch and began to climb. I was so shocked I just sat there, staring, Mother. The tall hat on her head didn't budge as she pulled herself up, stopping at a branch just below. She swung a leg over, grinning up at me.

'You're an Igorot, aren't you? I can tell by your tattoos. The papers said Igorots lived in trees, and here you are! And boy I'm glad you can speak English! How do you do?'

She reached up and grabbed my hand suddenly, squeezing it hard. She was wearing a glove made of deerskin. Lucky I was clinging to another branch with my other hand or she would have pulled me down.

'I . . . How do you do?' I finally managed to say.

'I – AM – FINE.' She grinned. 'Say, the view is great from here. I can see all the way across the lake! Is that why you're up here? To look at the view?'

I was still trying to decide how to answer her question when she suddenly said, 'I am so *RUDE*. I completely forgot to introduce myself! My name's Sadie. Sadie Locket. What's your name?'

I looked at her. The way she moved, the way she talked – she was unlike any American I'd ever seen. 'My name Luki.' I was surprised at how easily the words came to my lips.

'Luki. Luki. Luki. Hmm. Sounds like Looky, as in "Now looky here, it's an Igorot in a tree!"' Sadie said. 'Even with that coat on, I could tell you were an Igorot. I've read everything I can find about Igorots in the papers. Boy oh boy, I can't believe I've actually met one! I mean, that's why I decided to take Skyrocket for a little ride around the lake, I was hoping to catch a glimpse, you know?' She smiled up at me. 'Everyone in the United States of America wants to hurry over to Saint Louis to meet all you scary Igorots! But you're not scary at all,

131

are you? That's why I wanted to see you for myself. You never know if what the papers are saying is true.'

She laughed again, and this time I laughed with her, Mother, even though I could barely keep up with what she was saying. Before I knew it she was talking again. 'Oh and I just remembered something else! The papers say you Igorots eat dog for breakfast, lunch and dinner. Dog! How can you pet the creature one moment and then roast it over a fire the next? Is that true?'

Dog for breakfast, lunch and dinner? What was she talking about? Pet him one moment and then roast him over a fire? Is that what Americans thought we did?

I must have looked dismayed, because Sadie Locket was now regarding me with serious eyes. 'My golly. So the papers were lying, eh? I am very sorry I brought it up. I don't know beans about these things, and I am very sorry that newspapers in the United States of America are such a bunch of slimy, no-good scoundrels.'

She nodded her head so vigorously the tree shook. I suddenly realized how twiggy the branch she was sitting on looked. I tried to warn her. 'You . . . you . . .'

But she was talking again. 'Is it true Igorots don't drink milk? Maybe that's why you're so darn little! That's how you skittered up this tree with no trouble at all. This tree don't mind little ol' you but I'm sure it ain't too happy about an American girl like me, grown on milk—'

Now, the tree was groaning as if it was in pain.

132

'You . . . you . . .' I sputtered.

'Spit it out, girl, what do you wanna say?' Sadie said.

'You too heavy!'

Too late.

There was an almighty crack and the branch Sadie Locket was sitting on crumbled beneath her.

19

Sadie Locket

It was instinct that made me wrap my legs around my branch, instinct that made me swing myself upside down and grab her flailing arm. I didn't think about it at all. I just did it.

So there we were, me upside down, with Sadie dangling from my fingers, the tall hat still fixed to her head. The ground seemed an awfully long way away.

Terrified blue eyes stared into mine. 'Don't let me go! Don't let me go! Oh, lordy, what if you don't speak enough English to understand?'

She was wriggling like a fish, the weight of her pulling my arms out of their sockets. The tree groaned again and I darted a look at the branch I was dangling from. Was it strong enough to hold us?

Sadie finally seemed to realize the seriousness of the situation. 'Luki!' she whispered. 'What are we going to do?'

Eheh, tree! Are you going to send us crashing down? Or are you going to show us mercy?

I tilted my head towards a branch at her left. 'Feet!' I said quietly.

She looked at her feet and then at the branch. I tightened my fingers on her arms and nodded.

Sadie swung her legs towards it and, Mother, the branch beneath my knees screeched as if it was going to splinter into a thousand pieces. But Sadie had managed to hook the branch with one foot, pull herself closer, and sit herself down on it while I made my way down to her.

Moments later we were sitting side by side, dangling our feet over the sheer drop. Mother, she made me laugh. Her throat made words so quickly they tumbled out before she even knew what she wanted to say.

'You sure outsmarted this tree!' she cried. 'You saved my life! Do all Igorots climb trees like you?'

I laughed, remembering all the times I'd sat alone in a tree, waiting till sunrise to capture a boar. What was the English word for hunting? 'I . . . I go up tree when I hunt,' I managed to say.

'You hunt? Igorot girls go hunting?' Sadie looked genuinely amazed.

I shook my head. 'No. Not allowed,' I said. 'Everybody angry.'

Sadie looked at me. 'So girls are not allowed to hunt?'

I shook my head.

'What do you hunt with? A gun?'

I couldn't remember the word for spear, so I drew a spear's shape in the air and pretended to throw one.

'Oh my, a spear! Don't let anybody say that you aren't amazing, because you are! So did hunting get you into trouble?'

I nodded. 'They tell me become wife.'

And, Mother, to my surprise, Sadie's face fell, as if what I said was the saddest thing in the world. 'And did you get married?'

I shook my head so hard, she laughed and raised her hands. 'I get it, I get it. You didn't become a wife.'

I grinned at her. 'I come America!'

Sadie cheered. 'Well, bully for you, Luki! Hey, I was in exactly the same situation. My pa, he kept warning me. Sadie, girls don't ride, girls don't shoot. Sadie, he said, the best thing for you is to find yourself a nice husband! He threatened to sell Skyrocket if I didn't get married! And there was no way I was going to let him do that!'

I stared at her, open-mouthed. Her story was just like mine. I couldn't believe this vivid girl whose body seemed too small to contain such a large spirit had such a similar experience.

'Wait, let me show you something.' She planted both fists in her waist. I couldn't help staring at that narrow waist – it looked like a giant had pinched it in between his thumb and forefinger.

She seized my hand and pressed it against her side. 'Feel this!'

Under the thickness of her dress I could feel something rigid encircling her waist. It was not a giant's thumb and forefinger, but it might as well have been. 'It's called a corset!' she declared. 'Made of whalebone. We American women are expected to squeeze our waists to nothing. It's how we're supposed to look even though it's uncomfortable as anything. And did you see how I rode the horse? Side-saddle, we call it! No lady should be seen a-straddling a horse! So Looky, I know exactly how you feel. We women have a lot of expecting to cope with.'

Mother, it was so frustrating not to have the words ready in one's throat. There was so much I wanted to tell her. About constantly being told I was not behaving correctly. About wanting things that women weren't supposed to have.

But Sadie suddenly cried out. 'Lord almighty, Luki, why didn't I notice your feet before? Bare feet in this snow?'

I tried to explain that I'd lost my rubber boots, but Sadie had quickly unlaced one of her own boots and pulled it off, revealing a foot warmly sheathed in a thick woollen sock. She handed the boot to me. 'Hold this,' she said, frowning as she began to take the sock off. 'I can't give you my boots, but you can certainly have my socks.' She grabbed my foot and pulled the sock onto it. Then she put her boot back onto her bare foot and began to work on the other boot.

It was embarrassing, Mother, to have her dress my feet, but there was nothing I could I do but allow her to do it. 'You will let me do this, Luki,' she commanded, her deerskin gloves warm on my ankle. 'And we mustn't stay here a minute longer. Come, let us get down from this tree. Skyrocket and I will take you back to the Igorot Village. What is the name of your manager? How could he leave you shoeless in this weather? It's outrageous!'

I wanted to explain that the boot was somewhere under the snow, that it wasn't Truman Hunt's fault, that I had sneaked out of the Igorot Village while nobody was looking. But she was already climbing down.

On the ground, Sadie whistled and Skyrocket, who had wandered a few yards away, promptly came to stand next to the tree. 'Just climb straight onto Skyrocket, so you don't get your socks wet. That's it. Now put your leg over there.' There was a great knob on the side of the saddle, and she showed me how to hook my knee over it so that I could ride sideways like her. Then she took the reins and strode towards the bridge.

We crossed the bridge, and as she walked, Sadie pointed at a building to one side of the path. There was a sign, but of course I didn't know how to read it. 'It says "Negrito Village". I've read about them! I read they were going to perform a wedding ceremony every day. Will they be marrying each other over and over?'

We turned a corner and there was Truman Hunt, standing outside the Igorot Village gate with the guards. At the sight of me on the horse, his face turned bright red with anger. He ran

towards us. 'Where have you been? And who the hell is this?'
But then he did a double take and his face turned from red to
white. He swallowed. 'Ma'am . . . er . . . you're . . .'

I began to take the socks off, but Sadie stopped me.

'You keep them.' She looked over her shoulder at the
snowy path to the Igorot Village. 'You'll have to run. Those
socks will be soaked but they're better than nothing.'

Truman Hunt found his tongue. 'Ma'am. Miss Locket, such
an honour to meet you! I am one of your greatest admirers! I
saw you at that show you did in New York, you were superb!
I remained standing and clapping long after you had left the
arena.'

Sadie flashed him a look over her shoulder as she helped
me down from Skyrocket's back.

She threw her arms around me and gave me a hug. 'It's
been the greatest pleasure talking to you. Now, Luki honey, go
on indoors before you catch your death of cold while I have a
word with . . . ' She raised an eyebrow at Truman Hunt.

'Truman Hunt, ma'am.' He snatched his hat off his head
and clutched it to his stomach. 'I am the manager of the Igorot
Village. I am so grateful to you for bringing our Luki back,
we've been looking high and low for—'

Sadie interrupted. 'Mister Hunt, I found her in the forest,
sir, her feet were bare and near frozen. *Frozen!* You were
responsible for her and somehow you lost her. This is shocking
neglect. The Igorot people are our guests. If you're planning
to lay the blame on her head . . . well, let me tell you, it is not

her fault but yours. And if I discover you've punished her for this, you will be reading about it in the papers!'

I stopped by the gate and turned around. It's not his fault I ran away, I wanted to say. And it's not his fault I lost the boots!

But Sadie waved me on, her face stern. 'Go in, Luki! Git!'

She glared at Truman Hunt, mounted Skyrocket and rode away.

20

Tilin

'She's lucky you've had a lot of practice sitting in trees,' Tilin giggled when I told her about Sadie back at the cuartel. She seemed so well, laughing and joking and sitting up in bed with Sidong, leafing through her drawings. She looked like she had turned a corner.

But then the next morning I woke up to Tilin gasping for breath, her chest creaking like an old forest in a big wind. The other women in the room were sitting up, staring at her.

'Is she all right, Luki?' a woman nearby said as I hurried to her bedside.

She just needed to sit up, I thought. She would breathe more easily. But I couldn't wake her, and when I tried to sit her up, her head rolled to the side like an overripe fruit falling from a tree.

'It's them,' a woman named Ubey whispered behind me.

'The men who died on the train. They will feel so isolated here, in an invisible world that has none of their kin. They will want more souls to join them. That's why they've come for her.'

'Surely not!' cried another woman. 'Her life is not over yet. She said she wanted to raise her sister. She wanted to see the world.'

'But she is ill and weak,' Ubey said. 'They will take her just because it is easy.'

I realized she was right. The hairs rose on my arms.

The spirits like to choose who will live and who will die, the ancients always say. They will give you death when you've finished living your life in the visible world. They might also take pity on a sickly person and speed their death so that they can find comfort in the spirit world. But they are just as capable of robbing you of your time by forcing your death – when a person has somehow offended them, out of malice or anger or revenge. Or loneliness.

Sidong's eyes were wide with terror. 'Luki, you must do something!' she whispered.

'What can I do?' I looked around at the other women. But they knew as little as I did about resisting the will of the spirits. I tried to remember the words the ancients had chanted to beg the mercy of the spirits when someone was grievously ill.

'Spirits,' I cried out, my voice sounding too loud in the room. 'Let Tilin live. Please, she deserves to live a full life. Sidong needs her . . .' The tears spilled from my eyes. '*I* need her. Please, help my friend.'

Tilin's chest rose and fell violently as she tried to draw air. They were strangling her! I was using the wrong words. The spirits were not listening.

'Tilin! Tilin!' Sidong cried.

I could hear someone sobbing behind me. 'Get Truman Hunt,' someone said. 'He will have medicine for her.'

I actually ran to the door. But wouldn't it anger the spirits more if I begged an American's help?

'Samkad!' I said suddenly. Samkad kept faith with the spirits. He would know what to do. I shoved my feet into the rubber boots Truman Hunt had given me to replace the ones I'd lost and threw myself out the door. It was warm outside. The lumps and clumps of snow had vanished, leaving the paths puddled in mud.

I banged on the door of the men's sleeping room. 'Samkad! Samkad!'

He came immediately. Deep inside, I was terrified that after everything, he would be reluctant. But of course he came, Mother.

He listened to me with a melting compassion in his eyes. I let him take my hand and squeeze it. 'Let me see what I can do,' he said. 'I cannot promise that the spirits will listen to me. I am young, I do not have the wisdom of the ancients, but I will do my best.'

Tilin's face was as pale as dried grass, and her lips were almost the same colour, cracked and withered as a parched field. Her breath grated in her throat. Samkad fetched a small

143

bowl of rice and laid it on the floor. He gestured, and the other women joined us in a circle around the bed.

He took Tilin's hand, stroking it gently. 'Here, spirits, here,' he whispered. 'See, how we bring food. You do not need this girl. Leave her be.'

We followed Samkad's lead, Mother, chanting the words he needed. We told the dead men that it was unfair that they'd lost their lives before they had even had a glimpse of Saint Louis. We promised to take their corpses home to Bontok, so that their spirits could join the invisible world of their ancestors. We promised to always remember them, even though they were strangers to us, we would always offer them appeasements, we would remember their names . . . if only they would set Tilin free.

And then the door to the women's room banged open.

'What the blazes is going on here? Where is everyone?' It was Truman Hunt. 'Luki! Samkad! We are waiting for you outside. What are you up to?'

He peered at the bed. 'Is that Tilin?'

He strode to the bed and, shouldering Samkad aside, he stared down at her.

'How long has she been like this?' he demanded.

'Since early morning.' I said.

Truman Hunt bent down and pressed his ear against Tilin's chest.

Sidong grabbed my elbow. 'What is he doing to her?' she asked frantically.

144

Truman Hunt raised his head and looked at Sidong. 'It's all right. I am just trying to find out what's wrong with her,' he said. 'Hush now. I must listen.'

He bent over Tilin, closing his eyes as he listened to her chest.

'Can he hear her soul?' Sidong asked. 'Can he tell her soul to stay?'

He straightened. His face was grave as he took Tilin's wrist and pressed his thumb against it. He stood, quietly, as if he was listening to an invisible voice. Then he turned to us. 'I don't know what you were doing, but it is not going to help her. I am fairly sure she has pneumonia and that it's too far gone to be treated at the Reservation hospital. She will have to be taken to the big hospital on the other side of the fair. They will have the medicines she needs, and there will be doctors and nurses to care for her. As soon as possible. It is not too late to save her. I will arrange it now. Do you understand?'

Samkad looked at me. We had not finished the healing ritual. But Truman Hunt said it was not too late to save her. If we delayed, we could do Tilin more harm than good.

'We understand,' I told Truman Hunt.

'But you're not finished!' Sidong cried. 'The spirits will not leave Tilin alone!'

'Hush, Sidong,' I said, putting my arms around her.

A white van came, pulled by two grey horses. Men in white jackets strapped Tilin to a canvas pallet and carried her to the back of the van.

'Easy, easy,' Truman Hunt cautioned as they put Tilin into the wagon. 'And tell them I expect a full report as soon as possible.'

'Yes, doctor,' the men replied.

That was what Truman Hunt was when he first came to the mountains. A doctor. Mother, I remember when the ancients used to turn their noses up at his cures. But soon enough they began sending for him whenever their chants and rituals failed to get the attention of the spirits.

Such as when you died, Mother.

One moment, you were well, cracking jokes and nagging me to tie back my hair. The next you were writhing on the ground, the sweat rolling off your body as you burned from the inside out. Clearly, a vile spirit was kindling a fire inside you. Your dog, Kinang, licked your face, whimpering, and we had to drag her away to make room when the ancients came.

You were glazed with pain. They lifted you onto a pallet outside our house, covered you with a blanket – but the spirit inside you made you tear it off. The ancients began their usual chants and remedies, casting grain in the dirt around you, laying a trail of wine and dishes of meat leading away from the house to lure the spirit away.

But, Mother, the spirit would not be deterred. Your fever burned higher. You were shrivelling before our eyes. The ancients pushed me aside impatiently as they alternated between cursing and begging that vile spirit to leave. When they realized they could not persuade it, of course they sent for Truman Hunt.

He arrived, lugging a large leather bag.

Your head was thrown back, Mother, the tendons bulging, your shoulders tense, your fingers like claws. The vile spirit had you in a death grip, dragging you away from the world of the living.

Truman Hunt quickly pulled a bottle out of his bag, prised open your rigid mouth, trickled some dark liquid into your throat. The spirit inside you convulsed, Mother. For a moment, I thought Truman Hunt had succeeded in banishing it from your flesh. You arched and jerked and your arms flew out, knocking the bottle from Truman Hunt's hand.

'Mother!' I had screamed. 'Mother!' But your body lay splayed, half on the ground, half on the pallet, your eyes staring unseeing into the white sky.

Truman Hunt backed away from the pallet, shaking his head.

'I'm sorry. I . . . don't think I can help her,' he whispered.

'The evil spirit that is sickening her is stronger than the American's potion,' muttered Old Dugas, who was kneeling by Mother's feet.

'What can we do?' Old Pito cried, his voice high and quavering. 'If we don't get rid of it, she will be a slave to the spirit in the invisible world.'

Just then, your dog, Kinang, appeared. She scurried past Truman Hunt and nosed under my arm, sniffing and whimpering. She licked your grey cheek and your eyelids flew open. But it was the evil spirit that glared through your eyes.

You stared at Kinang in terror, struggling and whining like a beast, flapping your arms at the dog.

'The spirit fears the dog!' Dugas cried.

'The dog!' 'The dog!' 'The dog!' The ancients murmured to each other.

It was obvious, then, what they had to do.

They had me come forward. 'Call Kinang,' they said. 'She will come to you.'

I called, and Kinang came eagerly.

The ancients took Kinang, praying over her loudly, so that her spirit would have the strength to fight the vile spirit. I looked away when the knife descended. Kinang made no noise.

When I looked again, the dog's soul had already departed for the world of the Dead. 'Please, Kinang,' I whispered. 'Set Mother free.'

The ancients chanted, their eyes squeezed shut, their voices shrill as they urged the dog on. Mother, as they chanted, your body began to thrash, your eyes rolled to the back of your head and your cries cut the air like so many knives. It was painful, but I forced myself to watch.

And then, Mother, you arched one more time before your body slumped back into the pallet, your hands suddenly limp, your ankles soft, feet dangling. I threw myself on my knees next to you. Had Kinang's soul lost the battle? Were you trapped in the clutches of the spirit forever?

But then you sighed. Your body relaxed. All the tension in

your neck and arms diasppeared. You began to draw clean, free breaths.

I touched your cheek and your eyes opened. Joy leaped inside me. You were back! Looking up at me with soft eyes.

You smiled. 'Eheh,' you whispered. 'Luki!'

Kinang had done it. She had freed you from the vile spirit.

Your eyes were like pools of water. They shimmered and swirled as if Lumawig himself was stirring it with a finger. 'Daughter,' you sighed.

I kissed your cheek and you looked at me like you never wanted to look at anything else.

Then I watched as you died, your spirit gently leaving your body.

The ancients sighed with relief. You were free and safely in the arms of our ancestors now – and your dog, Kinang, was with you to protect you for ever.

'Thank you,' we all prayed. 'Thank you, Kinang.'

Later, we took the meat Kinang had gifted us with her death and shared it out. I parcelled up a small portion for Truman Hunt as thanks for his efforts.

But when I tried to give it to him, Truman Hunt shook his head. 'No, thank you,' he said. 'I do not eat dog.' And I wondered at the look on his face, the way his mouth curled and the way his voice came out like a frog's croak.

Older folk say the souls of some people are bound tightly together. Love, hatred, desire or guilt – any of these will draw one spirit to another. The bond continues even if one of them dies. The spirit of the dead would not be lost to the invisible world, but able to inhabit the body of their living partner and walk the earth again in borrowed flesh.

Did we ever have such a bond, Mother? After you died, I lay in my bed, calling on you to come, use my body, walk with me. But you didn't come.

The days passed. Every day, I asked Truman Hunt in my clumsy English whether Tilin was better. Were the American remedies working? When was the sickness going to pass? When could we go and see her?

Truman Hunt would only shake his head. *It takes time for American medicine to work, and, no, you know you're not allowed to see her. Besides the hospital is too far away. Tilin is getting the best care in the world. American medicine is the best in the world. It will save her.*

But how could I be sure?

21
Spicing it Up

Mother, after they took Tilin away, things changed between me and Samkad. I found myself welcoming his company. Neither of us marked it, we just let it happen. As if it had always been so. As if nothing had passed between us to push us apart.

It felt so natural, to sit with him at mealtimes, to talk in front of the fire, to play with Sidong together. Everyone noticed, of course, especially Truman Hunt, who, every chance he could get, would ask one of us, 'How are things with your *sweetheart*? You know what *sweetheart* means, don't you?'

But, Mother, we needed to be with each other. It wasn't that hard to ignore the winks and fake kissing noises. Anyway, people got tired of their own silliness soon enough.

It would have made Tilin unbearably gleeful to realize that her illness had brought us together. 'You've called a truce!' she would have teased. 'All this time, you secretly wanted to marry him!' But no, Mother, it was not so much a truce as an unspoken agreement to leave the future alone.

The Igorot Village was completed at last, and everyone moved out of the cuartel. The houses were bigger than we were used to, but there were houses for men and for women and we had everything we needed. Mother, I thought we would feel at home.

But it wasn't home. Everyone was nervous. Finally living in the Igorot Village only meant one thing: visitors were coming.

And oh, Mother, who could forget the hooting crowds that came to greet us in Tacoma and here in Saint Louis? At night, I dreamed of men reaching to grab my ear plug, of dirty fingers tracing the tattoos on my face, of crowds pouring water over my head and shouting 'Everlasting life! Everlasting life!' I woke up exhausted, as if I'd been running for hours.

When we spoke of our misgivings, Truman Hunt shook his head from side to side. 'No, no, no!' he cried. 'Translate, Kinyo! Nothing like that will happen. The visitors are coming to learn about life in Igorot Land. They want to see you at work. They want to see the houses you live in! They are *paying* to see you. They will come with a different attitude. There is nothing to worry about.'

And anyway, Truman Hunt added, we had guards to step in if anything went wrong.

I looked at the unenthusiastic faces of the Scouts and wondered if they really would.

And then, Mother, I had Sidong to contend with. Truman

Hunt had announced that all children on the Reservation would be required to attend an hour of school every day. The school was called the "Model School" and the teacher was called Miss Zamora, a Visayan woman with her hair rolled into a great loaf on the top of her head.

When Miss Zamora came to the Igorot Village to meet the children, Sidong cowered behind me like a pup afraid of being kicked.

'Eheh, Sidong,' I said. 'What's wrong with you? It's going to be just like Mister William's school.'

Miss Zamora smiled at Sidong. '*No hay nada que temer*,' she said softly. 'Don't be afraid, little one.'

'Yes, nothing to worry about,' Truman Hunt said. 'You will feel at home with the other wild children.'

Opening Day arrived, and to our surprise, Truman Hunt was right. The visitors were nothing like the mobs we'd encountered before.

There must have been a hundred of them, waiting outside the gate. But these Americans were quiet and shy to approach us.

Truman Hunt had spent the morning positioning us around the village. Samkad was with a group of men at the tiny rice paddy. The Suyoc women were sitting at looms. There was a group weaving baskets and another carving wood. I was with a cluster of women, each of us armed with a large wooden pestle to take turns pounding the grain in a large wooden mortar, even though the rice we ate came already pounded and packed in neat sacks provided by Truman Hunt.

As the visitors slowly walked around the village, each group got to work – planting rice, weaving, carving, pounding – as soon as they approached. And then stopped when they moved on. They didn't say much, these Americans, their faces were solemn as they touched the fabrics hanging on a bamboo rack. They picked up axes displayed in front of one house, tested the blades with their fingers. Then they walked out the gate.

We grinned at each other. When the next visitors came, we would just have to do it again. All that worry for nothing!

Then, Sidong and the other children returned from the Model School. The girl who had begged not to go was wreathed in smiles. 'We spent the whole time *drawing*!' she said. 'I love school, Luki!'

So, Mother, you couldn't blame me for being in a jubilant mood when Truman Hunt summoned us to the fire at the end of the day. In fact, *everyone* was in a jubilant mood.

But Truman Hunt looked grim.

'We've had complaints,' Kinyo translated.

Complaints? I almost choked. Weh! Those quiet Americans complained?

'Several people demanded their money back,' Kinyo continued. 'They complained that the Igorot Village experience was not worth the money they paid.'

Truman Hunt looked like an enormous boulder had crushed his dreams.

The complainers had said we were boring. Why couldn't we be more like Visayans, they said. Why couldn't we sing and dance? One complainer said we were not real Igorots. He'd read all the newspaper articles about Igorots and he had expected to see headhunters, not farmers.

Mother, we were so bewildered. The way those people had watched us did not give us any clue to their disappointments!

Truman Hunt sighed. 'Maybe we ought to change things around a bit. The fair will be running for six months, we have time to spice things up a little. How about singing? Or dancing? I've seen you dancing back home.'

Samkad looked like he'd swallowed a great lump of ginger. 'Sing? Dance?' he said. 'Translate this, Kinyo! We dance to thank the spirits of our ancestors. We sing to beg them for help. The spirits of our ancestors are not here in America. There is no reason to sing and dance.'

'The spirits of your ancestors are a selfish bunch,' Truman Hunt snapped. 'Surely they wouldn't mind you earning a bit of coin.'

'Coin we don't need,' Samkad answered in English before Kinyo had even begun to translate.

The next day, Truman Hunt ordered everyone out of the village and locked the gates behind us. Outside, twenty Scouts were waiting in the field. Truman Hunt ushered us into orderly rows of twos and threes, with the Scouts spaced out on either side of us.

'Today, I am going to show you the fair,' he announced. 'Let us forget about yesterday's disappointing start. It is time for inspiration!'

The fair! We were all suddenly agog with excitement! Watching that giant wheel turning tantalizingly in the sky, we'd all longed for this day.

And, Mother, walking out into the fair's extraordinary landscape of billowing flags and colossal white buildings and columns and domes and turrets and giant figures made of stone and jets of water shooting up and up and up, I was reminded of another time – that first time you took me into the forest.

I was so small and the forest was so big, the great green trees reaching up and blotting out the blue sky. They seemed to throb with a million thoughts and all I could hear was my heart pounding and their quiet whispering song as we followed a path between their moss-padded bellies. 'Beautiful, eh?' you'd said to me. I could only nod because I did not have the words to describe it.

And now I could feel my heart racing in my chest again, to the Fair's own belting song. I was clutching Sidong's hand so hard she suddenly cried, 'Ow!' and pulled away. Samkad grinned at me. He must have been feeling it too, like a door had been wrenched open and a new world revealed to us. I felt like throwing my arms into the air and screaming: *This is what I wanted! I wanted a chance to see this!*

We made quite a stir, marching in the middle of those

broad, broad avenues, our Scout escorts with their boots and flat-topped caps and straight backs making a stern barrier between us and the fairgoers, who stopped to gawk and point and take kodaks and I realized that we were just as much an attraction of the fair as all these fine buildings. It certainly made me walk a little bit taller . . . and when children waved, I waved back with my most gracious smile.

We saw the giant wheel, we saw a giant clock made of flowers, we saw several gigantic buildings, one lined with white columns, another one with pointy spires overhead. It was a shining world, Mother, and for the first time since we'd left Bontok, I felt that I had made the right decision to come to America.

And then Truman Hunt led us down another avenue, Mother, this one guarded by an alarming sculpture of four men on horseback – rough-looking men, with wild hair and grinning faces, firing guns into the air. It was so huge and so tall, we had to walk around it to see the avenue it guarded.

We could hear the thunder of voices, as oceans of people boiled down the street. We heard screams. And there, high above us, we saw a box cart rolling up a narrow track that suddenly dropped down into water with a mighty splash. And, Mother, I swear I also heard a wild beast's roar.

Sidong and I clutched at each other. We were terrified and we were thrilled.

'What is this place?' Sidong whispered.

'I don't know,' I whispered back.

Truman Hunt swivelled on his heel and waved his hat. 'This is the Pike, ladies and gentlemen.'

The Pike! What a strange name. But then it was a strange place. Here, there were no fairgoers strolling quietly, simply enjoying the elegance of the sparkling white city. Here, the pace was frenzied. Here, the people were loud. Here, they were fighting over who was first in the queue. Here, there were shouting men selling food from smoking carts.

The attractions were oddities. Here was a horse that could count by tapping his hoof on the ground. Babies that were kept in boxes. A miniature ocean with miniature ships doing battle. A man dancing on a high wire. A woman dangling from a string.

I could feel my eyes bulging out of my head, Mother. What is this? What is this? What is this? It was one amazement after another.

Truman Hunt gathered us close together. 'I want you to meet some people.' He grinned. 'This way to the Esquimaux!' We entered a large building. But inside, it didn't feel like a building at all. Craggy mountains rose to the rafters. There was a small blue pond. On a hill, there was a cave. And the entire jagged landscape was covered with snow. *Snow*, Mother!

With wide eyes, the Esquimaux watched all two hundred of us fill their space. There were men and women and little Esquimaux, all dressed from top to bottom in fur even though the day was warm.

Once they recovered from their surprise, they hurried forward, greeting us like old friends.

They led us to where other visitors were waiting by their fire, which turned out not to be a fire at all, but a red light under some logs.

The men suddenly began to pace with their spears, and we realized that they were hunting. Or acting at hunting, because it was not obvious what they were stalking. Even so, it was all very exciting. They dived into the caves, threw their spears about, crouched and stamped. We all clapped and cheered. The Esquimaux looked pleased.

Then the children dragged a cart out with long wooden blades instead of wheels and fastened six large dogs to it, like they were horses. They invited Sidong and the other children to climb in and they all laughed and squealed as the dogs pulled them in a circle, snow flying (the snow, it turned out, was not real snow, but some kind of man-made white flake).

When all that was finished, the women sat in a circle and sang a song in a tongue we couldn't understand, but it didn't matter because it was pretty and soon we were clapping again.

After that Truman Hunt took us to see more peoples at the Pike. There were the Japanese, with their ornate red building, their women with hair sculpted into elaborate towers on their heads. There were the Cliff Dwellers, who beat drums, danced in circles and sold baskets and clay pots. And then, on the Streets of Cairo, there were Egyptians and more singing and dancing, in addition to a man wrapped in the biggest snake I'd ever seen.

'It's a chance to see the world, without having to travel far,' I heard Truman Hunt explaining to Kinyo.

By late afternoon, everyone was exhausted and ready to sleep for a hundred years. Even the Scouts looked softer, their backs not quite so straight, their chins sunken into their chests.

'What a day!' Truman Hunt pulled his hat off his head and sighed. 'It's time to head back—'

'Wait!' I cried.

'Miss Luki, it's getting late, we'd better—'

'Wait!' And this time I threw myself on Truman Hunt's arm and dragged him round to face the giant poster hanging above our heads that was the size of three American houses set on top of one another. I pointed at the smiling face at the centre of the poster, the golden hair straying from under the tall hat, the waistline that looked like it had been pinched between a thumb and a forefinger . . . she was standing nonchalantly on the saddle of a galloping white horse.

It was Sadie Locket.

22

Sadie's Soft Spot

'SADIE! SADIE! SADIE!' The people were wild, banging their fists on the backs of the wooden chairs, stomping their feet on the boards. Mother, I felt every shout, every stomp, like little lightning bolts in my bones.

'SADIE! SADIE! SADIE!'

Sidong tugged my skirt. 'But why are they shouting?'

I shook my head. I honestly didn't know.

Truman Hunt chuckled. 'Everybody loves Sadie,' he said.

It was just the three of us now. Nobody else had the energy to see one more thing, not even Samkad, no matter how much I begged. Sidong only came along because she wouldn't be parted from me. In the end, Truman Hunt had taken pity on us. He'd sighed and said he'd take us in to see Sadie's show.

And now here we were in this throbbing mass of people. Hundreds of them, Mother. All seated on steep tiers of benches circling a great sandy space. Our benches were on the very front, which was elevated high above the performing ground.

The band at the edge of the ground played a loud fanfare. A man yelled through a tin cone, 'Ladies and gentlemen, Miss Sadie Locket!'

Out trotted a white horse ridden by a girl in a white dress. The crowd went wild. 'SADIE! SADIE! SADIE!'

I peered at the girl on the horse. Was this Sadie? The hair seemed too yellow and too curly. The cheeks were red. Her white dress was all flounces and she held a silly little umbrella . . . she didn't look anything like the brash girl who climbed up a tree with me!

Suddenly ten men on horses exploded from the paddock behind, riding around her at a furious pace, shouting and hooting. We were so close we could smell the dust and the beasty stink of the horses. Sadie looked tiny, like a bug ready to be squashed. Sidong clung to me, frightened.

Sadie calmly folded up her umbrella and tossed it to someone in the paddock behind her. She rummaged in the little white bag hanging from her shoulder, and produced a small pistol.

The horsemen immediately slowed their horses, circling her slowly, reaching for the guns at their waists.

But then Sadie fired so quickly, it seemed she wasn't aiming her gun at all – BANG! BANG! BANG! The men flinched as their hats pinged off their heads. Ten shots, ten hats. The crowd roared.

Sadie, smiling sweetly, jumped up onto the saddle of her horse and with one quick motion, magically stripped her frilly dress off to reveal boots, trousers, gun holsters, a checked shirt.

A boy had run into the arena and gathered up the hats. He tossed a white one up to her and she put it on. The crowd erupted again.

And then it was one amazing feat after another. Sadie shot at targets that got smaller and smaller. Then she performed tricks on Skyrocket, standing on the saddle as she galloped, hanging from the saddle with one leg, and then leaping over barriers that got more and more challenging – first a chair, then a man sitting in a chair, then two men sitting on chairs then a dining table with the men sitting on either end. It was incredible, Mother.

'SADIE! SADIE! SADIE!' The crowd went berserk as Sadie hopped up on the saddle. She bowed deeply, sweeping the white hat off her head. The show was over.

Sadie straightened, smiling, her arms spread wide.

And, Mother, she was looking straight up at me!

One twitch of the reins and Skyrocket was cantering towards us, Sadie still standing on the saddle, relaxed as you please.

And as the applause continued to thunder around us, Sadie Locket looked up at me. This close, I could see that her lips had been painted a brilliant red, and her eyebrows had been deepened to dark strokes, like one of Sidong's charcoal drawings. But there was no mistaking that this was the girl I had met in a tree. I glanced at Sidong. She was grinning from ear to ear.

'Hey, Looky!' Sadie yelled, and tossed her hat at me. I only just managed to catch it by its wide brim.

I felt Sidong tugging at my elbow. 'Did she just say your name?'

I smiled. 'Remember the snowy day? I told you about her. She's the girl I met. Here, this hat is yours now.'

Sidong hugged the hat, beaming.

Truman Hunt was looking at me with a peculiar expression on his face. 'Well, well, well, Miss Luki. I think Sadie Locket has a soft spot for you!'

Sidong put the hat on and struck a pose. 'Look at me, Luki! I'm Sadie Locket!'

Later as I put Sidong to bed, she whispered, 'I am going to draw a picture of Sadie Locket for Tilin. And a picture of me in Sadie's hat!'

I laughed, but Sidong was so exhausted she'd already fallen asleep. *Eheh, Tilin,* I thought, as I tucked the blanket around Sidong. *How long does it take to recover from pneumonia? When you're better, I am going to take you to see Sadie Locket, who pretends to be small and fluttery but can shoot and ride better than any man. And she does it in front of an audience of hundreds and there are no ancients to tell her this is no way for a woman to behave.*

I crept out of the House for Women. Outside, people were

164

still sitting around the fire, discussing the astonishing sights we'd seen that day. Truman Hunt was sitting on a low wall, looking pleased at the excitement. Kinyo sat near him, quietly translating what everyone was saying.

'No wonder those Americans complained!' someone said. 'The Igorot Village has got to do more.'

'More what?'

'How about if we did a hunt like the Esquimaux?'

'Can we get dogs and a sled?' There was much laughter. But some faces turned serious.

'We must dance!' a woman said.

Everyone cheered.

'No!' Samkad jumped up. 'No dancing. We dance to connect with our ancestors, we dance to honour the invisible world.'

'What's wrong with dancing to entertain some visitors?' someone said.

Samkad shook his head. 'If the spirits found out they would rain all sorts of punishments on us. If the ancients were here, they would never allow it.'

But then one of the older Suyocs rose to his feet. He smiled at Samkad. 'We understand your cares, Samkad, but this is not the first time we have danced to entertain.'

The Suyoc's name was Bayongasan. He wasn't old enough to be an ancient, but silver gleamed in his hair. He was the closest we had to an ancient, though, and since we'd arrived in Saint Louis, many of us had begun to rely on his wisdom.

'Son, listen to me,' he said. 'Many years ago, when I was a young man like yourself, I was taken to Spain by the Kastila. There they had another World's Fair, just like this one, with grand buildings and people from all over the world. Just like this World's Fair, we built ourselves a village to live in. There were carabaos, and we even created rice paddies that we planted up only to watch the rice wither and die in that cold climate. And while we were there, we were glad to dance. We wanted to show the Kastila who we were. The spirits of our ancestors were far away, but we knew that they would have been proud to see the crowds that came to see us dance. We were so popular that, at the end, we were even taken to see the most important Kastila in Spain, the Queen.'

All around Bayongasan, heads were nodding.

'Son, I will always be proud that we showed those people our dances. And let me tell you, when we returned home, none of us suffered any punishments from the spirits.'

Before Samkad could reply, there was a banging noise.

'Someone's at the gate,' Kinyo said.

'Who could that be at this time of the night?' Truman Hunt said.

In the distance we watched the flutter of the guard's kerosene lamp as he unlocked the gate. And then there was a loud creak. The gate swung wide open.

A horse trotted in.

Truman Hunt leaped to his feet. 'Who's there?' he cried.

'It's me!' Sadie Locket said. 'I've come to see Looky!'

Sadie Locket's face gleamed in the firelight, all the paint now washed off her face.

I clasped her hand. 'So good.' I said fervently. 'You. So good with horse. With gun.'

Sadie beamed down at me. 'I saw you right away, sitting next to that little girl. Your face, when you realized it was me! It was so funny I almost forgot what I was going to do next! I could hardly wait until my act was over so that I could ride right up to you! I would have been here sooner, but it takes so long to get changed, you know? It's hard, getting all that gear off by yourself, and then Skyrocket was a bit grumpy and needed a lot of talking and stroking. And then I thought maybe I should leave it, maybe it won't mean as much to her as it means to me, but I told myself, Sadie, there's no time like the present, and here I am!'

She paused to take a breath and Truman Hunt managed to speak before she resumed: 'So pleased to welcome the great Sadie Locket to the Igorot Village!'

'It's my pleasure.' Sadie looked around her. 'Oh, Looky, do you all do this every night? Sit around a fire and tell stories? I don't get to sit around campfires like this, I have to go back to my hotel every night and eat by myself, and even during the day it's just me in my tent. I used to have a girl helping me, but she fell in love with a boy at the last place we performed and didn't want to come to Saint Louis and so I'm all by myself at the moment, sorting Skyrocket out, dressing myself and running my own bath, and sometimes they send a boy to help out but I can't let a boy dress me so I have to make him sit outside the tent, which is utterly useless and it's just not the same as having a fellow female you can commiserate with and share all your thoughts and feelings.'

I could see that Kinyo had given up trying to translate what Sadie was saying to the others. He grinned at me. 'Can you follow everything she says, Luki?'

I nodded happily. When had my ears become so accustomed to English?

Sadie was speaking again. 'I was just getting Skyrocket into the stable for the night, and I tell you, Luki, I couldn't face returning to that lonely old hotel room, so I thought, why not visit? What was stopping me?' She threw an arm around my shoulder. I blushed to see everyone leaning forward to watch us closely.

It was Truman Hunt's chance to speak again. 'Is there anything we can do to be of service?'

Sadie's eyes seemed to flare in the darkness.

'Why . . . yes. There is something. I really enjoyed Looky's company that day it snowed. And seeing her again in the stands, just reminded me of how much I liked her. Look at us! We are like sisters! You know, I was telling you I am currently in difficulty because my maid fell in love. I've been looking everywhere, but all the girls in town have already got jobs at the fair. I was wondering, Mister Hunt, if you could spare Looky from her duties at the Igorot Village? To come and work for me? Lord knows I need help with my costume changes and my horse. It gets mighty lonely being the only woman at the Wild West Show.'

I stared at her, mouth open. Was I hearing her correctly?

'But, Miss Sadie, that is impossible,' Truman Hunt began to bluster. 'She is here on the invitation of the US government, and it is her duty to remain in the—'

'I will pay,' Sadie interrupted. 'I understand the inconvenience, of course. But I will pay Looky half a dollar a day to work for me.'

'I . . . I—' Truman Hunt was huffing and puffing and shaking his head.

'And I will pay *you*, Mister Hunt,' she continued. 'Half a dollar for Luki, and half a dollar for you. A day. For the inconvenience.'

Truman Hunt looked at me. 'Well, maybe, maybe,' he blustered. 'I'm mighty partial to the idea, but what will people think about—'

'—about Sadie Locket having an Igorot for a maid?' She laughed. 'They don't have to know. I'll dress you proper, Looky. And you'll just be *Lucy*, my new maid.'

There was a buzzing in my ears, I felt light-headed, looking at Sadie's smile. I could also see the gleam in Truman Hunt's eyes. The money pleased him. But I didn't care for the money, Mother. This was what I had been looking for when I left Bontok. Something that was outside my experience, outside my culture, outside my ordinary life. Oh yes, it would be such an adventure. Oh yes, it would be wonderful to spend time with Sadie. Yes! Yes! Yes!

But I had promised Tilin I would look after Sidong.

So I had to say no.

Part Three

23

My Country 'Tis of Thee

A few days after Sadie Locket came looking for me, we started our new programme.

While tourists were waiting outside the gates to be let into the village, the women on the other side sang a lullaby. Just loud enough to catch their attention. Just soothing enough to make them feel warm inside. And when the gates finally opened, a group of children were waiting. 'Good morning!' they cried. 'Good morning.' You could see that just hearing the children speak in English lit up the visitors' eyes. The children led them around the village. And yes, we were still waiting for them, planting rice, pounding grain, weaving on the looms. But this time we did all these things while singing lively harvest songs.

It made such a difference, Mother. Visitors walked around with smiles on their faces. They were utterly charmed.

Truman Hunt, standing and nodding under a tree, was grinning so broadly I could see the gap between his side teeth. And through it all I couldn't help thinking how Sadie could get her audience cheering with just the flick of one hand.

Then Bayongasan appeared, leading five other men, dancing in formation as they beat their gangsas. The guests gasped to see them, and I felt a tingle of pride. The rhythm they beat was one we have all known since we began to remember, and at Bayongasan's signal, we women started to dance too, holding our arms high like ripe stalks of grain. If I closed my eyes, I could imagine that I was home, surrounded by forests and rice terraces.

The song of the gangsas ended, we melted back to the sides of the clearing, and two men leaped into the centre with great shouts, each banging an axe on a shield. Soon they were leaping and swooping like two fighting roosters, twirling and thrusting and uttering bloodthirsty cries. The Americans watched open-mouthed.

And then, suddenly, the dance was over, and in the men's place stood a twelve-year-old boy named Anteng. He stepped forward and there was only his voice, high and sweet.

'*My country 'tis of thee, sweet land of liberty . . .*'

Our visitors seemed mesmerized. The men pulled the hats off their heads, clasping them to their chests. The women laid their hands over their hearts. They joined in singing the final lines:

Land where my fathers died
Land of the pilgrim's pride
From every mountainside
Let freedom ring!

As the song ended, everyone exploded into wild cheering.

One woman turned to Truman Hunt, tears streaming down her face. 'I have never been so proud to be an American. These poor people had been living in darkness and we have gifted them with civilization!'

'God bless you, ma'am,' Truman Hunt had replied, and I was surprised to see tears glistening in his eyes too.

That night, a parcel was delivered for me at the gate. I peeled off the brown paper wrapper, and stared at a pair of black shoes with heels and pointed toes.

They were from Sadie Locket. Again.

She'd promised to dress me in a way that would spare me from unwanted attention. If I wanted to work for her. But I had said no – so why was she, night after night, sending me something new. A long black skirt. A white blouse. A straw hat with a black bow. Gloves. Stockings.

I asked Truman Hunt to read the notes enclosed with them. It was always the same message. *Please change your mind. I need you.*

I didn't tell Sidong or Samkad that Sadie was still pursuing me. I hid the clothes from the other women. At night, I argued with myself. You want to, Luki. But you shouldn't.

What about Sidong? What about Tilin? And then my mind churned with fear and worry. Was I right to trust American medicine? Truman Hunt seemed so confident, then why was I so scared? As sleep finally shuttered my eyes, I told myself that Tilin was going to get better. She had to.

Mother, you might think that such troubled thoughts would lead to troubled nights. But no, in my dreams, Tilin was there, strong, healthy, enthusiastically performing by my side in the Igorot Village. Then suddenly, I would find myself on a tall white horse, wearing the long skirt Sadie had sent. On my head was a broad-brimmed hat and at my waist were crossed belts, with the shiny white handles of pistols poking out of the holsters. And then who should appear but Sadie, on Skyrocket. At Sadie's signal, my horse and I followed her, up and up and up into the sky.

And then I would wake up, happy at first, and then filled with remorse that I had enjoyed my dream.

It was not long before our visitors began to give us money. A silver coin for a turn at the mortar. Another coin for a go at the loom. Coins scattered on the ground like chicken feed after every mock battle and dance. When Anteng burst into song, the dollars fell like rain. Americans liked to show the measure of their pleasure in money and, Mother, I must admit, the money made us a little bit more eager for the start of the day. It made our shouts of 'Good morning' warmer, our smiles wider.

Truman Hunt promised to take us all shopping, and the

other women talked about what they would buy. Ubey, who was one of the weavers, said she would buy a hat, with flowers on it, like the ones our lady visitors wore. Kiwang, who shared Ubey's loom, said she had her eye on a pair of white gloves. Kinay, who was Suyoc, talked about getting a pair of American shoes.

I said nothing. I had all of those things hidden under my bed.

One evening, Sidong showed us a box of coloured sticks that Miss Zamora had distributed to the children. 'They are called Crayola.' Sidong beamed, prising open the flap of the small orange box to show me eight sticks in different colours – red, orange, yellow, green, blue, violet, brown and black.

Sidong drew a picture of Miss Zamora for us, her hair piled up in a brown anthill, her fancy Manila dress with the huge stiff sleeves, rendered in green and orange. Then she drew a picture of Sadie Locket. The hat, the bright yellow hair, the pinched waist, the hand on one hip, the smile that filled her face.

'Sadie Locket!' It was Truman Hunt, appearing out of no-where. 'What a coincidence.'

'What you mean, coincidence?' Samkad said.

'It means two events, with no connection whatsoever, happening at the same time,' Truman Hunt said. 'Here is a picture of Sadie Locket, and here, in my hand, is a letter from Sadie Locket, to you, Miss Luki.'

I shook my head. No. No. Not in front of Sidong. But

177

Truman Hunt had already unfolded the paper. 'Dear Mister Hunt, I have not heard back from Luki. Please would you be so kind and speak to her on my behalf. I do not know why she would turn down the job I offered her. It is such an opportunity for someone like herself. I am willing to pay ten cents more.'

'A job? With Sadie Locket?' Sidong's eyes were wide.

'What is the girl saying? My Bontok is rusty,' Truman Hunt said.

Samkad frowned. 'Why did you say no, Luki? That makes no sense. I thought you liked Sadie Locket very much.'

I made myself smile. 'Oh, but I have so much to do here.'

'What are you people saying? Speak in English,' Truman Hunt said.

Sidong made a face. 'You're not going because of me?'

I opened my mouth to explain, but Sidong went on. 'You should go. I'll be fine. Samkad can look after me.'

She turned to her book and continued to draw.

Samkad laughed. 'She's right. Let me look after her.'

'It's a lot to ask,' I murmured. Besides, we'd barely become friends again and I wasn't ready to owe him so much.

'Tilin's my friend too,' Samkad said. 'Don't think I'm just doing it for you.'

'Excuse me,' Truman Hunt said. 'Shall we all discuss this in English?'

I got to my feet. 'It's late, time for bed, Sidong,' I said.

*

That night, I crept out of the House for Women into the cool of the Saint Louis night. The electric lights that kept the World's Fair aglow in the evening had been switched off, and all our own fires had dimmed to embers. It was properly dark. I sank onto a log and buried my head in my hands.

Then, under the sighing of the trees, I heard a quiet tapping, and a voice, singing softly, somewhere in the darkness.

I recognized Samkad's voice. He was singing a song to comfort the dead. I knew it well, I myself had sung it to you, Mother, after your spirit had parted from your body.

In the gloom, I followed his voice to a stand of trees. I could see the gleam of rice in the bowl he was holding up to two figures perched on the branch of a tree. They had pebbles for eyes and their arms wrapped around their knees. Samkad had made spirit figures for the two men who died on the train. He was trying to show the dead that they were still remembered by the world of the living.

Mother, when I had placed your spirit figure alongside the figures of others who'd died before you, I had choked on my sorrow. I could barely sing. How could I comfort you when I needed comforting myself?

I found myself joining in Samkad's song.

Samkad's head jerked to one side in surprise. But he did not stop and we finished the song together.

We bowed our heads over the bowl of rice.

'We have been neglectful of the dead,' I said softly.

He nodded. 'It is only right we do this.'

He regarded me with soft eyes.

'I would like to accept your offer,' I began. 'It is a lot to ask.'

'No, it isn't,' Samkad said.

And I knew he meant it, Mother. I knew he was not offering to do it because he wanted to impress me. He really cared for Sidong and Tilin. He really wanted me to go.

At that moment, it was as if we were the people we had been before – before we'd come to America and before Samkad had asked to marry me. I could sense that Samkad was about to put his arms around me.

I stepped away from him.

'Thank you, Samkad,' I murmured. 'It will mean a lot to Sidong. And to Tilin.' And then I touched him on the shoulder, and returned to the House for Women.

24

Dressed

It was a pain explaining it to the other women. How I'd met Sadie. How I'd be working for her at the Pike. How I'd have to dress in American clothes. They seemed bewildered, then amused, then they wanted to examine every piece of clothing that Sadie had sent, arguing about which way was inside and which was out and whether the buttons were on the front or the back. But mainly they wanted to know why – *why you, Luki? Why would someone like Sadie Locket want* you?

I had no answers, Mother. I had asked myself that question. More than a thousand adoring people watched her show, twice a day. It was hard to believe that she couldn't find anyone else. Was it because I had saved her from a bad fall? We had hardly spent any time in each other's company.

But now that I had made up my mind to go, Mother, now that Samkad and Sidong had put my mind at ease, I really,

really wanted this. Sadie was like nobody I'd ever met. I was hungry to know her.

That first day was a warm day, Mother. Sweat was prickling all over my back as I stepped out of the House for Women to the boisterous shouts of the others (whose constant advice made dressing take twice the time).

I had thought the American clothes would not feel that different from a Bontok top and skirt, but the blouse was cut to fit closely, the collar reaching around my neck like a pair of strangling hands, and the heavy skirt, hanging all the way to the ground . . . it was like dragging a blanket around.

The stockings kept catching between my toes. And what about the shoes? The other women told me the shoes were pretty and swore they would all wear shoes if they had the chance. But Mother, they felt like a punishment, pinching my heel, squeezing my toes with every step.

Samkad had been given permission to take Sidong to visit the carabaos by the Visayan Village before she had to go to the Model School. Off they went, Sidong without even a backward glance. It left me just a little bit miffed that she wasn't more bereft. But only for a few seconds. As I made my way to the gate, I had this strange sensation, as if the slight morning breeze was blowing not just on my face, but inside me. It made me smile, Mother. Sidong was going to be very happy in Samkad's care.

Truman Hunt had said I wasn't allowed to walk around the fair on my own. It was not safe. I needed a companion. When they weren't playing with the band or marching on the marching grounds, the Constabulary men had to make themselves available to do errands and small jobs on the Reservation, so Truman Hunt requested an escort to take me to and from the Pike every day.

Mother, had you been alive, I would have made a game of getting you to guess the identity of my companion. But of course, being dead, you already knew.

Waiting for me by the gate was none other than Johnny, the boy who found us in that park in Manila. I recognized him immediately, though somehow, the crisp, grey uniform made him look taller and broader of shoulder. He clutched his hat to his chest and his short cropped hair caught the sparkle of the morning sun. He looked like he'd been rolling in gold.

I took my straw hat off, but he still didn't recognize me. '*Buenos días, señorita*. I am your escort.'

'Johnny.' I grinned at him.

He looked shocked to hear me say his name. Then his eyes began to blink rapidly as he remembered. '*¡Sé quién eres!* You are one of the lost Igorot girls!'

I pointed at myself. 'Luki. My name Luki.'

He bowed. '*Señorita* Luki, you look so different in those clothes!'

I was tempted to twirl, like I did the night before for the women when they made me try on the clothes. But I resisted

'How is your *amiga*? Your friend?' he said. 'What was her

name?' He paused, pursing his lips. 'Tilin! She was called Tilin! And how is her *hermanita* – uh . . . Sidong? *Sí*, it was Sidong.'

It was astonishing. He remembered me, he remembered Tilin, he remembered that Sidong was Tilin's little sister.

I searched my throat for the right American words to explain what had happened to her. 'Tilin . . . Hospital,' I said. 'Pneumonia.'

He stopped walking, and shook his head. '*Lo siento mucho*. I am very sorry.' And he looked at me with such sorrow, Mother, that it almost cracked my reserve. I had to bite my lips to stop them wobbling. '*La pulmonía* . . . it is very bad.' He raised two fingers. 'We have two Constabulary boys *hospitalizados también* with the *pulmonía*. And you know the school in the Philippine Reservation? *El maestro*, one of the teachers, died of *pulmonía* before opening day!'

Mother, he said it, and then he was suddenly crestfallen and full of apologies. '*Ay*, I was not thinking! Of course it will not happen to your *amiga*! The *maestro*, he was old. Probably already sick!'

I smiled. He was so kind to worry that the news would make me feel bad. But the truth was, just talking to Johnny had made me hopeful, Mother. It was so easy. He was patient with my English, giving me time to rummage for words and put them on my tongue. When I got something wrong, he just giggled and gently told me the right way to say it. Listening to him, I made myself a promise, Mother, to put more American words in my throat. Then I could go anywhere and be understood by everyone.

Johnny and I walked contentedly side by side, as if we'd been strolling through Saint Louis all our lives. I copied how Johnny threw his shoulders back and held his head high, showing his face to the world. If it had just been me, Mother, I would have pulled my hat down and tucked my chin into the collar of my American blouse.

The air was fresh against my face, I felt bold. Free. There was nobody pointing fingers and shouting 'Igorot!'. People seemed only to see my American clothes. To them, I was just another tourist at the World's Fair.

I felt so wide awake, every sound was knife-sharp, the bells, the *clop clop* of horses' hooves, the distant strains of music, while all around us colossal things loomed in their own giant forest. The wheel, the statues, the buildings – everything seemed to reach for Saint Louis's blue sky.

And then, for the first time in a while, I thought of President Roosevelt. Truman Hunt said he would be visiting the Philippine Reservation at some point, but nobody knew when. I had been disappointed when he wasn't on hand to meet us on our arrival. But now I'm glad, Mother. Because when we had arrived, I did not possess an imagination big enough to take in this World's Fair. And now, I knew better. Meeting Roosevelt would require much more than a welcoming fire and a shared bowl of tapuy.

We entered the Pike, and it was like the giant forest was

suddenly on fire. In fact, there was smoke everywhere, all the stalls selling refreshments busy frying food at the same time. The crowds were already in place, clumped around each entrance listening to men announcing the merits of each show.

'Ride the Magic Whirlpool!' one man shouted. 'See the sixty-foot waterfall and the Enchanted Lake!'

'Enter the Chinese Village!' another yelled. 'Restaurant! Tea House! Temple!'

'Paris! See the Bastille complete with reproduction guillotine! Perfumes, lace, champagne!'

'They're called barkers,' Johnny said.

'Barkers?' I frowned, trying to remember whether I had heard Mister William use the word in American School.

'Bark!' Johnny said. 'Like: *bark, bark, bark!*'

Like a dog! Mother, the idea made me snort!

Johnny read the sign above another great archway to me. 'Wild West Show. This is us.'

The Wild West Show's barker was dressed in deerskin trousers, his face and chest painted with bright red stripes, a huge hat of feathers on his head. He grinned at me. 'Miss Sadie told me to look out for you.' He pointed through the arch to a path that skirted the arena where Truman Hunt had taken us to watch Sadie's show.

'Follow that until you get to a big paddock where you'll see some horses grazing. The tents are in the big field beyond. The redskins live on the right and it's whites-only to the left.

You can't miss Sadie's tent. It's got a little wooden porch and a rocking chair.'

'Redskins?' I asked Johnny as we made our way.

'He means the Indians, like that man,' Johnny said, pointing to a man leading a horse in the paddock. He was dressed in an American shirt and trousers and had his long dark hair tied back neatly. 'They call Indians redskins because of their *piel roja*. Their skin is red.'

The man didn't look red-skinned at all. He was the same shade of brown that I was. In fact, it was the barker, standing in his feather hat, whose skin had turned a vivid red in the sun.

The fields behind the paddock were neatly fenced. To the left, were boxy grey tents. Then there was a large fenced off area with horses chomping grass. To the right were a different kind of tent. Tall conical shapes, draped with hairy animal pelts.

'This way.' Johnny led me to the boxy tents. The barker was right. There was only one tent with a wooden platform out front. A slight breeze made a chair on rockers ever so slightly move to and fro. Johnny pointed at some writing along the front of the plank floor. 'See, this says, "Sadie Locket".'

He knocked on the wooden floor, calling, '*Buenos días*, Miss Locket! I have Miss Luki from the Igorot Village for you.'

'Come in!' a voice replied from inside.

Johnny smiled and gave a small bow. '*Hasta luego, señorita*. I will return at four this afternoon to take you back. *Buen día!*'

187

My heart was suddenly pounding. But I just smiled and waved and drew the tent flap to the side.

It took a moment for my eyes to adjust. The tent had a wooden floor partly covered by a thick carpet with a faded flowery design. In one corner was an iron stove and a tin trough about the size of a large boar. In another corner there was a battered looking wardrobe. Most of the light came from a lamp on a table with a large mirror attached to it. Sitting at the table was a girl.

'Sadie?' I murmured.

The girl turned. She had dusty brown hair that was cut close to her head. Her face was heavily freckled. When she stood up, I saw that she was wearing baggy blue trousers held up by braces.

It wasn't Sadie.

Johnny had taken me to the wrong tent.

'Sorry, sorry,' I backed away.

But the girl threw herself across the carpet and hugged me.

'Looooooooky! It's you!'

25

Shape Shifting

The brown-haired girl picked me up and whirled me around, once, twice, three times. Her arms were hard and wiry. The freckles on her face glittered. This was Sadie? But she didn't look anything like her. Not even like the poster outside the Wild West entrance.

She put me down. 'Here, sit on this stool over here. Oh my, but you look real fine in those clothes! Did you notice I didn't send a corset? Do you even know about corsets? Well, I figured it wouldn't agree with you. Look at you – you look like you've dressed like this all your life!' The stream of words sounded like Sadie. I squinted. Maybe she did look like Sadie. But what had happened to the yellow hair?

Mother, she sat herself on the stool facing the mirror, and slowly turned herself into the Sadie I knew. She opened a box filled with thick sticks, like Sidong's Crayolas. She rubbed them on her skin covering up all the freckles. Then she took a rag and smoothed and flicked and stroked until the all the colours ran together and slowly Sadie Locket's face emerged.

'Don't look so shocked! I should've had my face on when you arrived, but Skyrocket was a-snorting and a-calling me back to give her one last rub, and by the time that was done it was too late.'

When she'd finished smoothing out her face she took a red stick and painted it delicately over her lips. Then she leaped up and threw the doors of the wardrobe open.

Mother, the wardrobe shelves were lined with heads! Not real heads but carved wooden ones, with no faces. A row of them wore hats. Another row wore heads of hair in different styles.

She handed me an armful of hair. 'Here, take this. Nobody is going to pay to see Sadie Locket without her golden hair!'

It was called a 'wig', she said. Sadie showed me how to pin it onto the shorter hair on her head.

'Well, I don't blame you for looking so shocked! Did you think I was going to grow my hair in time for the eleven o'clock show? This way, I don't have to spend hours getting ready!' she grinned at me in the mirror. 'I'm so glad you're here. I really need a lot of help, I'll tell you what to do as we go – you'll see. It's easy, but it's a lot. You'll need to help me get into my corset and the rest of my costume and then we'll go over to the stable and get Skyrocket ready too.'

I did all that, Mother. Helped her put on her stockings and

then a loose white dress. Over that went a pair of short, wide trousers called drawers. And then an unbelievable thing called a corset that girdled Sadie's waist. She made me pull a string and instantly her body changed into that pinched middle, with a flaring top and bottom. I had to lace her into it tight, so that her body wouldn't plump out again.

'It hurt?' I cried, but Sadie just laughed.

'Don't worry, see this under-dress? It is called a shift. It stops it pinching too badly. But hey, as it gets tighter and tighter I can feel it turning me into someone else. It doesn't just change me on the outside, it changes me on the inside. Once I'm in it, I can do everything that I have to do.'

And it was true. Before my eyes, she had transformed from a rough, freckle-skinned girl to golden-haired, pearly complexioned, tiny waisted Sadie Locket who could outride and outshoot a band of men.

It was frantic: getting Sadie ready for two shows, keeping track of all the things she needed for her performance, making sure her hat and umbrella and gun didn't get forgotten in the rush, and then, while Sadie settled Skyrocket in the paddock, I had to fire up the stove and heat enough water to fill the boar-sized tin trough for Sadie's bath.

It was not difficult work. But not work I would ever have found in Bontok.

At the end of the second show, when Sadie took the shift off, her pale back was covered with rosy welts from the corset. Her arms and legs were blue with bruises from the stunts she had performed on Skyrocket. She groaned as she lowered herself into the warm bath, until the water closed in over her head. Then she sat up, her short hair now wet and slicked to her head. She looked like a child.

She closed her eyes with a sigh and leaned her head back against a rolled towel. 'People always call me talented, Looky. But nothing that I do is down to talent,' she murmured.

She opened one eye. 'I work darn hard, wake up before sunrise to lift dumbbells and twirl juggling pins. Practise shooting every chance I get. I do every stunt a million times until it's perfect, then I do it a million times again.'

I knew exactly what she was talking about. I did not become a good boar hunter without spending many hours practising with a spear.

Sophie sat up and pointed at the table. 'Fetch me that pamphlet!'

The pamphlet had a picture of Sadie and Skyrocket on the cover. 'It's my life story!' She grinned. 'We sell it for the bargain price of two cents.'

I knelt by the tin trough and Sadie began to turn the pages. It was filled with line drawings of Sadie's incredible life. 'See here, I grew up in such a poor family, I had to learn to shoot so I could hunt for food. Oh, and here I am fighting a bear. And here's me on a train being attacked by train robbers. I outgunned them all!'

I stared at her, open-mouthed. Sadie giggled and flicked water at me.

'None of it is true, silly,' she said. 'I never killed a bear. I was never in a train robbery. But that doesn't stop the newspapers reporting it as fact. It's all good for getting thousands of people to turn up for my shows. The truth is . . . I grew up in a happy family. We had no trouble finding food to eat. I didn't grow up anywhere near the Wild West. I learned to ride and shoot on my uncle's ranch. That's it. I was nothing special.'

I pointed at her. 'You are! You special!'

'Why thank you, Looky,' she sighed. 'I think you're special too!'

At the end of the day I made my way to the entrance to meet Johnny but he wasn't there and, Mother, I was so tired, and there were so many people walking and talking and laughing with great big mouths that I pressed myself against a wall, remembering Truman Hunt's warning that I was not safe on my own. And then I spotted a circle of girls, in their great spreading skirts and feathery hats and I realized that the boy standing in their midst, like the dark eye of a flower, was Johnny.

'Luki!' he called. He bowed to the girls and hurried over to me. One girl broke away from the others and tugged at his sleeve. Johnny blushed as she handed him a slip of paper. 'Write me,' she whispered before she rejoined her friends.

'She like you!' I grinned.

'*Ellas son maestras* – teachers,' Johnny looked shy. 'I met them when they were touring the Philippine Reservation.'

We set off, and I wanted to ask Johnny if he liked the American girl? And did she like him? Was it even possible for an American girl and a Visayan boy to become friends? But it was too complicated, I didn't have enough words, and anyway Johnny was trying to say something to me in a sad voice.

'What do you think about the new clothing rules at the Igorot Village?'

Clothing rules? What was he talking about?

He took a piece of paper out of his pocket and unfolded it to reveal a newspaper. 'So many people are complaining.'

Complaining? But we fixed the problem didn't we? The other women told me that visitors burst into tears at Anteng's singing so reliably that the men were betting on which tourist might cry first.

'What newspaper say?' I said.

Johnny stopped to read. '*Should the Filipinos be exposed to the American public in their dusky birthday robes?*'

I frowned. 'What mean?'

'Dusky birthday robes – birthday robes means naked skin. And dusky refers to *su piel oscura*, their dark skin. The article is saying the American public doesn't like that Igorot men *están desnudos*, um . . . are naked.'

Naked? But they weren't naked, they were dressed in breechcloths! Seeing the expression on my face, Johnny explained. 'Look at the Americans, see how they dress, they cover their necks, their arms, their hands . . .' He lowered his voice, as if he was telling me a secret. 'So to them, Igorots look naked.'

194

He straightened the paper and continued to read. '*At the very least, the men should be wearing short trunks under their breech clouts.*' He grinned. 'They want Igorot men to wear *pantalones* – trousers! They have written a letter to the President asking him to step in.'

I smiled. Good. President Roosevelt would dismiss these foolish ideas quickly. How many times had Truman Hunt said that Roosevelt was pleased with the progress we'd made in the Igorot Village? That he was excited to come and visit? If our men began wearing trousers, they would look no different from the Visayans!

But, Mother, Roosevelt did no such thing. Johnny left me at the gates of the Igorot Village and I entered to find the men completely transformed.

Their shoulders were now draped in long shirts that dangled down to their bums. Their heads were covered with straw hats. And under their breechcloths, they wore loose trousers that hung down to their knees.

Mother, I admit I have looked at Samkad and wondered what *he* would look like in American clothes. Kinyo had looked odd at first but everyone quickly got used to it. But these looked nothing like American clothes.

Samkad wore a shirt that dangled from his shoulders like wilted swamp cabbage. The trousers were loose and cut below the knee, making him appear shorter and bow-legged. The hat looked like a nest some forest creature had built on his head. 'My head won't stop sweating, my armpits itch, and look.' He walked a few steps. 'It makes me move like a frog.'

Kinyo looked even more dejected. He had, of course, immediately offered to wear his own shirt and trousers. But Truman Hunt shook his head. 'You have to be dressed like everyone else, son.'

In the days that followed, the blue of the sky deepened and the trees looked a fresher green as the weather warmed. But at the Igorot Village, it was as if all the heat had leaked away. In their new outfits, the men turned into sad, hunched creatures who couldn't look anyone in the eye.

Later, Samkad told me the dancing had become so listless, visitors were walking away before it was over. Even Anteng lost the sweetness of his voice, stumbling over the words as if weighed down by his baggy shirt. The rain of dollars ceased. And visitors began to complain again.

Bayongasan tried to cheer everyone up by telling more stories of his time at the Spanish World's Fair. The same thing had happened in Spain, he said, they too had been ordered to wear trousers for their meeting with the Queen. 'We must do it out of politeness,' he said. 'Our visitors are shocked by the sight of our bare chests and legs. Our hosts deserve our respect.'

And he was right, Mother. Why else do I wear this hat, blouse, skirt and shoes when I go to the Pike?

But one of the younger men retorted, 'Why don't *they* take *their* clothes off as a small politeness to *us*?' Which got a big laugh and left Bayongasan shaking his head.

I was surprised though when Johnny told me not all

196

Americans were agreed. '*Todos están discutiendo*. Everyone is debating it!' he said. 'Some people want the Igorots in trousers but others say no, no, no – *¡no es auténtico!* This is not what the public wants to see. They want to see *real* Igorots.'

Sadie was sympathetic. 'Of course they hate it. It's not *natural* for your men to wear trousers is it? If they're used to having their legs bare all the time, it will feel like a prison.' She turned back to her mirror. 'But, Looky honey, in this business, you gotta please your audience. If I have to erase my freckles before every show, then maybe your men have to put on some pants.'

And then it was over as suddenly as it had begun.

Johnny collected me from the Pike one day waving another newspaper. '*Dice que el problema está resuelto* – the problem is resolved,' he said.

'What happen?' I said.

'*Presidente* Roosevelt ordered a stop to it,' Johnny replied. 'No more trousers, he said. Roosevelt said *el público no lo quiere* – Americans don't want to see Igorots in trousers, they want to see them in *su traje nativo!*'

And everything settled down. The men stretched out their bare legs and stood tall again. Weaving and dancing and husking and fighting got done. Tourists wept when they heard Anteng sing and reached into their purses. Coins glinted in the grass, like stars.

People wanted Sadie Locket to have no freckles and a pinched waist. And they wanted Igorots without trousers.

26

Cakewalk

Sidong drew a picture of Samkad in his American clothes and, Mother, I laughed so much that water squirted out of my nose. Never laugh while drinking water.

Sidong's ledger was almost full. She couldn't stop herself. She just had to draw. She'd used up so many pages of the thick ledger that she'd begun folding the pages in half to fit more scribblings in. I wondered if Truman Hunt could find us a ledger. I'd seen him writing in one. He must know where to get them.

I opened to the first pages all smudged and black with drawings made with charcoal from the fire. There we were walking down a steep mountain. There was Truman Hunt, holding that tattered lowlander flag. She'd even remembered to draw the strange little face on the flag's yellow sun. There was the round window next to our bunks on the *Shawmut*, streaks of ocean leaping about outside. And there was our train window, the great white mountain of Tacoma leaning in against a black sky.

In her most recent drawings, Sidong had begun to add colour. Red to a night fire. Blue to Samkad's hair. Green to a tree.

'I drew this for Tilin,' Sidong whispered into my shoulder when we came upon a picture of Samkad, me and Sidong holding hands. Samkad looked handsome, his chest tattoos picked out in blue. His breechcloth in red and white. 'Can we ask Truman Hunt to take it to her? Do you think he will do it?'

'Of course!' I said promptly even though I wasn't sure.

'And please can we ask him again to let us visit her?' she whispered.

'Yes,' I replied without any conviction, which Sidong didn't notice.

The thing was, what with working for Sadie, I had not mentioned Tilin to Truman Hunt all week.

I pulled the drawing carefully out of Sidong's book and the next morning, took it to Truman Hunt's office, which was in a wooden hut behind the ticket sellers. It was a tiny room, only big enough for a small table and a chair. Everything was piled high with paper. Truman Hunt sat there, smoking and pushing a stack of them around the table as if he wished they were somewhere else.

I handed him Sidong's drawing and made the request.

'Hell's bells, the girl drew this?' he murmured. 'I've seen her scribbling in that book of hers. Didn't realize she was this good. And in colour too! Where did she get the colours?'

'Miss Zamora give them to her,' I said. 'It called Crayola.'

'Ah, yes, I've read about them. Coloured wax crayons. Clever new invention.' He sighed. 'Miss Luki, you know I'm busy, but I will do my best to get this to Miss Tilin.'

I suppose I should have said something else. Like, *This means a lot to Sidong.* Or, *Promise!* But I didn't.

Instead, I asked, 'And visit Tilin? When we can visit her?'

He shook his head. 'I told you before. Strictly no visits are allowed. You understand?'

Mother, I could have protested. I could have said, *surely there must be a way.* I could have been sorrowful and made him feel bad about saying no. I could have been angry.

But I didn't do any of these things. I just nodded and said thank you and then hurried to the gate where Johnny was waiting to take me to Sadie.

At the end of that week, Truman Hunt handed out brown envelopes, clinking with coins. When he handed me mine, he shut one eye then opened it again, so quickly, I thought I had imagined it. I knew what it meant though. I'd seen Americans wink at each other before. Mister William explained that a wink meant we shared a little secret. Which was true. The money inside my envelope was more than double what others were paid, because Sadie had paid me too. And that meant

Sadie had paid Truman Hunt, which was what he was so pleased about.

Everyone in the village had money now. Even Sidong received a little brown envelope, which she handed to me because she was busy drawing in her ledger. I watched the other women fuss over their envelopes. They were pleased and proud. They now had the money to buy all those things they liked to talk about at bedtime.

I took my envelope and pushed it to the bottom of my pack. Then I pushed the pack deep into the darkest corner of the House for Women. I didn't want anyone to realize that I was making more than they were. But even with the money out of sight, I couldn't stop thinking about the brown envelope that would be coming my way next week. And the next. And the next. I couldn't stop thinking about what the money would soon be able to buy. Certainly, new drawing things for Sidong. And how about a kodak, with a tripod, so that I could take photographs of everything and never forget. Or maybe a guitar, so that I could learn to make lovely music like the Visayans.

The following week the walk to the Pike was as usual, Johnny chatting away, me peeking at the shining world around me from under the brim of my straw hat. But I had put a few coins in my pocket, and it made all the difference. I was no longer someone from elsewhere, observing the people in the Pike. I was one of them. I too could stop and buy some sweet thing from one of the vendors. I too could buy postcards with pictures of all the grand buildings. I too could buy a fifteen-cent ticket to ride the Magic Whirlpool, and see all the waterfalls and lakes its barkers boasted about.

When I got to her tent, Sadie asked, 'Did Hunt give you the money I sent?'

'Yes!' I grinned, holding out some coins from my pocket.

'Goody.' She clapped her hands. 'I was worried, honey. I thought that man Hunt might keep it from you. He strikes me as some kind of grifter.'

I didn't know what a grifter was, but from the look on Sadie's face, it couldn't have been anything good. Why did she dislike him so much?

'Truman Hunt not bad,' I said.

But Sadie just made a face, and then there was no more time to talk. Between us, we had to lug a heavy wooden box from her tent to the paddock where Skyrocket was waiting. Her eyes followed us from under her blonde fringe as we struggled across the dusty ground. I swear, Mother, sometimes that horse looked so human.

We set the box on the ground and the horse whickered crankily. 'Patience, my darling!' Sadie sang gaily as she dropped down on her knees. She lifted the lid and began to turn knobs, fitting pieces together. She took out a metal cone longer than my arm and twisted into one end, so that it stuck up like a carabao horn. She unfolded a handle and cranked it round and round. Cylinders began to turn and she cupped one hand behind her ear. 'Listen to this, Looky!'

Mother, it was a music box! But this one didn't skip or crackle or make scraping noises like Mister William's music box back at American School. A bright voice announced: 'Cakewalk, performed by the Ragtime Minstrels, Columbia Record!' And then strong rhythmic music began to play.

Sadie grabbed my shoulders and turned me to look at Skyrocket.

The horse was moving her front feet to the music. Left foot, right foot, left foot, right foot. Then her back feet began to move too. She was dancing!

'It's our new number: it's a dance called the cakewalk! Everybody's crazy about it.' Sadie giggled. 'The audience is going to go wild!' Then she bounded over the paddock rails and, taking Skyrocket's reins in one hand, she began to dance next to him, her steps in perfect time to the horse's forward and backward prancing. The dance ended with Sadie and Skyrocket face to face. Sadie curtseyed and Skyrocket bowed, bending on one knee.

She showed me how to crank the music box and then they began to practise. The sight of them was irresistible; people from all around hurried over to watch. Cowboys left the horses they'd been tending, Indians left their fires, and the tourists who'd paid to enter the Indian camp all crowded to the fence, nodding and tapping their feet. Soon a number of children climbed over the fence and began to strut behind Sadie and Skyrocket, copying their moves. People roared with laughter, and suddenly everyone was over the fence and dancing along, heads thrown back, knees raised high. When the music ended, there was much clapping and whooping and Sadie had to hold tight to Skyrocket's reins, while I shooed the crowd out of the paddock.

Later, making our way back to Sadie's tent with the music box, I felt as light as a butterfly. Bontok seemed a million miles away . . . and I was glad. I was glad I didn't marry Samkad. Glad that I wasn't tilling a rice paddy in Bontok. Glad that I wasn't wondering when we would have our first baby. I would never have had this much fun. And I would never have known what I was missing.

'What is it?' Sadie was watching me. 'I saw something in your face just now.'

And, Mother, I couldn't help myself. I told her what had spurred this mad impulse to sign up to go to the World's Fair. I told her that I was afraid that I had made the wrong decision. Samkad was a good man. We loved each other. We were the best of friends. We were always meant to marry. But today I knew I had not made a mistake. And it was hard, explaining it, Mother, because my tongue was too thick and heavy to speak the English. But Sadie was patient. She listened. And she waited until I'd found the right words.

When I finished, she reached out and took my hand. 'I can't believe it,' she whispered. 'The same thing happened to me. Someone back home asked me to marry him. He was tall, handsome, he had money, and he was about to set up his own ranch. I liked him. Heck, maybe I even loved him. But the choice was: marry this sweet boy and never do trick riding again, or get out of there and become who I was meant to be. It hurt my heart to say goodbye to that boy, but when I hear the crowd cheering and chanting my name, I tell myself, no regrets! Sadie, you made the right decision!'

She threw her arms around me. 'Looky, you did right! And I'm so glad you're here! Now, how about we play the phonograph and I teach you the cakewalk?'

Sadie and I must have paraded arm-in-arm around the inside of her tent a hundred times doing the cakewalk. Walking home that afternoon, I could feel the thump of the music in the soles of my feet, and it was all I could do not to gather up my skirt and high-step my way back to the Igorot Village.

'¿Que pasa?' Johnny laughed. 'Are you humming the cakewalk?'

I giggled. I had not realized I was humming. Johnny began to hum too. He raised his knees high for a few steps and offered me his hand. We made an amusing sight, humming and dancing all the way back to the reservation. We crossed the bridge to find the Constabulary Band already rehearsing at the bandstand.

'¡Uy! They started without me!' Johnny broke into a run. '¡Adiós, Luki!'

I laughed and waved goodbye. I didn't mind walking the rest of the way by myself. Despite the rising band music, the cakewalk continued to drum in my head and then as I entered the Igorot Village, I realized it wasn't in my head at all because somewhere inside there was a music box playing. A group of visitors were doing the cakewalk, in the open ground in front of the jail, heads thrown back, fingers snapping.

And there, right in the middle, was Kinyo, knees punching high, as he danced with a large American woman, his hand tucked into her gloved hand.

27
Fair Play

The dancing continued past closing time. And then all the visitors filed out, humming and high stepping, the music still thumping in their blood just like it had been in mine when I left Sadie. Oh, Mother, the coins that dropped into Kinyo's hands – there was so much he had to put them in his straw hat. 'Thank you.' He beamed. 'Thank you.' And hearing him speak in English, his admirers threw even more coins into his hat.

That night, when the last kerosene lamp had been extinguished in the House for Women, Kinyo was on everyone's lips. *Did you see? Did you see? He was holding that woman's hand!*

Sidong whispered into my ear, 'They liked seeing him dance their own dance!'

'Yes, they did,' I whispered back, remembering how people shouted and whooped to see Skyrocket dancing the cakewalk.

'Well, that was more applause than we've ever had for one of *our* dances,' I heard Ubey muttering in the far corner. 'Maybe we should do the cakewalk instead of pretending to husk rice.'

'Weh! Didn't Truman Hunt say we still needed to come up with one more attraction? Maybe it should be the cakewalk!' Kinay said. 'Think of the money we'll make!'

The other women cackled like hens and then someone began to hum the cakewalk song and then, of course, we all joined in, tapping the beat on the wooden floor under our sleeping mats with our heels and knuckles, and we all pictured the astonished faces of tourists who had come to learn about Igorots only to find us doing the cakewalk.

But Kiwang had to spoil it all. 'Truman Hunt's not going to allow it, you know,' she said. 'I heard him say he would only allow it today – Americans don't need to learn the cakewalk from Igorots.'

'Heh, maybe he didn't like seeing Kinyo making all that money,' Ubey said.

'What has this got to do with money?' I said.

'Haven't you seen the sacks of money they make in the ticket booths? Those visitors are paying a fortune, and we are getting none of it!'

'But we're getting paid!'

'Sure we are. But not much compared to what people pay to come and see us.'

And then, Mother, they began to argue about who was getting all the ticket money. Truman Hunt? President Roosevelt?

About who amongst us deserved the most gift money. They talked about the fairness of it all. They began to measure the worth of what we were doing according to the number of coins we'd received. Did the dancers get more? Did the weavers get their fair share? Did the warriors receive too much?

At some point, Sidong fell asleep in my arms. And listening to the quiet in and out of her breathing amidst the accusations and recriminations I thought, but it wasn't about money or who deserved what or how to get more money. We were here, in America. We were seeing things that we would never have seen in Bontok and none of it had to do with money. After this, how could we go back to our ordinary lives?

It was the one thing I knew for sure. My life was definitely never going to be the same again.

I tried asking Johnny if he would take me to the hospital to see Tilin. I had this idea that perhaps we could do it without Truman Hunt ever finding out.

Johnny was most sympathetic. 'Your poor friend,' he said sadly. 'But I would get into trouble if I did that. I am sorry, I cannot help. If Truman Hunt agreed, I will be happy to take you.'

But I didn't get another chance to talk to Truman Hunt, as I became more engrossed in the Wild West Show.

The first part of the show was all about sweaty, rough-looking Americans called 'cowboys' fighting Indians. That's what the cowboys called them anyway, even though I could see from their hair and clothes that they must have been several different peoples.

I said, *Sadie, Indian don't look like one people*, and Sadie said, *No, they're not, but it's easier just to call them Indians*, and I thought, *Oh, just like it's easier to call us all Igorot!*

I managed to watch a couple of the battles, and they were very exciting. The cowboys would be working or minding their own business or just riding quietly along, and then the Indians would gallop into the arena on their powerful horses, all scary whooping and shouting and waving small axes, and at first the cowboys looked outnumbered, but they always managed to pull out their guns in the end and shoot the Indians dead. Pretend dead, that is. Because after a few minutes lying on the ground, they always got up and tidied their things from the arena.

The second part of the show had the cowboys shooting guns, tying up cattle and riding horses, which was boring, after all the bloodthirsty Indian battles, but then Sadie came on and it stopped being boring. Especially when the band began to play and Skyrocket suddenly began to dance the cakewalk!

It was always very busy in the back, where everybody had horses to handle or gun tricks to practise or hats to count, so people didn't usually pay me any mind. But, several times, a cowboy got close enough to see the tattoos under my hat and the plugs in my ears, and it always made them laugh and shout things at me in English that I didn't understand. Luckily, by this time, Sadie would be making her way out and she had the right words to make them back away with their hands held high, as if she was about to draw her little pearl-handled pistol and shoot them dead.

One afternoon, Sadie asked me to make her bath hotter than usual. 'I'm aching all over, Looky. I came out of that somersault the wrong way and caught the edge of my saddle.' There were blue bruises blossoming all over her shoulder and she winced as she got into the tub. With a long sigh, she sank deep into the water until her hair pooled around her head.

'Is right?' I murmured, dipping an elbow expertly into the water. I knew it was perfect even before Sadie nodded because, Mother, I had become very good at this job, which I could never have imagined had I stayed in Bontok.

I put away Sadie's wig and hat and gun and rope and hung up her clothes, then I grabbed the broom and swept the tent's plank board floor. Sadie's eyes followed me around the room.

'Say, Looky, one of these days, you oughta come back to the hotel with me. We could have dinner at the restaurant. Ever been to a restaurant? I imagine not. You'll love it. We'll sit at a table and all these fancy waiters will bring you your food covered in silver domes.'

I smiled, but really, Mother, did she really think Truman Hunt would allow me to go off to a restaurant with her? I didn't say anything, though. And I liked imagining us sitting opposite each other, with great domed plates on the table. Of course, there was the matter of how to use a knife and fork, but I could just follow Sadie's lead. How hard could it be?

'Looky, did you hear what I said?'

I blinked.

Sadie was sitting up in the water, smiling.

'You were off in your little dreamworld, weren't you? You didn't hear a thing! I just asked you: what are you planning to do, after this?'

I gestured vaguely out the door. 'Later . . . Johnny fetch me—'

'No!' She laughed. 'I don't mean what are you doing today. I mean what are you doing when the World's Fair is over! Have you got plans? Have you even thought about it?'

I just looked at her. Mother, my only plan had been to get away, to escape Bontok. And doing that had been so enormous, I had not even begun to think of the future.

Sadie sat up sending water streaming down the sides of the tub. I rushed to wrap a towel around her.

'Well, you may not have been thinking about the future, but I have. A lot.' Her voice was suddenly low and shy. 'I . . . I really like being with you. I . . . When the fair is over, I don't want you to go back. Not to Bontok. Looky, what I'm saying is . . . stay. Bontok doesn't need you, but I do. Stay with me, here in America. Be my companion and friend. I need you, Looky. And, oh, Looky, someone like you deserves a much better life than the one you have in Igorot Land. You can be anything here in America. And you will have me to look after you. Please. Stay.'

I couldn't speak. Sadie wanted me! Me! Me! Me!

Mother, my heart was pounding. Stay, she said! Live *here*,

in America! Like an American. That meant wearing shoes and a dress and a hat. That meant becoming like Sadie, going any-where, making things happen. I could make horses dance. Make audiences cheer. I could build a new life.

'Looky?' Sadie said.

Sadie's voice seemed a long way away. The booming of my heart made my ears ache. Stay, she'd said! But did I even know how? It was strange enough, being in this fair. And what about Sidong? What about Tilin? What about Samkad? What about Kinyo? I knew nothing about America, and my whole life was in Bontok. But wasn't this what I had been looking for? Isn't this why I came? To discover something beyond anything I could ever imagine in Bontok?

'Looky, are you all right?' Sadie was watching me as she dried herself. Quickly, she pulled on the robe that I had laid out for her on a chair.

'You said . . .' I reached for the word in my throat. 'Stay.'

'Yes.' Sadie smiled. 'I think you will be happy here. We will be happy together.'

I looked at her and she looked at me.

I turned and grabbed my coat from the stand. I put it on even though it was too hot. I put on my hat.

'Looky?'

I smiled at her. But under my coat, I was trembling all over.

'See you tomorrow.' For once, I said it perfectly, as if I'd been saying it every day of my life.

Then I pulled the tent flaps open and left.

28

Mabel

Outside, everything looked the usual. The horses grazed in the paddock, tourists strolled around the Indian encampment, the stable boys shovelled hay. At the entrance, the barker had finished for the day and sighed as he took off his fur hat with the tail of some stripy creature that didn't exist in Bontok. But there was nothing usual about the turbulence that Sadie's invitation had stirred inside my belly.

Mother, I was happy. Mother, I was sad. 'Yes, Sadie,' I wanted to say. 'Yes, I want to leave everything behind and step into your shining new world.' But all the things I would have to leave behind! Could I really do it? I knew what Tilin would say, 'Of course you can. You just crossed a massive ocean to get here.' And then I became angry with myself for not trying hard enough to get permission to visit her.

I tried to spot Johnny's dark grey uniform in the crowd.

Today the Pike was this shrill, shouting thing, and the crowds were taller than usual so that it was hard to see the sky. There was a man in a head wrap, walking a huge grey creature called an elephant from the Hagenbeck Animal Paradise down the street. It was so big it made everyone shriek. And then a small group of men from the China exhibition walked by, so close I could see the tiny bristles on their shaved foreheads.

Johnny was standing under the massive gateway to The Creation, the biggest attraction at the Pike, where, Johnny said, you could tour the grandest cities of the world in a boat. The arch was covered with tiny writhing human figures. He stood under a giant horse, rearing up on its hind legs.

'Johnny!' I called. 'Here I am!'

He turned and I realized he'd been speaking to someone. It was the girl – the one who'd asked him to write.

'Oh, Johnny, there she is. There's Luki,' she said, as if she knew me.

Johnny turned red. 'Luki, this is my friend, Mabel.'

Mabel was wearing a dress so white that it made me squint in the strong sunshine. Even the flowers on her straw hat were white. She lowered her head to peer more closely at my face. Without thinking I pressed my hands over the tattoos on my cheeks. She looked away.

'Delighted to meet you!' she said. 'I was just asking Johnny if I could walk with you back to the Philippine Reservation.'

Johnny smiled at her in that way boys smile at girls they liked. If Tilin were here, her elbow would be digging deep into my ribs and she would be making secret kissing noises behind my ear. He liked her, Mother! And she liked him. Why else would she be walking with us?

The three of us made our way through the Pike and out to the great avenue lined with palaces and I found myself walking slower and slower, watching Johnny talking to Mabel, his Kastila flowing into his English. Mabel didn't seem to mind, she flashed little pink-lipped smiles and touched his elbow when she laughed, showing very white teeth and a white throat.

'I'm so looking forward to your concert tonight!' Mabel was saying. 'I read in the papers that Sousa thought the Philippine Constabulary Band was the best he'd ever heard.'

'Sousa?' Johnny looked impressed, so Sousa must have been someone important.

'Band very good,' I said loyally.

'Thank you,' Johnny said. But he said it to Mabel.

'I'm so silly, I didn't realize people played modern music in the Philippine Islands,' Mabel was saying. 'I thought there were only tribes and wilderness and that maybe some of the natives were just imitating music they'd heard from America. But here's you! A proper musician!'

'I studied music in Manila,' Johnny said. 'My family are just farmers, but I learned to play the piano in church and then I played in our town band and then my father would not hear of me working in the fields; he sent me to Manila to study. The whole town took up a collection to pay for my expenses.'

'Oh, how wonderful!' Mabel cried. 'And I was so impressed to hear you speak English too! When I visited the Reservation, every other Filipino seemed to speak a different language.'

We were nearing the bridge to the Philippine Reservation and I was waiting for Johnny to bid Mabel goodbye, when Mabel suddenly threw her arms around him, screaming.

I rolled my eyes. Tilin once did this to Samkad, when a tiny lizard ran over her foot. As if. Tilin was lucky I didn't punch her.

'What's wrong?' Johnny cried.

'Pygmies!' Mabel said in a strangled voice. 'That sign says the Pygmies are just over there! Oh, it frightens me to think they are so nearby!'

Mother, the Pygmies were people from Africa. Tourists at the Igorot Village were always comparing us. *You dress just like the Pygmies! Are Pygmies headhunters too? Igorots are exactly the same size!*

'The Igorots are much better than Pygmies,' Truman Hunt always responded, and I wanted to ask him, how are we better? Is it really possible for one people to be better than another?

'It's OK,' Johnny soothed Mabel. 'They're still a way off.'

'Will you look at that.' A low, menacing voice. 'A gugu holding a white girl.'

Mabel and Johnny jumped apart.

Two men clad in the blue wool uniforms of Jefferson Guards sidled towards us. They were broad and tall, towering over Johnny, with thin lips and angry eyebrows. Mabel backed away from Johnny as if he'd suddenly burst into flame. Johnny's face was a mixture – he was fearful, but he looked angry too.

'Gugu?' Johnny said. 'That's what you Americans called us during the war.' He spat on the ground. 'Isn't that right, sir?'

Mother, *he spat on the ground*. And the way he said 'sir'! It was practically a challenge.

The guardsmen looked at each other.

'It speaks, Ed,' one said. 'It called me "sir".'

They burst out laughing.

'Look, we weren't doing anything,' Mabel said, her voice was sullen. 'You boys can just leave us alone.'

'My pal Joe and I just want to know why a white girl like you would be hugging this gugu,' the one called Ed said.

'Sir,' Johnny said. And this time, he said it softly. 'She was frightened. She thought the Pygmies were nearby.'

'Is that true, miss? You scared?' Joe asked Mabel. 'Well, Ed, I s'pose there's plenty to be scared of in these here parts, what with Pygmies and redskins and Igorots everywhere.'

He suddenly turned to me, his nose twitching. 'Look at this one. All dressed up like a human being!'

He peeled up the brim of my hat. 'Hell's bells! Look at them tattoos!'

Johnny snatched the American's wrist away. 'Don't touch her.'

The one called Joe stepped up to Johnny. He was a full head and shoulders taller. 'Allow me,' he said. He grabbed Johnny's arm and twisted it until Johnny cried out.

A man and a woman were walking by. 'Help!' I grabbed the man's elbow. 'Help us.' But the man shook me off and the two of them hurried away.

'Look at that uniform, Joe,' Ed said. 'Philippine Constabulary, right? I seen you gugus marching around with your noses in the air like you think you belong here. I fought in the Philippine War. See this scar?' He pointed at an angry pink stripe along his jaw. 'Got it from a gugu with ideas above his station. Hated that war. Hated the jungle. Hated the heat. But most of all, I hated the stinking savages.'

He grabbed Johnny's other arm and pinned it behind him.

Joe pushed his face against Johnny's. 'We don't like gugus touching our women.'

Johnny turned a dark red. '*¡Es mi amiga!*'

'Amiga? She's your *friend*? No white woman would be *friends* with a gugu. Am I right, Joe?'

'You're right, Ed.'

'Mabel, tell them stop hurting Johnny!' I cried.

But Mabel just stood there.

'You are right to be scared, ma'am,' Joe said. 'Nobody's safe with savages around.' He unhooked a wooden truncheon from his belt. 'Hoo boy, you're in trouble, gugu. Attacking a Jefferson Guard like that!'

'He no attacking you!' I shouted.

'Says who?' Joe said, looking at Mabel. Mabel shook her head and looked away.

And he would have beat Johnny up, Mother. But he did

not expect me to step into the gap between them. He did not expect me to be so strong when I grabbed the end of his truncheon and twisted it, wrenching his wrist in a sharp, awkward angle. He did not expect me to follow that with the full weight of my body behind my fist, thumping hard on that twisted wrist.

He let go of his truncheon with a scream. His friend Ed was so startled, Johnny was able to swivel from out of his grip. They grappled. Ed easily forced Johnny to the ground.

I felt huge hands around my neck. Joe squeezed the air from me, pushing me down to my knees. I tried to pry his fingers off, but he was too strong. He laughed. 'We weren't going to touch you, were we, Ed? Didn't seem worth the effort. But now . . .'

And there we were, Johnny and I, with those two great beasts on top of us. Useless Mabel was wringing her hands and making puppy whimpering noises, when who should suddenly turn up behind the two thugs, but Lieutenant Loving, the bandmaster.

'ATTENTION.'

Mother, I had not heard Loving speak before. Back when Johnny had found us lost in the park, he'd whispered his orders into Johnny's ear. I'd seen him waving his baton to keep his band in time . . . but I'd never heard him speak. His voice was strong, sharp and heavy with gravel. It hit the men like a gunshot. The two guardsmen sprang up instantly, heels together, chests out, stomachs pulled in, arms fixed to their sides. 'Sir!' they yelled in unison. They were facing the wrong way and couldn't see Lieutenant Loving's slate face getting even darker with anger.

Johnny struggled to his feet. 'Lieutenant!' he cried, his hand flying to his forehead in a salute.

'What the hell is going on here?' Loving barked.

'Sir, this gugu was touching that girl . . .' Ed began to turn to face the lieutenant.

'EYES FORWARD, JACKASS,' Loving barked. The two men froze, continuing to face away from the bandmaster. Loving allowed a long minute to pass before he spoke again. 'I know what I saw,' he drawled. 'I saw two boneheads roughing up an Igorot girl and a defenceless Constabulary soldier.'

'But, sir—'

'Shut up, soldier.'

It amazed me to see the two men, who had been unworried about bullying Johnny in the open just a moment ago, so cowed by Loving's arrival.

Johnny bit his lip. 'Lieutenant, they didn't hurt me, sir.'

Joe and Ed grinned. Why was Johnny letting them off?

I glared at him. 'But they did!'

'Yes. I know. I saw it all,' Loving said.

Joe said, 'Sir, we were only—'

'ONLY about to lynch an official guest of the World's Fair? Do you know how many thousands of dollars it cost to bring these people here? And have you considered what this is going to look like on the front pages of the newspapers tomorrow?'

'But, sir—' the guardsmen wriggled, desperate to turn around.

'EYES FRONT,' Loving roared. Then he took a small pad and a pencil out of his pocket. 'Now give me your names so that I can write you up.'

'But, sir—'

'NAMES!'

'Private Joseph Graham, sir.'

'Private Edward Hammond, sir.'

'Let us see what your commander has to say about this. Meanwhile, I want you hayseeds to march yourselves as far away from the Philippine Reservation as you possibly can. You understand?'

'Yes, sir.'

'EYES FRONT,' Loving yelled. 'DISMISSED.'

The men threw themselves down the path, racing away from us. At the brow of the hill, they glanced back and, Mother, the looks on their faces. Their jaws dropped open as if they'd seen a ghost.

Loving chuckled. 'I guess they've just realized that they were following orders from a coloured man.' He cleared his throat and yelled after them. 'What did I say? GET OUT OF MY SIGHT.'

But now that they'd seen him, their faces became sullen. They dawdled, glaring at us. Then to my relief, they shrugged and finally walked away.

Johnny grinned. 'Phew, you saved us, boss!'

But Loving interrupted. 'You, boy, are an idiot. What were you doing, stepping out with this white girl?'

Mabel suddenly broke her silence. 'How dare you talk about me like that!' She stamped her foot. 'You have no right—'

Loving turned to her with a withering look. 'Ma'am. This boy don't know how we do things here in America. But *you* do. I don't know what game you were playing, but Johnny here is in my charge and I plan to get him back to his country alive. So may I respectfully ask you to stay the hell away from him.'

Johnny shook his head. 'Boss, Mabel *no tiene la culpa*—'

The lieutenant put a hand on his shoulder: 'Son, look at your skin. Look at hers. You're coloured. She's white. In America, coloured boys don't get to walk with white girls. Those two morons were about to lynch you. Do you know what a lynching is, son? Do you read the papers? There's one in the news every day. First, they beat you until even your own dear mother don't recognise you. Then, they shoot you. Then, they hang you from a tree. Then they burn you until all that's left of you is charcoal. Then they stamp on the charcoal until it turns into black dust. She's not worth it, boy. You stay away from her. *¿Entiendes?*'

Mabel gave a small shriek of frustration: 'Mister, you can't tell me what to do. My friends and I can step out with any boy we like.'

The lieutenant peered down at her. 'Your friends are stepping out with other Constabulary boys?'

Mabel glared up at him. 'Yes, they are, and they wouldn't

care for your opinion either. How dare you talk to me like that. That uniform doesn't give you the right—'

Loving turned abruptly away from her. 'Johnny, are you feeling fit enough to play tonight?'

'Yes, boss.'

'Well, if you don't escort this young lady back to the Reservation now, you're not going to be playing in the concert.'

'Yes, boss!' Johnny nodded for me to follow him.

As we left, we heard Loving say quietly to Mabel, 'You and your friends stay away from my boys. You're going to get them killed.'

29

Just Performing

Johnny strode ahead of me, his face carefully turned away from mine. But now and then I caught glimpses of his reddened eyes and the grim set of his jaw. We barely said a word, and when we got to the Igorot Village, his gaze slid everywhere as he nodded goodbye, as if he was afraid of what would happen if our eyes met. He turned to leave, but I grabbed his wrist. I wanted to say something to console him but before I could find the words, he gently prised my fingers from his wrist.

'*Lo siento*,' he muttered, and there was such torment in his eyes that I flinched. 'We are fools. I should never have agreed to see Mabel. We should never have come to this country.'

He turned on his heel. Cheerful strains of band music wafted across the ground from the cuartel where his fellow musicians were already preparing for the concert. I found myself thinking of Sadie. I had been so happy that I hadn't trusted myself to speak when she had asked me to stay. How had everything changed so quickly?

Now, dread churned inside me and my eyes jumped in my head, fearful of spotting the uniform of a Jefferson Guard.

There was a burst of laughter over my shoulder. It was closing time at the Igorot Village and the last visitors were strolling out. Seeing that one of them carried a spear, I drew back instinctively. *They don't mean you any harm, girl*, I scolded myself.

I hurried in.

'*Hola*, Luki,' one of the Scouts manning the gate called, but I could not reply. I was suddenly remembering the guardsman's meaty fingers closing around my throat. *Look at this one, all dressed up like a human being*.

'Luki!' Suddenly Sidong's arms were wrapped around my legs and her face pressed into my skirt.

'What's wrong, little one?' I cried, and lifting her chin I saw that her face was smudged with tears.

'Come, come, little girl, no need for that!' boomed a voice. Truman Hunt? With Sidong?

I stared at him in disbelief. When had Truman Hunt ever bothered with any of the children? And yet here he was, touching the top of Sidong's head lightly with his fingers. 'It's not that bad, dear!' he coaxed.

Sidong was bawling like a baby. 'Sidong!' I cried. 'What happened?'

'She's overreacting. She's crying over nothing.' Truman

Hunt clumsily tried to rub her back. I slapped his hand away.

The way he looked, the way his eyes couldn't meet mine . . .

'What you do?' I snapped. He sucked his bottom lip.

'He . . . said . . . no more . . . drawing.' Sidong could barely speak, her breath jerking. 'He . . . took away . . . my drawing things.'

'What is she saying?' Hunt said. 'Kid, say it in English.'

Only then did my vision clear, Mother. Guilt. That was what I was seeing in Truman Hunt's face. And that was Sidong's book tucked in his armpit. And Sidong was straining away from him, as if she thought he was going to take something else from her.

'Give that back!' I screamed, setting Sidong down and snatching the book from under his arm.

'Hey!' he blustered. But I could see that he was nervous.

'You have Crayola,' I said. 'And pencil. Give back to Sidong.'

He pulled the pencils and colouring sticks from his pocket and handed them to her.

'Look,' Truman Hunt said in a reasonable voice. 'I had to take them away. The kid has been so obsessed she was not joining in. She has a job to do. All she has to do is sing with the other children once Anteng gets everyone going. But no, she just wants to draw! It looks wrong!' Then he tried to take the book again.

I grabbed his wrist, but he snatched it back.

'What you mean, wrong?' I demanded.

'Her, drawing all the time!' he blustered. 'It looks wrong! It is not Igorot!'

Not Igorot? The blood was beating hard in my ears.

'I want to draw!' Sidong wailed.

I stared at him, this American, his waist spreading under his jacket, his mouth twisting. Oh, Mother, how could I have been so blind? I had trusted him. I had believed him when he called himself our guardian. I had defended him when Samkad questioned his motives. But he was not interested in who we were at all. He was trying to turn us into some kind of amusing version of ourselves. It was all for show. And Sidong drawing did not fit into that show.

He smirked at me.

Sadie had not trusted him and now I could see why.

He smirked.

What had Sadie called him?

'You . . . you are a *GRIFTER*,' I said.

He turned a bright red.

I took a step towards him, and he took a step back, uncertain. I flicked the hat off my head and pushed my face into his.

'You see my tattoos, Truman Hunt?' I snarled. 'They show I am woman with honour. They say I am Bontok woman. They say I am Igorot.'

Truman Hunt looked terrified.

I opened Sidong's book and held it up to his face. 'You see this book? Sidong make these pictures. You cannot tell her no more drawing. You cannot tell her who she be.'

I took Sidong's hand. 'Let us go, Sidong.' I said quietly.

As we walked away, we could hear the smack of Hunt's lips as they opened and closed like those of a fish plucked from the river.

We had only taken a few steps when I stopped.

'Sidong,' I said. 'Where is Samkad?'

Her tearful face looked up into mine.

'Samkad is in jail.'

When the Americans came to rule us, they built many things. Chapels for the missionaries who came flooding into our villages. Schools. And jails.

The ancients had protested bitterly. *This is not our way, we have no need for jails. We have dealt with wrongdoings since we have begun to remember. We have our own ways.* But the Americans declared that old ways would have to sit with new ways, that a jail meant security and safety. *Whose safety? Whose security?* The ancients demanded. Now there were jails up and down the mountains. It was only a matter of time before the ancients would have to let the Americans build one in our village too.

And now Samkad was locked in the pretend jail in our pretend Igorot Village.

Sidong tried to tell me what happened, but the tears came again and I comforted her and took her to the House for Women, leaving her in Ubey's care so that I could hurry to the jail. And even in the white glare of my turmoil, I noticed how the people I hurried past looked away as if they knew where I was going and they had reason to be ashamed for it.

Samkad was sitting on his heels behind the jail's iron bars.

He rose to his feet. 'It's all right,' he said. 'I am unhurt, I am fine.'

'You are not fine,' I said. 'This is not right.'

I turned. Three men were approaching, stiff-legged, shoulders bunched, like young boars girding to attack a smaller hog. I'd seen Samkad laughing with these men. I thought they were his friends.

One of them called, 'Samkad, what kind of man are you to summon a woman to your rescue?'

Samkad sighed. 'No need for that. You've already put me in jail. Leave Luki out of it.'

But I planted my fists into my hips and faced them. 'What is going on here?'

They glared at me resentfully and talked over each other in their rush to speak. 'Your beloved deserves to be in jail.' 'Always so full of himself. Always telling us, you're doing it wrong! That is not the way!' 'As if we didn't have minds of our own. As if we couldn't decide.'

'But what did he do? Tell me!' I cried.

'He wrecked our performance.' Kinyo appeared behind me. He shook his head and clicked his tongue as if he was sorry to see Samkad in such a state. Then he looked me up and down. 'Every time I see you in that dress, I marvel at how it suits you.' He grinned. 'Should we expect you to continue to dress like an American once we've returned to Bontok?'

'Was it Kinyo who put you in jail, Samkad?'

'Oh, you can't blame me,' Kinyo said. 'Everybody wanted to see him punished. He's finally managed to annoy everyone.'

I clenched my fists. 'Punished for what?'

Kinyo looked at the other men. 'Shall I explain?'

They nodded.

'We have a new attraction. A feast. You're never here, so you wouldn't know all the effort that went into planning it. We were just getting ready, setting up. Some visitors had already begun to gather, curious about what we were going to do. And Samkad . . . well, he disapproved! He'd been objecting to our plans from the beginning, but was overruled. So when it came time for us to do it, he decided he would stop us with force. He kicked our cauldron over. He stamped on our tools. He poured water over our fire.'

One of the men pointed at a blue bruise under his eye. 'He punched me, right here.'

I looked at Samkad. His head was bowed. When he spoke there was a sob in his throat. 'You've left something out, Kinyo. Tell her what kind of feast you were preparing.'

Kinyo's eyes flickered. But then he glared at me defiantly. 'We were recreating the dog sacrifice.'

'What dog sacrifice?'

'You know, when we send a dog's soul into the invisible world. When we kill a dog and then feast on it.'

I gasped. They killed the dog to feast on it? I remembered how we sent your dog, Kinang, to protect you in the invisible world and to ease your passing, how careful the ancients had been to say the right words, and how we'd thanked Kinang for accompanying you into death. *We can only do this rarely and for the right reasons*, the ancients had explained to me. *Otherwise we might upset the equilibrium of the invisible world.*

'Oh now, don't tell me, this is upsetting you too? We were lucky there were no newsmen today or Samkad's temper tantrum would have been in the newspapers in the morning!'

'Killing a dog for no reason is wrong,' I said. 'The ancients would never agree to this.'

'We had a reason. It was a re-enactment. It was for the education of our visitors.' Kinyo held a finger up. 'And there are no ancients to forbid it! And anyway, these are American dogs. Who's to say they have souls?'

I could feel the blood rushing to my face, Mother. I would have quarrelled with him, but Samkad shook his head as if to say, *don't get into trouble as well*.

Kinyo reached through the bars and patted him on the shoulder. 'Samkad, you've got to try harder to get along. Everyone's tired of you looking for things to fight about all the time.'

Samkad said nothing.

And then they left us, Mother, and I sank to my heels and held Samkad's hand through the bars, and Samkad whispered, 'Please don't worry, they should be letting me out in the morning. I shouldn't have lost my temper. I should have approached them more carefully, tried to persuade them.'

And then he told me how the idea for the dog feast came about.

It was Truman Hunt's idea. He had been looking for just one more strong attraction, and he'd suddenly remembered the day we had asked him to help with you, Mother. *A dog feast!* Truman Hunt had announced. *It will be a great success! Americans will come for miles around to see it!*

And when Samkad said, *There is no such thing as a dog feast*, nobody would listen to him. All they could hear was the clinking of coins in their imaginations.

I could not stay with him long. Sidong needed me.

'Don't worry about this, Luki. Everything will be fine,' Samkad said.

I nodded, but he knew as well as I did that that wasn't true.

30

Power Cut

That night I dreamed of your death all over again, Mother: there were the ancients crowding around, calling on the spirits, there was your hand lying limp on the ground, there was your beloved Kinang whimpering, and then, when it was all over, there was Truman Hunt, shaking his head: *No thank you, I do not eat dog.*

I sat up, my fists pressed against my pounding heart, I could feel the grief, fresh and sharp inside me again, as if it had been mere moments since you took your last breath. The ancients say a dream this real is not a dream. It is a message from the invisible world. Was it you, Mother? What were you trying to show me?

Now, I laid myself down, breathing deeply to calm my heart. I closed my eyes trying to look inward, picturing your death again. What did I not see? I forced myself to look away from the harrowing sight of you, on the floor. I made myself look at Truman Hunt, watching from the side. I could see his sadness, that he had not been able to help save you. And then, as Kinang was brought forward, his bewilderment. And then his shock as the ancients killed Kinang to send her soul to your side in the invisible world. And then something else. He was fascinated, Mother. And then, as the ancients began to sing, and the women began to keen, his eyes widened, he moved in close, he smiled. He was enjoying it.

While we had laboured to protect your spirit in the invisible world, Truman Hunt had experienced your death as an entertainment. And now he was determined that other Americans would do the same.

A soft giggle. My eyes flew open. There were people talking quietly in the dark.

One was Kiwang. 'Ubey,' she whispered. 'Did Truman Hunt ask you to join his travelling show?'

There was a pause before Ubey answered. 'Yes. So he asked you too, eh?'

'Eheh, I haven't agreed to go yet.' Ubey's voice turned conspiratorial. 'Not until I find out what the other showman is offering.'

'There's *another* one?' Kiwang whispered, incredulous.

'There are three of them, secretly approaching people in the village.'

Kiwang clicked her tongue. 'Like Truman Hunt said, America can't seem to get enough of Igorots!'

And, Mother, my stomach began to churn as their secret chat turned to the amounts of money the showmen were offering, the numbers they were recruiting, the number of months they would have to agree to.

'We'd only have to do what we're doing here,' Kiwang whispered.

'Dancing and singing and *feasting on dogs*?' Ubey snorted, trying to stifle her own giggles. I could hear the two of them gasping at the thought of America believing that there was such a thing as a dog feast.

And when at last Kiwang and Ubey went to sleep, I lay awake, staring into the darkness. *America can't get enough of Igorots*, Truman Hunt said. But it was his idea of Igorots that he wanted America to see.

They set Samkad free and when he joined us at breakfast time, Sidong wept to see him, and then she wept for fear of losing him again, and then she wept because she did not want to go to school.

Yesterday's events had put a fear into her, and I knew exactly how she felt because I too now had a fear inside me. For the first time, I was afraid to leave the village for fear of running into a Jefferson Guardsman.

People were still resentful towards Samkad, and as we ate together, he had to endure their pointed looks and snide comments. He put his arm around Sidong and tried to comfort her, even though he looked utterly exhausted from his night in the jail.

Sadie had given me a taste of what it would be like for America to become my home, and I had loved it. But yesterday, two Americas had been revealed to me.

One that was unafraid of change, that offered all kinds of choices and adventure and exciting possibility. Sadie's America. She had shown me a way of being that I could not have imagined on my own.

And then there was the other America, the one that didn't think Igorot children would like to draw with Crayolas. An America that could turn a solemn ritual into entertainment. An America that despised the sight of me – *Look at this one, all dressed up like a human being*.

I could live in the first, but how could I endure the second?

It shouldn't have been such a shock. Hadn't Americans invaded our shores? Hadn't they overwhelmed our homes? Hadn't they tried to change our ways? Somehow, I had pushed all this evidence into the shadows.

And now? The danger was inside *us*. We were forgetting what mattered. *I* was forgetting what mattered. Oh, Mother, I should never have agreed to work in the Pike. Sidong needed me. And Samkad too.

It broke my heart too when Samkad presented me with a smooth, untroubled face and told me not to worry, he would be able to manage with Sidong while I went to Sadie at the Pike. I thanked him and dressed for work. I didn't tell him about yesterday's troubles with the guardsmen, and I didn't tell him about Sadie's offer.

There was no need.

I wasn't going to be gone long. Today, I was going to tell Sadie I could no longer work for her. And, of course, that meant I would not be accepting her offer to stay with her in America.

The Scout on duty at the gate waved me through, but I had to pause to swallow my fears before I put one foot in front of the other to exit the village. I spotted Johnny immediately, waiting for me just on the edge of the parade ground.

My plan was clear. I would ask Johnny to wait for me outside Sadie's tent while I said goodbye. And then he could escort me safely back to the village. Safely? After yesterday, I wondered if I would ever feel safe again.

'Johnny!' I called.

He turned and I cried out in shock. Mother, his face was black with bruising. Swelling around his eye and mouth made him almost unrecognizable. His nose was covered by a large white dressing.

He smiled through distended lips and spoke slowly as if his tongue was too big for his mouth. 'Last night, after the concert, the guardsmen . . . *me golpearon*. They beat me up.'

Mother, I felt an icy finger run down my spine. I had been calling myself foolish to feel this leaping terror of the guardsmen. But I was right to be afraid. The guardsmen were not going to allow their humiliation to pass unavenged. And now it turned out that other guardsmen were happy to join in.

They must have known that the Constabulary band were tasked with folding away the chairs after every concert.

They'd waited until Johnny was alone, on an unlit path, grabbed him, gagged him, and dragged him to a deserted corner where they'd beat him soundly.

'*Fue tarde*, the boss was calling the roll when they realized that *yo no estába* – I was missing. They found me in the parade ground—'

'He was a mess.' Loving stood to one side, shaking his head.

'Boss!' Johnny saluted.

The lieutenant looked tired, his eyes smudged and the lines deeply etched around his mouth. He sighed. 'After what happened at the concert, I should have realized they were up to more mischief.'

'The concert?' I looked from one to the other. 'Something happen?'

'Sabotage,' Loving growled.

'The lights went out in the middle of the concert,' Johnny said. '*Un apagón*. A power cut.'

'Obviously, the work of those bastards,' Loving said. He grinned at Johnny. 'But you men did good.'

'We kept playing.' Johnny smiled. 'Right to the end! And when we finished, the audience was so impressed they began to cheer and throw their hats in the air.'

'Hah, that must have hacked them off.' Loving laughed. But then he sighed, his face serious. 'It made them thirst for more blood, unfortunately.'

Johnny shrugged. 'I think they would have beat me up, whether or not their sabotage worked.'

'President Roosevelt,' I said. 'You must tell him. He will stop them.'

Johnny and Loving exchanged glances.

'What?' I looked from one to the other. President Roosevelt had invited us to America. He would not stand for any of this.

'I . . . ah . . . well, I think right now, the most important thing to do is get Johnny off the streets. We have it on good authority that the guardsmen and their friends are looking for him.' The grim lines returned to Loving's face. He turned to me. 'That is why, with regret, today is the last time Johnny will escort you to the Pike. It is too dangerous.'

I nodded. I was expecting it.

'If I had my way, he wouldn't be doing it at all today. But he felt that he owed it to you.' He turned to Johnny. 'I've spoken to Professor Kovacs at the Anthropology Building and he is willing to take you on as a messenger boy, but only if your English is good enough. I assured him it was, but he wants to hear it for himself. Just a short interview, he said. You must be there in an hour.'

'Yes, boss,' Johnny said. '*Gracias*, boss.'

Loving left us then, and it was my chance to explain to Johnny that this would be my last journey to the Pike as well. I needed him to wait while I talked to Sadie, and then take me back. We agreed that he would take me with him to his appointment at the Anthropology Building. It wouldn't be long, he said. I could wait outside while he showed Professor Kovacs that his English was good enough for a messenger boy.

As we made our way through the familiar avenues to the Pike, Johnny told me how the band managed to continue playing after the lights were turned off.

'We all grew up playing in bands in small towns. Our music was the centre of any important event – *una celebración religiosa o fiesta*. We used to duel against other bands to see who could outplay the other, without having to read the notes on sheet music. Sometimes the battles lasted for many nights, we played until one of the bands forgot their music first, or faltered from exhaustion. It's called *tambakan*. So when the lights blinked off last night, the men whispered to each other, "*Tambakan! Tambakan!*" and played on.

'And the boss!' Johnny laughed. 'When he realized what we were doing, he pulled out his *pañuelo* – it's a white cloth – tied it to his baton and waved it around as the audience clapped in time! Ah, Luki, it was beautiful! I can still hear *el aplauso*, the people were cheering and stamping their feet!'

His bruised face stretched into a smile. 'I had five brothers. We were farmers. My older brother taught me how to play his guitar. We used to attend a church with two *padres*. One to celebrate the mass, and the other to play the piano and lead the singing. One Sunday, I sneaked back into the church after mass. I wanted to try playing that piano. I could remember the notes the *padre* had played, and I found that I could easily pick them out on the keys. The *padre* found me, and he insisted on teaching me how to play, and how to read music. And later, Loving found me, in my music school in Manila, and signed me up to the Constabulary Band. Johnny isn't my real name,' he said shyly. 'It's Juan. I changed it because Americans couldn't pronounce Juan.'

31

Ignorant

Johnny settled himself down on the fence opposite Sadie's tent. I promised I wouldn't be long.

But there was no sign of Sadie, so I decided to prepare her dressing table. It was the least I could do. I opened the vanity box, packed with small tins and jars. Then I laid out the sticks of greasepaint on a piece of paper in the order Sadie needed them alongside the freshly washed pads and brushes for the face powder she used to blend the colours on her face. I brushed out one of her wigs, working my way up from the edges to carefully remove tangles, the way she taught me. It didn't take long at all.

'Looky! Look what've got!' Sadie burst in like a sudden ray of sunshine, holding something up high in each hand. 'Ta-daaaaah!'

Before I could say a word, she'd already put one of them in my hand.

It was some kind of food. It was a crunchy kind of biscuit rolled into a cone with something inside, something cold. Was it a ball of snow?

'Lick it like this.' Sadie stuck her tongue out and flicked it over the snowball.

I did the same.

It was delicious! It was creamy, like milk, and sweet. I licked it some more, imitating the way Sadie was slurping on hers, nibbling the cone and licking the snowball.

'It's called ice cream!' she said, between licks. 'Isn't it good? One of the Arab food stalls make this thing called zalabia. They've been rolling it up and selling it with ice cream. Eat up, Luki, before it melts!' She pushed the last bite of ice cream and zalabia into her mouth.

I would never have thought of combining a crunchy sweet thing like zalabia with ice cream. But this was the sort of impossible thing that could happen at the World's Fair. I rolled the last of my ice cream around in my mouth and swallowed. And then, to my dismay, I began to cry.

'Looky, what's wrong?' Sadie's eyes widened.

I tried to hide my face but my hands were sticky with the ice cream, and to my shame Sadie had a good look at my streaming face and my ugly downturned mouth before I managed to turn away.

I felt a warm arm over my shoulders. 'Is there something on your mind, Looky, honey?'

I tried to tell Sadie everything. But though English came

more easily to my throat now, it wasn't enough to soften my message. My heavy tongue could not add any kindness, could not show Sadie my sadness and regret. I might as well have been a boar grunting in the woods.

At first she looked confused and then she just looked irritated.

'Looky, I thought you were my friend! How could you do this? How could you abandon me? You can't imagine how lonely it is being the only woman in a camp like this! I thought you understood me! I thought you saw how much you meant to me!'

I tried to tell her that I did not come to this decision lightly, Mother. But the more I tried to explain, the angrier she got.

'You would rather leave,' she said, her voice rising. 'You would rather sleep in a mud hut or whatever you Igorots live in than lead a civilized life in America. You would rather dress like a savage than wear the clothes I gave you. You would rather have *NOTHING* than something.'

My eyes were blinking fast with the effort of trying to remember the words for 'sorry' in English. But I couldn't find them. The last sorry I'd heard had not been in English. '*Lo siento,*' I said, remembering how Johnny had said it, even though it hadn't been his fault that he had been attacked by guardsmen.

'What the heck does that mean? Why are you talking gibberish? Looky, I took you in! I met you and I liked you and I saw your potential and I gave you a chance – and I persevered even when you turned me down the first time. And now . . .' She kicked her dressing table and all the pots and brushes I'd laid out came crashing to the ground. 'We've become FRIENDS! Why would you do this to me?'

I opened my mouth to say, *But I'm not doing this to you. You* are *my friend. My dear, dear friend!* But I was too slow. Sadie made a strangled noise, pulling at her hair.

'I was looking forward to it, Looky!' The paint on her lips had faded and there was a drip of ice cream on her dress that, had I stayed, I would have washed out carefully. 'I thought we could travel together to all the Wild West Shows and I thought we would see America together. I thought we would have a laugh!'

I tried to explain, about the Jefferson Guards, the way they talked, and how it was not safe for me to be outside the reservation. But Sadie, in her fury, was not prepared to listen.

'I was doing you a favour! I thought you deserved better than life as a savage! I saved you! I'm not the villain here!'

I had often wondered why Sadie had chosen me. Why had she invited me into her life? Just look at the Pike, Mother, all those people. She could have picked anyone, but she picked me.

She paused for breath.

'I . . . cannot . . . stay,' I managed to say. 'I need . . . go . . . home.'

'HOME!' Sadie threw her head back and laughed harshly. 'From everything I've read – and believe me I've been FASCINATED, reading everything about the Philippine

Islands that I can get my hands on – based on everything I've read, *you're not going home to much*. It's hot, stinky and stupid. It's the *armpit of the world*.'

'No!' I cried. 'No! No! No!'

Sadie sneered at me. 'Looky, if you weren't so *IGNORANT* you would try to think more like an American. Look for opportunity. I thought I saw something in you, but I was wrong. You're just like the rest of the savages.'

'I need go back!'

'To what? Planting rice? Or maybe you miss eating *puppies* for breakfast.'

My heart contracted. I couldn't breathe. For a moment everything went black.

But then I heard the swish of the tent flaps sweeping open. Bright sunshine flooded in.

Sadie staggered backwards in shock.

I heard Johnny's voice. 'Miss Luki, it's time to leave.'

'How dare you!' Sadie raged. 'This is a private tent!' She reached for the nearest thing, a coffee cup and threw it at him.

It fell, harmlessly to the floor. Johnny took my arm. *'Vamos. She doesn't deserve you.'* His bruised face was dark with anger.

I barely managed to grab my hat and coat before he pulled me past Sadie.

'Come back here!' Sadie sobbed. 'I'm not finished with you!'

'But *she* is finished with you,' Johnny said, as he marched me out of her life.

32

Heads

Eheh, Mother, my heart. It roared inside my chest like a violent monsoon. I was shaking. My feet, in their clumsy American shoes, somehow carried me away from Sadie, howling and ranting behind us like some kind of night beast. I tried to focus on Johnny's voice – *Vamos, vamos, vamos* – until we reached the gate, and there was the Wild West Show barker, up on his perch, today covered in Indian feathers, his bare chest bloody with red paint again.

He flashed his teeth as we hustled past. 'See ya tomorrow!' forgetting to move his mouth away from his tin horn and blasting the words down the street.

'*Adiós*,' Johnny muttered.

We entered the heaving street, Johnny pulling me behind him. When Samkad and I were little, we used to catch geckos to tow them along on the end of a string. That's how I felt,

Mother, like one of those geckos, trailing behind Johnny, my feet moving without knowing where they were going.

I had thought of Sadie as my friend. But to her, I was only someone to be saved from mud huts and dog eating. She just wanted to see if I could be turned into someone else. The way Truman Hunt was trying to turn us into his idea of Igorots. What a fool I'd been.

'*Estamos aquí*,' Johnny said. 'We are here.'

I gazed up at the red-brick building, confused. And then I remembered. Johnny had promised to meet someone at the Anthropology Building before he took me back to the village.

I rubbed my eyes, took my hat off, tidied my hair. Johnny watched me with gentle eyes. '*Bien*,' he said. 'You made the right decision to leave that woman.'

I shrugged and tried to smile.

'Now, we must find Professor Kovacs,' he said. 'The entrance is this way, I think.'

We ascended the stone steps, entering through huge double doors into a musty room with a lofty ceiling. It would have felt cavernous had it not been crammed with cabinets and glass boxes. Making our way down a narrow alley between cupboards, we peered at the cups and bowls and plates on display.

'Hah, people actually like looking at these things?' Johnny said. He pointed at a sign on the distant wall. 'It says the offices are down that way, in the basement.'

Some stairs led to a cool, tiled corridor. 'You'll probably have to wait outside while I speak to him,' Johnny was saying.

'It shouldn't take any time at all. He will hear how good my English is as soon as I open my mouth.'

A door to one side opened. To my surprise, Bayongasan and five other Suyocs wandered out. 'Luki!' He smiled. 'I thought we were the last Igorots to be measured?'

'Measured?'

'Ah, I forget that you work at the Pike! They have been taking measurements and tests of everyone at the Reservation. Height. Weight. Measuring the sizes of our heads and parts of our bodies. Also strength, breathing . . . it feels like they've tested everything. Is that why you're here?'

I didn't answer right away, still trying to process this measuring business. What for? But I gestured vaguely at Johnny. 'Johnny just needs to talk to somebody before we go home.'

Everyone nodded politely to Johnny. They had all seen him collecting me at the gates every day.

'Well,' Bayongasan said. 'Perhaps you are not too late, and they can take some measurements while you're here.'

I tried to look agreeable, even though it sounded like the last thing I wanted to do. As Johnny and I continued down the corridor, I could feel their eyes boring into the back of my head.

We found the right office and Johnny knocked on the door even though it was open. A brown-haired woman behind a desk seemed alarmed to see us. She stared at Johnny's swollen face and then at my tattoos. Johnny tried to smile. 'Sorry, I had a fall the other day, I don't look my best. I am Johnny. Professor Kovacs is expecting me.'

But the woman couldn't relax. She kept eyeing me as she said, 'Yes, you can go right in.'

'I am escorting this lady to the Igorot Village. Can she wait here with you while I speak to the professor?'

The woman actually looked terrified.

Johnny bit his lip. 'I can take her in with me, I'm sure the professor will understand.'

The woman looked relieved. 'Oh, that's all right then.'

She stood up and knocked lightly on another door. 'Professor Kovacs, the boy is here.' She pushed the door open and then leaped back to allow us to go through.

I hung back, worried that Kovacs would not want me there.

'Ah, Loving's boy. Johnny.' The voice was light and pleasant. I relaxed and followed Johnny into the room. 'Loving told me what happened. It's a rough business, eh? So many of those guardsmen are veterans of the insurgency. You never know what men like that would do when provoked. And what have we here?'

The room was large and lit by low lamps. A thin glaze of sunshine filtered in through high windows. Behind a large desk sat a pale man whose thin face was covered by thick spectacles.

'Yes, I am Johnny, Professor Kovacs, sir. This is Luki from the Igorot Village. She's been working at the Pike. I am escorting her home today. Your secretary said she could come in with me.'

'Quite right,' Professor Kovacs said, staring at me intently with his over-large spectacle eyes. 'Does she speak English?'

Mother, I was offended. Is that crazy? I mean, I barely spoke English. But here was a stranger talking about me and staring straight at me. I considered saying something, but after today, I just couldn't be bothered. I left Johnny to reply, enthusiastically, I noticed, *Oh yes, we have conversations, etc. etc.* while I had a good look at the room around me.

Their voices subsided to a dull murmur as I examined shelves, stuffed with books and objects, teetering right up to the ceiling where, I was startled to see, a row of white faces peering down at us. I was relieved to see they were made of some kind of white pottery, with small paper labels stuck over their hairless pates. Scanning the next shelf, I was shocked to see human skulls, looking pitted and dirty next to the pottery heads.

Mother, the room was packed with heads. Even the walls were papered with pictures of them: kodaks of heads facing front and sideways, diagrams, sketches of skulls, tiny writing covering every page, like bird scratchings.

The two men continued to talk. *I learned to speak English at the Music Conservatory where I was studying the piano*, I heard Johnny say. *There are music conservatories in Manila? How interesting!* Professor Kovacs replied.

On the large mahogany table at the centre of the room were perhaps twenty more heads, life-sized ones this time, made of plaster. Their eyes were all closed, as if whoever had sculpted them had done so while they were asleep. I recognized Bayongasan from the Igorot Village. And I recognized another as a Pygmy. I had seen his picture in Sadie's official

252

catalogue of the World's Fair. Sadie had been quite dismissive of the Pygmies. *The Pygmies are from a place called Africa, just as backward as the Philippine Islands. But see, now I have got to know you, Looky, I think you Igorots are far more advanced – look at them, dressed in grass skirts!*

But looking at the Pygmy's head with his broad nose and full lips, he looked just like us.

Kovacs had risen from his desk and was pointing at some of the writing pinned to the walls. *We're taking measurements of everybody, including intelligence, memory, hearing, sight, movement and agility. Not just the indigenous people, but the tourists too. It's called anthropometry. The data will allow us to compare and classify the different races.*

He bent down to lift a huge glass jar from the floor to the table. It was filled to the brim with a clear liquid. Inside floated a soft-looking, greyish mass of convoluted folds. It looked like a loaf of bread, but I knew what it was. A brain.

There have been several deaths already, which is to be expected, what with there being thousands and thousands of participants in the fair. The fair hospital has allowed us to harvest specimens from the dead . . . like skeletons and these brains here. He bent down again, to lift up a second jar with a brain in it. And then a third. *This one is the most recent.* The jars had large white labels with thick black writing on them.

Mother, I had helped attend the dead many times since I was a girl. But seeing these human parts separated out from the whole, made my stomach churn. I looked away.

'Sir, I must say *adiós* now, sorry,' Johnny suddenly said. 'I must take Luki back to the Igorot Village.'

It was so abrupt, I whirled round to stare at him. Beads of sweat trickled down his face. Were the brains making him queasy?

Professor Kovacs must have noticed it too, because he laughed. 'It's all right, son, I understand. You'll get used to it. And don't worry, your job here will be to deliver messages, not brains!'

'Yes, sir,' Johnny murmured. He grabbed my hand and dragged me so roughly out of the room, I thought perhaps he might be needing to vomit. But he ushered me rapidly through the secretary's anteroom, up the stairs and out of the building. When we finally emerged, he just stood there, looking at the sky.

'Are you all right?' I asked.

He shook his head. 'It's . . .' He bit his lip. 'So many dead.'

I felt an icy gust blow on my neck. He was right. That room was a tomb.

I remembered how puzzled the ancients were when they learned that the Americans called us headhunters. They had tried to explain. *We take the heads of our enemies to stop them continuing to torment us from the invisible world. It is the right thing to do, the moral thing, for the sake of our people.* But the Americans told us it was disgusting. It made savages of us.

And yet here they were, splitting open the heads of the dead to possess what was inside.

Who were the headhunters now?

33

The Hospital

Johnny finally got tired of staring at the sky and turned his gaze on me. He stared at me so intensely, I had to look away. 'Miss Luki,' he said softly. 'We must go somewhere. Now. I promise to explain later.'

'Explain now!' I said.

But Johnny shook his head. 'I will explain when I am sure.' His face crumpled – oh so briefly, I might have imagined it. And then he smoothed his expression and when he spoke again, it was to say, *¡Vámonos!*

Vámonos. Vámonos. Vámonos. The word echoed in my head like a ritual chant. Johnny looked so grim, I didn't dare press him for more explanation. But a cold dread was now sitting in my belly like a stone. A terrible thought threatened to take shape in my mind, but I pushed it away. Surely not, Mother. Surely not.

We walked across a plush green square, and then a vast

courtyard of shining white stone, and then we strode past a great glittering basin, so huge the boats upon it looked like scattered leaves. Then an avenue lined with trees, their canopies tamed into neatly clipped balls. Above us, the palace rooftops were gaily decked in striped American flags.

Soon, we turned into a narrower street, with smaller, plainer buildings devoid of monumental columns and turrets and domes.

Johnny bounded up some steps and pushed the large door open.

We entered.

After the sun shining so bright and white in the sky, I was blinded by the darkness. As my eyes began to adjust, I saw that we were in a high-ceilinged lobby. The tiles were green under my feet. The woman standing in front of us in a small white cap was grimacing.

'You should not come in here! Out! Out!'

Johnny was clutching his hat to his chest. '*¡Lo siento!* Ma'am, we didn't know!'

The woman just glared at him. She pointed at the door. 'The coloured entrance is down the side. You can't miss it.'

Johnny took my arm and led me out again, hurrying me down another path. 'That entrance was only for white people,' he explained.

White people. *A gugu holding a white girl! No white woman would be friends with a gugu. What were you doing, stepping out with this white girl?* My gorge rose in my throat. But I must have looked dumb or something, because Johnny pulled his sleeve up and pointed at his arm. '*¡Mira!* Look. We are coloured. And that woman, she is white. In America, white and coloured do not mix. And so we must use *this* door.'

A white entrance and a coloured entrance. *White and coloured do not mix.* Lieutenant Loving had said something similar to us the other day after he ordered the guardsmen away. *You're going to get them killed.* It seemed mad to divide the world according to skin colour.

Johnny began to push the door open. Then he stopped and turned to me, as if he was about to say something. Mother, his face was so haggard I felt a shiver of fear. Then he closed his mouth and opened the door. We entered.

There was a corridor, with an assortment of people sitting on benches on either side. The smell of tobacco smoke mingled with a sharp odour that made my eyes sting.

I recognized two men from the Chinese Village. They sat, glum and silent, their shaven heads bowed. There was a grey-haired Indian man puffing on a pipe – at least I think he was Indian, Mother, his hair was tied back in a long plait even though he was wearing American trousers and an American coat. A small boy from the Esquimaux Village sat on the lap of a woman who might have been his mother. He held up a hand bound up in a thick bandage and cried bitterly as the woman kissed his hair. The furry coats they wore at their village were in a pile beside them.

We must have looked lost because the Indian leaned

towards us, tapping his pipe on the back of his hand and letting the ashes fall on the floor. 'You looking for a nurse? There are no doctors here.' I was surprised to hear a voice as American as Truman Hunt's. 'There's a nurse in the ward over there.' He nodded towards a closed door.

We entered timidly into a long room. Small, barred windows let in a sickly light. Crumpled figures lay in iron beds, so many of them, jammed against the walls. The smell became pungent.

Something in my belly turned. 'This is a hospital!' I cried.

Johnny nodded. 'We are here to see your friend.'

I peered into the beds. Tilin? Tilin? But the dark faces that returned my gaze were strangers. Such a lonely looking place, all these strangers, each on their own in this foul-smelling room. I cursed Truman Hunt under my breath. How could he have put Tilin here, all by herself? *There will be doctors*, he had said. *It's the best place for someone this sick.* It looked nothing of the sort, Mother.

'What are you doing here?' An angry woman in a white cap and white dress came rushing towards us (a *white* woman, I told myself).

'Tilin!' I said. 'We need see Tilin.' My heart was pounding. I was excited.

She just looked at me, uncomprehending. Johnny stepped forward. Seeing his bruised face she shied away, but he held both hands up in supplication and began to speak. *An Igorot woman. A month ago now. Pneumonia.* And as he spoke, she shook her head and shook her head and my heart beat louder and louder. When she spoke, I couldn't hear her for the banging in my chest.

But I saw the blood drain from Johnny's face.

The woman fetched a thick book filled with writing. She flicked through the pages and held it up, open for Johnny to see. And then she was pushing me, her hand hard on my shoulder. Past the beds, out through the door, and into the aching light of day.

The woman slammed the door shut behind us.

Johnny sat on his heels and covered his eyes with his hands.

'What is it? What did she say? Tell me!' I begged him.

Johnny stood, his head bowed. He took a deep breath. 'The brains on Kovacs' table, they had labels,' he said. 'The first two had written on them: *IGOROT, MALE, PNEUMONIA*. The date was soon after your arrival in Saint Louis.'

I gasped. The brains belonged to the men who died on the train! Johnny grabbed my hand and held it tight, his eyes glistening with compassion.

'But the third brain, Luki. The third one was labelled: *IGOROT, FEMALE, PNEUMONIA*. And there is only one woman who's fallen ill in the village, isn't there? Only one.'

No. No. No.

I wanted to pull away but Johnny wouldn't let go.

'I asked the nurse. She looked in her book. The nurse, she said . . .'

No. No. No.

'She said Tilin died a month ago.'

No. No. No.

Johnny folded me in his arms and held me, until I could scream no more.

Part Four

Part Four

34

Mourning

How could this be? We had walked down the mountain together, fled our tormentors in Manila's stony streets, sailed that boundless ocean, and crossed America by rail. How could Tilin's journey end like this, in a smelly iron bed, surrounded by strangers? American medicine had not saved Tilin. And I had betrayed her by leaving her to die alone.

I tried to put myself there, in that bed, enduring the tinctures and cures and potions of American healing. That nurse wouldn't have known the right words to ease her spirit into the invisible world. I tried to feel Tilin's soul, curled up inside her, sticky with congealed phlegm, desperate to free itself from the shrivelling darkness of her flesh.

And when her body finally released her spirit, what was it like to be alone, without your people to sing the songs that would comfort you, without anyone there to bid you goodbye, to tell you they would see you in the invisible world when they too reached their deaths.

Nobody had been there to sit with her, to honour her, to demonstrate to the world of the spirits that she was precious, someone who deserved their love, someone that they should welcome.

When we reached the village gates, I looked up at Johnny, at the whites of his eyes gleaming from under his visor's shadow. He was saying something, but somehow I could not make out the words. He patted my shoulder, but I felt nothing. I was numb with grief.

When Johnny left, my heart felt like a trapped bird beating its wings feverishly in my chest. How could everything continue to be so ordinary? The sounds of life on the Reservation drifted on the slight breeze – distant trumpet blasts, the crunch of marching feet, laughter and song from the Visayans, and the soft chatter of visitors still wandering about.

I became conscious of a sound, like barking. It was Truman Hunt chasing after me as I entered the village gates. He waved a small piece of paper. 'What did you do?' he cried. 'Sadie just sent me this note to say you're fired and she's terminating our deal.'

Sadie? Mother, I almost laughed to remember how devastated I'd been earlier today. It seemed so trivial now. I'd had no idea of what was to come.

I looked at Truman Hunt. I felt like I'd turned into smoke. One gust of wind and I might disappear. Could he see right through me? But my voice, when I spoke, was solid.

'Tilin is dead.'

The words had an extraordinary effect. Truman Hunt's face collapsed into itself, his eyes seemed to wrinkle and implode, the corners of his mouth drooped right down his jaw. It was like his skin had suddenly turned inside out.

But I knew he was just shocked that I'd found out. Because if he had truly cared about Tilin, Mother, he would have told us about her death as soon as it happened.

I could have accused him, Mother . . . said, *How could you?* or *Why did you not tell us?* But I didn't see the point. I was not interested in the answer.

He began to bluster. 'We did not think she would die . . . and then I couldn't think of a way to tell you. And I was so busy running things here, I couldn't . . . I couldn't . . .'

I began to turn away.

'Where are you going? Are you going to tell the others?' Truman Hunt said. 'Please. Don't tell them. We had important news just now. News we've been waiting for. The President is coming to visit tomorrow. *President Roosevelt himself!*'

It amazed me, Mother. Had Truman Hunt mentioned this last week, I would have been leaping about in excitement. But the last few days had changed me. I could summon no interest in the President's visit.

'You can't tell anyone about Tilin!' Truman Hunt was saying. 'They've got a lot of preparation to do for tomorrow and I don't want them distracted! You can't just turn up and . . .'

Mother, I walked away then. I could feel rage building inside me, but why waste my feelings on Truman Hunt? I needed to be strong. I had to tell Sidong. I had to tell Samkad. I had to tell the others. And then we had to build a death chair for Tilin. We had to show her that her spirit did not deserve to be alone.

Oh, Tilin. You had surprised me into becoming your friend. I was determined not to like you, but we had more in common than I had realized. And now, you were gone.

As Truman Hunt had said, everyone was preparing for President Roosevelt's visit. A stage was being built on the other side of the pretend fort. The President would be seated on the stage, and one by one, the different peoples of the Reservation were going to perform in front of him. Kinyo and a group of men were practising a pretend battle with axes and spears. Several women were practising a dance. And Anteng walked past, humming *My Country 'Tis of Thee*.

Samkad and Sidong were sitting under a tree, and as they turned their smiling faces towards me, I flinched, knowing that I would soon be plunging them into darkness.

I told everyone.

And we did our best, the men beating their gangsas and the women singing ritual songs. We did all the things necessary to guide a spirit to its new life in the invisible world. But how could it be right to hold a funeral without a body? How could we help Tilin into the invisible world when a month had already passed since her spirit had ebbed from her corpse? Who was listening to our comforting words? How could Tilin's spirit find her way back to the Igorot Village?

It was unbearable to think of Tilin in America's invisible world, all alone amongst the spirits of utter strangers. Everyone knew this, and by the flickering light of the fire, the furtive looks did not escape me. We were going through the motions for our own comfort. But was any of this going to be of use to Tilin?

And, Mother, through it all, Sidong said nothing. Mother, she just bowed her head and sat silently, her fingers lacing and unlacing in her lap, listening to the funeral.

That night, when the fire had died down and the last of the songs had been sung, Sidong and I prepared for bed in silence. If we'd had Tilin's corpse, resting in that death chair, we would have stayed up, sat the night through with her, talking to her, telling stories, reminding her of the life that she had had. We would have kept her company until her spirit was ready to join the world of the dead.

But we didn't have Tilin's corpse. We didn't know where Tilin's spirit was.

Sidong snuggled into my arms, lying on my shoulder like a baby; I could feel her tears rolling wetly down my arm. We adults are here to protect children, to comfort them, to answer their questions. But, Mother, there was nothing I could do for her.

Sidong raised her head and whispered, 'She cannot die *here*, Luki.'

'I know,' I whispered back, holding her closer. But she pulled free and sat up. In the darkness, I could feel her eyes boring into me.

'What happens when we leave? What will happen to her spirit? We cannot leave her here! Would she know how to find her way to us?'

I had wondered the same thing. If only there was a way to take her spirit back to Bontok with us.

Sidong sobbed into my shoulder. 'Tilin! Tilin!'

The other women in the House for Women sniffled and sighed, listening helplessly as the child wept for her sister.

I held her until she fell asleep, and then I lay there in the dark, feeling too hot, then too cold, listening to the twitchings of insects in the thatched roof overhead and the sleep rumblings of the other women.

I rolled out of bed and carefully groped my way to the door.

Outside, the stars pressed down from the sky, the young trees stretched up to the moon, and the coals died quietly in the ash heap. The white city beyond the tall bamboo fence had switched off all its lights, and the observation wheel was now just a vague smudge on the horizon.

I lowered myself slowly onto a log outside the House for Women. A mist began to rise, glowing white around my feet, like it did every morning in Bontok. But this was not Bontok, I reminded myself. This was Saint Louis.

I thought of death. I thought about losing you, Mother. I thought about how I'd longed for you to walk with me again.

The air grew cold. It flowed around me in a small current, causing my skin to prickle where it touched.

I felt a pressure in my ears, the kind of pressure you feel when you're walking up a steep mountain trail. Up and up and up and your head is suddenly expanding fit to burst . . . until, suddenly . . . pop!

The pressure was gone, my head empty and clear again. But Mother, I could not move. It was like I had been left unbalanced, the weight of muscle and sinew and bone pushing me down onto the log. I tried to move, tried to raise my hand, waggle my knees. But nothing. My will somehow seemed unconnected to the physical part of me. And then I felt myself bend forward, I felt my hand close around a stick, stirring the coals, so that it flared into a weak, guttering fire.

My vision began to waver. It was as if I was looking at the world through a screen.

Mother, I didn't understand what had happened until, suddenly, I rose to my feet. And it wasn't me that willed myself to stand. I took a deep breath, and it wasn't me that inhaled. And then it wasn't me that took one step, and another step, put my feet together then hopped. I laughed out loud, but it wasn't me that made the sound.

'Your body feels good,' I said. 'So strong.'

I didn't speak, Mother, but the words came out of my mouth. There was another spirit that had crowded into me, pushing mine aside, taken control of my physical self.

Tilin? I whispered.

'Shh,' I said. *She* said.

I picked up a bottle of water, tilted my head back and drank. It wet my parched throat. 'Did you feel that too? I haven't had a drink like that in a long time. So refreshing!'

Tilin. You can't do this.

'Stay down,' I said. *She* said.

And then in the blackness, I saw Samkad emerge. He trudged towards me, his face haggard.

'Couldn't you sleep, Luki?'

Tilin shook my head.

'I don't blame you.' He sat down buried his head in his hands and began to weep.

Tilin sat me down, put my arm around his shoulder and rubbed my cheek against his hair. *Tilin!* I begged. *Stop it!*

'I wish I had never come to America,' Samkad said. 'I came because I thought you needed me to protect you. But I have not protected anyone!'

Tilin put my arms around Samkad and I could feel his body shaking as he sobbed wretchedly.

Please, Tilin.

'Brother!' It was Kinyo. He bent over us, rubbing Samkad's back. 'You are grieving for Tilin. I am so sorry, brother.'

Samkad pushed Kinyo's hand away, jumping up. 'Take your hands off me!'

Mother, he glared at Kinyo as if he wanted to run a blade through him.

'Kinyo. I realize now that you are right. You are no brother of mine.'

'I am sorry I said that. I was angry. Now you are angry too,' Kinyo said softly. 'Luki, help me calm him down.'

I would have. But I couldn't move. Tilin kept my body absolutely still. Kinyo sighed and tried again. 'Brother, I know you're upset . . .'

'I heard you talking to Truman Hunt,' Samkad said. 'I heard you cheering when he invited you to join his travelling show. You disgust me.'

'Luki!' Kinyo's eyes begged me to say something kind, something to defuse Samkad's anger. But I just looked at them, silent and unblinking. Kinyo shook his head. 'Brother, I am not going to argue with you. You need time to mourn.'

'Yes, Tilin is dead! And she wouldn't be dead if we had stayed in Bontok! Roosevelt might as well have strangled her with his own hands.'

Kinyo sighed. 'Brother, we belong to America now. You have got to get used to it!'

'NEVER!' Suddenly Samkad had his hands around Kinyo's neck.

And, Mother, I wanted to pull Samkad off his brother. But I just sat there, trapped in Tilin's grip.

There was shouting. Several men appeared. They tried to pull the brothers apart, but Samkad had become a wild animal, hitting and biting and strangling.

271

CRACK. One of the men brought a clay pot down on Samkad's head. He dropped to the ground, dazed.

'To the jail with him,' one shouted. 'And this time, he's not getting out.'

They each took an arm and dragged him away, leaving Kinyo looking downcast. He shook his head. 'I'm sorry, Luki.' he murmured before he walked off in the direction of the jail.

And still Tilin, filling every space inside me, held me absolutely still.

Tilin, you cannot do this to me.

'I am not staying long,' I said. *She* said. 'I just wanted to tell you something.' My voice was dwindling, as if the spirit could not pass enough air out my throat. 'Don't leave me here, in America. Take me back to Bontok. Please.'

And only then, Mother, did I feel her weight lift. I raised my hand and touched my face. My body was responding to my will again. Tilin was gone.

35

The President

It was unfair, I knew, to want everyone to stay sad, to continue to grieve like I was grieving. Truman Hunt looked harassed as he lined us all up and then ushered us out of the Igorot Village to the parade ground. He made no comment about the funeral singing and the empty chair made of branches we had built the night before. Except to say – quietly, so the others couldn't hear – *Why couldn't you wait? Why did you have to tell them? Now look – they've all turned into ghosts! I needed them lively for the President!*

He was right. They were all in a strange mood. The other women, who knew Tilin well, had been shocked and unhappy to know Truman Hunt had kept her death a secret. And yet, apart from a few sharp glances, none of them took him to task. The men, who did not know Tilin, were sombre but just as silent. It pricked me, Mother, to see this. Perhaps they were conflicted by Truman Hunt's secret plans to take them on tour across the United States.

But the gloomy mood lifted once we were out on the wide open parade grounds, where a large platform festooned with red, white and blue ribbons had been built, where the Constabulary Band was playing a series of cheerful tunes in one corner and the Scouts were marching in another.

I couldn't be resentful, Mother. It was exciting to be gathered in one place with all the different peoples of the Reservation. Hundreds of tourists watched us from behind a rope barrier. They cheered as we took our places in front of the stage – encouraging the Visayans to burst into song. The Mangyans and the Aeta men, whom Americans labelled Negritos, were dressed in breechcloths like our own men, except for one, who wore an American suit and tall hat.

We had seen the Aetas, Mangyans and the Visayans on the ship, but being confined to the Igorot Village, it was our first time to meet the peoples who had arrived later.

The Moros shuffled in behind us and quietly sat on their heels to wait.

'Mind them, they're bloodthirsty,' Truman Hunt whispered. But there was nothing menacing about them in their shiny purple, green and gold clothing and head wraps.

There were also a people called the Bagobo, the men with long hair down to their waists, and dressed in beautiful beaded costumes.

It was exciting. But it was also profoundly sad. It felt so full of life, and yet I couldn't stop thinking of the dead. *Tilin, my friend.* I thought. *I don't want to leave you. But how can I take you with me? Tell me, Tilin.*

And then there was Samkad, still sitting in jail, the cut on his head bandaged, with two bored Scouts guarding him. Mother, I wondered whether to tell him what had happened to me last night. But when I went to see him in the morning, he just turned his face away and stayed that way until I left. *He's not ready to know about you, Tilin,* I thought. And it was just as well, it would have just depressed him even more to see how easily our fellow Igorots had cheered up.

All the school children had to gather around Miss Zamora, because they were going to sing for the President. Sidong didn't resist when I led her to the teacher, who was sitting on a chair, her large skirt fluffed out like a giant mushroom, the embroidered sleeves of her lowlander costume looking stiff and uncomfortable. Sidong crouched at Miss Zamora's feet, opening her drawing book and taking out her box of Crayola, as I quietly explained that Sidong's sister had died. Miss Zamora was nodding sadly when Truman Hunt appeared.

'What did I tell you, kid? No more drawing.' He grabbed Sidong's Crayola box and drawing book and handed them to Miss Zamora. 'You hang onto these, miss.' He tipped his hat and left us. Sidong sobbed at Miss Zamora's feet.

The teacher reached into her bag and pulled out another

box of Crayolas. She handed the book and the two boxes of Crayola to Sidong, then turned to smile at me.

'Don't worry. She will be fine.'

I made my way back to the Igorot group. The sky was blue overhead. Around me, faces were smiling. *Tilin*, I thought, *can those in the invisible world enjoy the world of the living?*

I felt the briefest of touches on my shoulder. 'Miss Luki.'

'Johnny!'

Though his hat visor cast a strong shadow on his face, I could see that the bruises had faded. His swollen eye was almost fully open. He smiled at me.

'*Yo quiero* . . . I just wanted to talk to you again before . . . There is something I wanted to tell you.'

He touched my shoulder again and, Mother, there was a look in his eyes that made me want to take his hand in mine, but I didn't dare. I could imagine how excited the tourists watching from behind their rope barrier would be to see a Constabulary Soldier and an Igorot woman holding hands.

Johnny took a step closer and bent his head closer to mine, keeping his voice low. 'I told you about my father and my brothers, about my town being so proud of me. I didn't tell you that my father and brothers, many in the town – they died in the war. *Están muertos. Todos muertos.*'

I felt his pain like a dagger to the heart, Mother. All this time I had thought Johnny's soul was light, unburdened by misfortunes and cares. He had been carefully keeping this secret, terrible sorrow hidden behind an amiable mask.

The band practiced some tunes and the crowds laughed, but I heard only Johnny's voice. And though I was surrounded by extraordinary sights, all I could see were his eyes, glittering with unshed tears. 'There had been a successful attack on an American garrison on our island. In response, the American commander ordered his men to kill and burn. Turn the place into a howling wilderness. Those were the words he used, Luki. *A howling wilderness.* And they did what they were told. My father had dreamed that I would lift the family up with my music. But now I had no family to lift. When Loving asked me to join the Philippine Constabulary Band, I had a crazy idea. I thought, somehow it would give me an opportunity to avenge my family. I would be inside the American system. I could strike from within. But I found myself enjoying the music, enjoying my life with the band and admiring Lieutenant Loving . . . I forgot about revenge.' His jaw hardened. '*Te digo esto,* I am telling you this because . . . I am going to do something today and when I'm done, I don't want you to think me mad. Or evil. I want you to understand why I had to do it.'

He lifted the flap of a pocket. There, solid and black, was a pistol.

I took my place with the other Igorots, dazed and apprehensive. I watched Johnny return to the bandstand, smiling and nodding at his fellow musicians. He took up a rag and studiously began to polish his trumpet.

He told me President Roosevelt always shook hands with band members before he took his seat on any stage. That was when he would get his chance.

Thinking of Johnny's father and brothers and all the people the Americans killed, their corpses slowly turning into earth in mass graves, how could I tell him no? The ancients say that when a man dies by the hand of another man, his spirit cannot enter the invisible world. It must live another lifetime trapped in a lonely, twilight existence. And only when he had finished this nothing life could he join his ancestors in the invisible world.

Johnny had suffered greatly. It was obvious to him that Roosevelt deserved this comeuppance. But did he?

And then it was too late to do anything, Mother, because the crowd began to cheer, Lieutenant Loving raised his baton and the band stood up and began to play.

The President had arrived.

We could hear him above the clamour. 'Bully!' he cried. 'Deeeeelighted!'

It was a big voice, a voice that matched the portrait that hung above our heads in American School back home: Roosevelt the hunter.

The crowd was cheering, Mother, and I realized that I was excited too, to finally meet President Roosevelt in the flesh! And then I remembered what Johnny was going to do, and I began to shake.

The band began to play. I watched Johnny blowing on his trumpet. His fingers pushed on the golden buttons, his cheeks puffing in and out. This might be his last song. What were they going to do to him after he murdered the President? Would they kill him? Or put him in an American jail? Whatever happened, his life would be over.

I felt the crowd around me tense. Bodies began to turn. I could hear someone above the music shouting: 'Make way please.' 'Mister President!' 'Mister President!'

Roosevelt was coming closer.

And then there was a shift, the huge notes subsided to a trill and each bandsman put down his instrument and lifted up another. Johnny had told me about this. How the Constabulary Band would switch from traditional band instruments to finer instruments. It was what set them apart from all the other bands at the World's Fair. Johnny's second instrument was a stringed box called a violin. I watched him tuck it under his chin and begin to draw a wooden bow across it.

The music changed, the sound soaring and sweet.

The crowd erupted into cheers.

'Bravo! Bravo!' That booming voice again. It was much closer now. Children were lifted up high and the wall of people opposite us parted. 'Make way for the President,' someone said.

I felt cold. I could not breathe.

'This way, Mister President!'

'Make way!'

'Hold on!' the President's voice boomed from somewhere nearby. 'Allow me to congratulate the band first.'

This was it.

I saw a large hand reach out over the heads of the crowd. Lieutenant Loving saluted before leaning over the balustrade and shaking Roosevelt's hand.

'*¡Señor Presidente! ¡Señor Presidente!*' The bandsmen crowded closer, their faces perspiring and excited. Johnny's face looked pale and strained amongst them.

The great hand stretched towards them, shaking each brown hand in turn. 'Deelighted!' Roosevelt thundered. 'Deelighted!'

The crowd was bouncing up and down in excitement.

It was Johnny's turn. He leaned out. One hand extended towards the President. The other was in his pocket, ready with the gun.

'Deelighted!' I heard the voice shout from below the bandstand. 'Deelighted!'

I saw a long arm reaching out. A great hand wrapped itself around Johnny's. Johnny grimaced as if he was in pain.

But there was no sharp report. No gunshot.

The President moved on.

'Deelighted! Deelighted!'

Johnny, eyes suddenly red, face gaunt, stumbled back to his seat and sat down. The other band members closed in front of him, waving and cheering.

I couldn't see Johnny any more, but I could feel his shame.

36

Surrender

I was relieved.

I had not wanted Johnny to do it.

I had not wanted the President dead.

I could hear Roosevelt exclaiming as he made his way up the stage. I could hear him, but I could not see him. He had no idea that his life had been spared.

And then the day moved on. I could not see the President, but I could just see the heads and shoulders of performers. The Visayans sang something that ended in a great shout. There was bamboo dancing, I remember white smiles, hands raised high, the sharp clacks as the dancers dipped their feet between clashing bamboo poles. I remember the Negritos lining up with their bows and shooting arrows into the sky, though I don't remember where the arrows landed. I remember the children in a row and Miss Zamora using her fan as a baton as they sang a song with the lines *O say can you see, by the dawn's early light*. I remember Truman Hunt hissing. *You'd better get things right, for Pete's sake.*

And then it was time for the Igorots. The men went up, the stage first to do their mock battle, Kinyo proudly clutching the axe that Samkad's father had given him, the one he had taunted Samkad with.

I could hear the men up on stage, grunting and shouting, and banging on their shields. The audience gasped appreciatively.

And then, suddenly, screams and shouts. Shrill voices. 'What in blazes?' I heard Truman Hunt shouting.

The crowds were in turmoil. *Assassin, assassin! He's killing the President!*

The sea of faces around me were all teeth and glaring eyes, twisted with shouting and excitement. They were excited about the possibility of death.

I couldn't believe he'd done it. *Johnny, don't throw your life away!*

But I had not heard a gunshot. There was still time. I pushed past the Visayans and then it was a short sprint to the staircase leading up to the stage. I raced up, diving under the elbows of the men crowding around the President.

'Move, girl!' Truman Hunt? What was he doing behind me? I felt his meaty hands on my back. He shoved me aside. But I kept going. On my hands and knees, I found gaps and gaps until I was in front and I could see . . .

282

Johnny wasn't there.

It was Kinyo, face down on the planks, his arms spread out like tree branches. On the floor in front of him lay the axe that he and Samkad had quarrelled over, its blade almost touching the polished boots of the man sitting in a chair. President Roosevelt. This was not an attack. It was a display of surrender.

'Well, I'll be danged!' People were not angry. They were laughing.

'Aw, leave the wild man to his worshipping! I think the President is enjoying it!'

Kinyo lifted his head slowly, his eyes darting nervously from side to side under his fringe. He was waiting to see if one of the guards would remove him. But nobody did. So he rose to his feet, holding his arms high. His lips trembled into a hesitant, nervous smile. He spotted me then, down among the trouser legs and he wavered for a moment as if he might change his mind. But turned his back on me resolutely and faced the man in the chair.

'Mister President! Sir! Here is my axe. It is yours now. I am headhunter no more . . . I am savage no more.' He was using a deeper voice than his normal speaking voice, as if he was trying to sound bigger than he was.

'Once upon a time I live in dark,' Kinyo intoned. 'But you, Mister President, you bring me here, to –' Kinyo's hands were still upraised and he stretched his fingers wide apart – 'the great America. My axe . . . it belong to you now.'

The mood changed. People were shaking each other's hands and slapping Kinyo on the back.

One of them turned to the crowds and raised a barker's horn to his lips. 'Ladies and gentlemen, one of the head-hunters has yielded his axe to President Roosevelt! He said he was living in darkness but now sees the light. He says that America has saved him and he has commended his people to the United States. God bless America!'

There was a thunder roll of clapping. Hats were flung into the air and the Constabulary Band began to play a heroic march with roaring drums and lightning crashes.

Behind me I heard someone say, 'Well done, Hunt!'

I turned in time to see Truman Hunt in mid-shake with one of the men.

'You pulled it off,' the man was saying. 'I think the President loved it.'

He was beaming, his face shiny and pink. 'Thank you.' He smirked. 'It took a lot of work to make sure the security detail knew not to grab my boy. I thought it would add a little excitement to the President's visit.'

And, Mother, I couldn't bear it. I couldn't bear that self-satisfied look on Truman Hunt's face, I couldn't bear the way the men were patting Kinyo on the back as if it was all an amusing joke, I couldn't bear that look on Kinyo's face, so eager to be praised, so keen to please. I couldn't bear the celebrations of the crowd. And I couldn't bear the loneliness of Kinyo's axe at Roosevelt's feet. *Brother, we belong to America now*, he'd said to Samkad. *You've just got to get used to it.* There was a clamouring in my head, but it wasn't the noise of the crowd.

Suddenly I was standing between Roosevelt and Kinyo. I pushed Kinyo aside and bent down and picked up his axe.

Somewhere, far away, I might have heard Truman Hunt scream my name.

'What is the meaning of this?' A booming voice. Roosevelt.

I turned to face the President of the United States. And Mother, my blood stopped its rushing, the dull roar of the crowd stilled, and everything dawdled to a strange lull, as I finally looked into the face of the man in the chair.

Here he was at last, Theodore Roosevelt, a man whose domain girdled the world.

He wasn't what I had expected, Mother. He didn't look at all like the tough young adventurer dressed in furs on Mister William's wall. This Theodore Roosevelt was not young. Sitting, he did not look tall. His body was soft. It sank into the chair, remoulding to its shape. The small round panes of glass that perched on his large nose had fogged to white. The eyes glaring at me were an intense blue, like the colour of the Chico River after a strong rain. A dark brown moustache sprouted thickly from his nostrils, drooping like the feathers of a bird soaked in the rain. There were crumbs on the moustache from something he'd eaten. His chin disappeared into his neck. Teardrops of sweat rolled down the shiny white forehead.

No, he didn't look like his picture.

He didn't look like much.

We belong to America now. It enraged me to remember Kinyo's words. It enraged me to remember Samkad, forlorn and wounded in that cage. It enraged me to think of Tilin's lonely death. And it enraged me that I had ever believed America would change my life.

I blinked. The moment resumed its momentum. My heart began pounding again. Around me, I felt thick, warm bodies closing in. 'Luki! Get away from him!' Truman Hunt's voice cut through the tumult.

I took a deep breath and pushed my face right up to Roosevelt's. His eyes widened. His body tensed and recoiled from me. But he could not get away. His glasses were cold against my face. I searched the watery blue of those eyes before I spoke, for once, the English coming swiftly to my throat.

'You cannot have this axe,' I said.

His body relaxed and he scowled, straightening his glasses. I felt hard fingers curling around my shoulders.

'You cannot have us!' I screamed.

'Get her off the stage,' Roosevelt muttered, and some-one jerked me away. I didn't take my eyes off him as rough hands dragged me away. He didn't even bother to see where they were taking me. He sighed, slumping a little in his chair. Then raised a hand to his mouth and yawned. Quickly, surreptitiously. Then he put a broad smile on his face, as he stood.

'Bully!' he cried. 'Deelighted!'

37

Time to Leave

They put me in the jail with Samkad.

I was in no mood to speak, Mother. I just sat there, staring stonily through the bamboo bars until Samkad gave up asking me what had happened. He retreated to the rear of the jail, watching me thoughtfully from behind his long fringe.

He yawned, Mother. Roosevelt had yawned. The big voice, the cries of 'Bully' and 'Delighted', they were all part of his own show. I had thought of him as a benevolent father, inviting us to come to America so that he could meet us for himself and hold us close. None of this was true, and I felt foolish to have believed it.

From inside the village we could hear the rise and fall of voices on the bullhorn. And then the band played *The Star-Spangled Banner*. The crowd sang. *The land of the free . . . and the home of the brave.* I clapped my hands over my ears, but the crowd's great voice continued to filter into my hearing.

I'd had enough, Mother, of the Igorot Village, the World's Fair, America. I wanted to go home. But did I have a home to go to?

Home is a mother and a father. Home is the familiar. Home is love.

I had no mother or father. And the familiar? It had angered the ancients that I would not be moulded into a good Bontok woman. And love? I glanced at Samkad, whom I had cowed into a corner of the jail with my belligerence. Look at what I've done, Mother! He chased after me, wanting to protect me, and what did I do? I led him into a trap – yes, Mother, that is what the World's Fair is – a trap! It turned everyone into distorted versions of themselves.

At the end of the day, after Roosevelt and the crowds were gone, Truman Hunt took the two of us into his office and began to rant. *Did I realize what a serious thing I had done? Did I realize I could have been shot by the President's guards? Oh, Kinyo was not in trouble – Kinyo would not have come to harm. He, Truman Hunt, had warned the guards about what Kinyo was going to do. There was never any danger! But you, Luki, you were not part of the plan, you arrived on the stage uninvited and you were lucky the guards were confused and didn't reach for their guns. And now look what happened!* Instead of praising Truman Hunt for Kinyo's act of submission, Roosevelt had called him to one side and told him to keep his people under control.

And that, Truman Hunt said, was why he had come to a decision.

'What happened today has made it clear to me that you two are a danger to the Igorot Village,' he said. 'You, Samkad, you could have killed your brother! And it's not the first time the two of you have fought! And you, Luki, I had high hopes for you, but now it's clear. You are just a troublemaker. There is no place for you here. We are better off without you. I have no choice but to send you back to Bontok – Sidong too, because, unfortunately, there is nobody here to look after the child.'

I did not know what to say, Mother. I did not want to stay in America, and yet, this dismissal . . . it felt like failure.

Truman Hunt smirked. 'You won't leave empty handed – your contract provides for an early exit. You will be paid your wages. And you will be safe on your journey – I'll get one of the Philippine Scouts to escort you most of the way,' he said.

'And Tilin?' I said.

He looked uncomfortable. 'Er . . . I will be speaking to the hospital and I will make arrangements for the remains to be sent back to Bontok. Er . . .'

But I had already begun to walk away.

A Philippine Scout was soon contracted to take us home. His name was Stanley and when he came to visit us, I was surprised at his youth. No bristles sprouted above his lip, his cheeks were as smooth as fresh fruit, his teeth glowed white, and his English was almost as good as Johnny's. He was very agreeable to Truman Hunt's questioning. Yes, he would look after us. Yes, he understood it was important to attract as little attention as possible. Yes, he would put his uniform away and come dressed in ordinary clothes. Yes, he was happy to do it, in fact he couldn't wait to get back to his hometown. He had packed a large suitcase full of presents from America for his family.

It didn't take long for other arrangements to be completed. Truman Hunt sourced American clothes for Samkad and Sidong to wear on the journey, and I already had the clothes Sadie had given me. I had asked Truman Hunt whether I should return them, but he just looked at me like I had lost my mind.

It gave me a pang, Mother, to realize that Sadie was in the past now. I was never going to see her again, never going to speak to her again. In the same way for Samkad, Kinyo was no longer part of his future.

On our last days in the village, there was no talk of forgiveness, and the brothers studiously avoided each other. Johnny, too, was now in the past, but not because I willed it.

I saw him several times, marching in the field with the other Constabulary men and playing in the band. I tried to catch his eye, but he turned his face away. He didn't want to see me, and even if he did, what was I going to say, Mother? Sorry you failed to kill Roosevelt?

They were all as good as dead to us, Mother.

Except, of course, the real dead liked to make their presence felt.

I found myself constantly arguing with Tilin in my head (and sometimes apparently, aloud, based on the startled looks people were giving me). *How can you expect this of me, Tilin? What do I know of the world of the dead? How would I know how to move a spirit across a continent and an ocean back to Bontok? Do you somehow climb into my pack? Do you hide yourself under my hat? And do trains and ships have special tickets for the souls of the dead?*

To which Tilin's response was always the same. An invisible whisper, deep in my head. *Don't leave me.*

Had Sadie still considered herself my friend, she would have told me my guilt was lingering in my belly like food poisoning. And she would be right – I did feel guilty.

I was tempted to tell Samkad, Mother. Samkad, who was always so obliging to the ancients, surely had picked up some wisdom about the dead. But what if he said we should not leave? What if his answer was that we would have to wait for some supernatural help that would never come? You see, Mother, I couldn't wait to leave, and I didn't want to risk jeopardizing our departure.

Sidong, still grieving for Tilin, seemed unsurprised by the news that we were leaving. The only thing that seemed urgent to her was to ask Miss Zamora for more boxes of those coloured crayons. When Miss Zamora found out about our imminent departure, she brought not only Crayola, but a large drawing book. 'I was going to give this to you at the end of the fair,' she told Sidong. 'You are a most talented young artist. God bless.' And, Mother, the look on Sidong's face, the way she held the book against her thin little chest, I was so grateful I was tempted to throw my arms around Miss Zamora, despite all her scratchy clothing.

And some time after that, Mother, the ghostly whispering in my head stopped. It worried me. I tried to summon her in my mind. *Tilin? Tilin? Where are you?* But all my entreaties were greeted with silence. Had she given up on me? Had she changed her mind?

38

The Way Back

We left quietly, before anybody was awake. We were ready, all dressed up in our American clothes when Stanley arrived, crisply clad in a striped suit, his hat slightly askew on his head. Truman Hunt appeared, rumpled and red-nosed and smelling of liquor, to bid us a terse goodbye and check that Stanley had all our tickets.

I glanced back as Stanley led us through the deserted Reservation. Truman Hunt was standing by the open Igorot Village gate, his face a pale smear in the darkness.

Our train didn't take us to Tacoma. It took us to a different shore, San Francisco. This way back, we saw none of the mountains and ravines that had rolled past our windows on our way to the fair. Instead, we saw dust and scrub and great brown fields under a great blue bowl of sky.

We arrived in San Francisco where we boarded a waiting

steamship. I was amazed at how swiftly life on board became humdrum, as if we had always lived in its floating world.

As before, Sidong and I retired to the women's room in steerage, and Samkad and Stanley slept in the men's steerage. Stanley immediately fell in with a group of Filipinos and they spent the month at sea playing cards in the men's quarters, while Sidong, Samkad and I spent the days walking on the deck and staring out at the endless horizon. This journey was warmer than our earlier crossing, the ocean mostly calm. And the temptation was great to shed our uncomfortable American costumes and put on the clothes we had brought from Bontok. But we knew better.

In fact, Mother, I couldn't help thinking about how much more I knew now than when we were making our way over. It was like I'd developed magical new senses. Once in a while, when passengers came down from the cabins reserved for white people, I knew to keep my distance. I understood now that it was not curiosity that made them look at us the way they did, but fear. I knew to wait for the other women in steerage to finish with the toilets before Sidong and I took our turn, in case we did something quite acceptable in Bontok, but disgusting for someone from elsewhere. I knew to ask Samkad not to take his gangsa out, not to follow the usual rituals of leaving and journeying. He did not ask me why. He knew too.

At night, I waited for Tilin to creep around my dreams and freshen all my regrets. But, Mother, no such thing happened.

I slept deeply and woke up restored, with no memory of anything untoward. Perhaps it was all part of the numbness that had settled on me over the journey. I felt no excitement about our imminent return to Bontok. I wasn't even anxious about what the ancients might say, how they might interpret our early return. Sometimes I tried to picture Bontok in my mind, to remind myself of the place I was returning to. But, Mother, I could only summon a green flicker, so tenuous I couldn't make out if I was picturing the side of a mountain or the canopy of a mossy forest.

Stanley had been efficient on the train journey, knowing which platform to wait on, who to hand our tickets to, which seats to take. Once in a while he would join us on deck, pressing us with questions about the fair. Had we seen the tiny babies born too soon, kept alive in glass boxes? Had we seen the wild animal display? What about the cascades all lit up every night? Had we spoken to the Indian chief Geronimo, who signed your hat if you paid him a few coins?

Samkad and I replied in monosyllables, but Stanley didn't seem to care. Sometimes he brought out a newspaper to show us. He had spent his months at the fair collecting newspapers to take back as souvenirs. Once, he read aloud from one. 'The appearance of the Igorots at a theatre last Sunday night was offensive to a lot of the women folk in the audience. There is a difference between seeing these little dark men on their own "diggings" at the World's Fair grounds in open air, but then to behold them seated in an enclosed box in a theatre in a costume that, according to no form or fashion, can be considered even fairly proper.'

Stanley laughed merrily. 'If only those Igorots were dressed up like you are now, there wouldn't have been a problem!'

I glanced at Samkad over Sidong's head. His jaw was tight. 'Maybe you do not understand the English. You understand, yes?' Stanley asked, perplexed at our lack of response.

I nodded. I understood everything now. Especially when words were being spoken at our expense.

'Stanley,' I said. 'What is your Filipino name?'

He looked surprised. 'Estanislao. How did you know I changed it?'

I just knew.

It was a relief, Mother, that Sidong was so completely entranced by her drawing things. On deck, she would often settle down in some sheltered spot to draw.

Which left me with Samkad.

At the beginning of this long journey back, Mother, there were only silences between Samkad and me. Neither of us wanted to speak, really. There was so much bitterness and grief in our throats, there was no point allowing any words to escape.

But as we walked the ship's deck together, our heads touched, bending over one of Sidong's latest masterpieces. Something between us was changing. When we heard snatches of music from the upper decks, I knew Samkad was remembering the sweet strains of guitar and violin that drifted from the Visayan village, night and day; or maybe the thump and glory of the Constabulary Band. And one day, when I was staring at the waves galloping high, I realized he was watching me. He knew I was thinking about the Wild West Show, the cowboys fighting pretend battles with the Indians and how Sadie was a better rider than any man there, even if she had to ride side-saddle.

And then he asked me, 'Do you remember?'

'Remember what?'

He sighed. 'Do you remember what Bontok was like? I've been trying to, but . . .' He shook his head. 'It's hard, it's as if the World's Fair was so loud and flashy it's made me forget.'

I stared at him. This was exactly how I felt. But not wanting to admit it, I said, 'Sure you remember. The smell of wood fires, every morning.' And to my surprise, I could smell it, Mother, the fragrance of pine burning.

'And the forest, Samkad, can you remember the scent of the trees after a rain.' I closed my eyes and there were the trees leaning into each other, vines tangling everywhere, beards of dripping moss and the rich, dark smell of earth, the sudden barks of monkeys in the tree canopy and the surprise of sunlight spearing through the green wilderness.

I opened my eyes. Samkad was gazing out at the ocean. 'And the rice terraces,' he said in a soft voice. 'The mountains.'

I followed Samkad's gaze and there, in the gently undulating water, I saw the rise and fall of mountains carved into great, green paddies, the splash of the waves became the laughter of women planting rice, and the thudding of the sea against the boat turned into the beat of the gangsas, celebrating the abundance of life.

Samkad and I looked at each other.

'Luki.' His voice was low. 'I thought following you was the right thing to do – the *honourable* thing. If I truly believed that we should be together, I told myself, I should be a man: fight for you, win you back. But instead . . .'

His mouth worked to find the words. 'What a fool I was. Always so sure I knew who I was, and who I was going to become. And now?' He shrugged.

Samkad was clutching the ship's rail so tightly, his knuckles were white. I smoothed my hands over his, peeled them away from the rail. He watched hopelessly as I rubbed his hands between mine.

'I have not been blind to your yearning for a different life, Luki,' he said. 'I knew that you needed more – that you *deserved* more. You say I was not wrong to follow you, but neither were you wrong to leave. You had to.'

'You were not wrong to want a life for us together, Samkad,' I whispered.

'If we were in Bontok,' he said, 'we would be asking the spirits of our ancestors for guidance.'

'Can we do that now?' I asked.

He looked at me, confused. 'But we are in the middle of an ocean. We have no ancestors here.'

'How do we know that?'

Samkad seemed confused. 'But what about . . .' He looked around us, at the sailors lounging in the sun, the Americans leaning over their balcony, the other passengers strolling on the deck.

I smiled at him.

So the two of us returned to our respective quarters. I took off Sadie's blouse and skirt and stockings and shoes and put on my Bontok skirt and top. And Samkad shed his American clothes and put his breechcloth on.

We returned to the deck with Samkad's gangsa and together, we beseeched the spirits of the ocean to help us find our way back to Bontok.

39

Home

Mother, we could feel the ocean's song trilling in our bones long after we stepped off our steamer's tilting deck onto Manila's solid ground. But we made ourselves put one foot in front of the other, lurching ungracefully like toddlers until the ocean ceased its singing, the rollicking of the waves ebbed from our limbs and we could walk steadily again.

One foot in front of the other.

Many months ago, our contingent of two hundred had walked the distance from the highlands to Manila – there were too many of us for Truman Hunt to put us on boat or train. But now, with just the three of us in tow, Stanley led us onto a train that took us swiftly to a small port town where we boarded a tiny steamer that took us along the coast to the foothills. What had taken us a week to cover on foot only took two days by train and boat. But I couldn't help feeling nostalgic about those nights walking by the light of the moon, surrounded by endless rice paddies or weaving between slender trunks of coconut trees made of shadows.

Stanley bid us goodbye at the port town. A smart salute and he was gone, taking the little steamboat back to Manila with his suitcase full of newspapers and memories of the fair.

The up and down trek to our valley was tougher than I remembered; our penned-in existence in the Igorot Village had weakened my muscles and I was surprised to find myself easily out of breath. But it was a comfort at night, when we rolled out our blankets, to fall asleep to the familiar chirrup of the crickets. Soon enough, we found ourselves striding along the banks of the Chico River. After America, everything seemed strange and familiar at the same time – the river water burbling contentedly below us, the colossal boulders on the banks, the extravagance of flowers everywhere, and, of course, the sweet green rice terraces climbing the mountainside.

One foot in front of the other.

Sidong was enthralled. It was as if she had forgotten that all this had been so ordinary to her before. 'Has that always been there?' 'What is this flower called?' 'That boulder! It has a face!' 'How green is the rice!' It struck me that all the wonders of the World's Fair had not excited her to chatter this way.

Whenever we stopped to rest, to eat, to get away from the sun, out came her book and pencil. She would sit, sketching furiously, her face intent, as if she was afraid everything

301

around us would evaporate into nothing if she did not fix them onto paper.

One foot in front of the other.

Once, we saw a wild dog watching us from a tangle of bushes. I thought about Kinyo and the others butchering American dogs for Truman Hunt's dog feasts. The ancients need never know, Kinyo had said, as if the only problem was the disapproval of the ancients.

The dog darted from the bushes and disappeared behind a stand of bamboo. There was a rustling and then a great lizard raised its head exactly where the dog had been. It was as if the dog had transformed itself into a lizard! After that, Samkad could not stop smiling. Perhaps the dog had reminded him of his own dog, Chuka. A long time ago, Chuka was a wild dog with no name. But she had chosen Samkad, followed him home into his sleeping room, and lay down by his side. Once he had named her, they became inseparable. It was a testament to his feelings that Samkad had left Chuka behind to win me back.

One foot in front of the other.

In the months that we had been gone, a new road had been scraped through the jungle. It took us one day to scale what had taken us three days to walk down. Gazing at the valleys ranging below us, we saw that several more roads had been carved into the side of the mountain. Great chunks of the jungle had been felled. And the clusters of villages we passed now bristled with the spires of new wooden chapels.

So much change! But I should not be surprised, should I, Mother? *We* had changed too. None of us were ever going to be the same again. I looked across at Samkad. He was walking hand in hand with Sidong. They were laughing about something.

I had left the village because I did not want to become a wife, and now I was returning with a daughter. I breathed deeply, filling my lungs with the sweet mountain air.

One foot in front of the other.

We were in the mossy forest now. Then there would just be the long green slope up to the village, the banana grove that sprouted up out of nowhere, and the path made of small boulders that lifted us up to the sun.

And then we would be home.

I felt it then, Mother, as we began to leave the forest. My invisible wound revealed itself. I had managed to keep it hidden until now, but the sight of those thatched rooftops at the top of the mountain stripped away all my defences. The pain was so sudden and so intense that I sank to my haunches.

'Luki!' Samkad let go of Sidong's hand and ran back to me. 'What is wrong?'

'I'm all right,' I said. But strange croaking noises came out of my throat. My chest was tight, I could not breathe. My sight dimmed.

Samkad knelt and put his arms around me. Sidong, not knowing what else to do, threw her arms around us.

Slowly I managed to fashion words from the rough noises in my throat. 'Tilin. I shouldn't have left her behind.'

I felt Samkad's arms tighten. But there were no words he could say that would comfort me. So he said nothing.

I felt a soft hand in my hair. 'Don't cry, Luki,' Sidong whispered. 'We didn't leave Tilin behind.'

I just looked at her. Her optimistic delusion both cheered and saddened me. I remember what I was like when you died, Mother. Death is a busy time and there was ritual and song and this and that and so many people wanting to talk to me. And then suddenly it was over and I was alone. And, oh Mother, how many times did I wish your spirit would come back and take me with you into the invisible world? It was a desperate, desperate time.

Sidong stroked my hair. There was so much love in the touch of those slender fingers, that even more tears came to my eyes. I straightened up, pushed Samkad away and rubbed my eyes with the back of my hand. 'I'm not crying!' I declared. But Sidong could see the fresh tears streaming down my cheek.

'We didn't leave Tilin behind,' she said again.

Samkad and I exchanged glances. Throughout the journey, Sidong had been so peaceful, I had attributed it to the new drawing book and crayons. But now, I realized there was something more to it. I swore to myself. What kind of mother was I going to be to Sidong if I could miss something like this? I opened my mouth but it was as if my throat had filled with sand.

'What do you mean, Sidong?' Samkad said, his voice light.

Sidong clapped her hands. 'Come!' she said. 'Come and see!'

She hurried to the flat stone where she'd set down her pack and her drawing book. 'See, see!' She opened the book.

Samkad helped me to my feet and we sat on our heels on either side of Sidong as she began to turn the pages.

I recognized many of the drawings. The early ones were heavily smudged, created with sticks of charcoal from the fire. Sidong had recorded our journey obsessively. But I recognized the mountains, the long stalks of coconut trees lining the road, the shabby huts and endless flatlands. There was one of Truman Hunt on his horse and the column of tired people following behind. Tilin sleeping under a tree. Then came Manila, the wide open windows with shutters glazed with seashells, the women squatting by their baskets, the carabaos blocking the road. Me, looking grumpy, sitting on the river bank. And Tilin pointing at a raft made of coconuts as our launch took us to the ship. The drawings on the ship were finer, Sidong had drawn mainly with pencils. There we were sitting on our heels watching the sea, Tilin fast asleep a ray of sunlight on her face, the steerage bunkbeds making untidy shadows around her. And then there was Tilin and me sitting with our heads close together. We looked like we were sharing a secret. Soon the drawings were of the train, the bright rectangles of light shining on rows of sleeping heads. Tilin and me having some sort of argument. Samkad, playing his gangsa after the two men died. And then there was Saint

Louis, and now the drawings had touches of waxy colour from the crayons Sidong was given at the Model School. Sidong overlayed red and yellow in an attempt to capture the colour of Tilin's complexion. My heart caught in my throat to see Tilin, smiling, lying sick in bed. And, Mother, Sidong had also drawn Sadie Locket, waving her white hat, her golden wig streaming behind her in crayon yellow. More studies of Tilin, as Sidong sat at her bedside. Smiling, sleeping, pensive.

Sidong turned to us. 'See?'

I was confused, Mother. What was she trying to show me?

'We did not leave her behind,' Sidong said firmly. She turned the pages and I realized that Sidong had not stopped drawing Tilin after her death. There we were, the three of us dressed in American clothes. And there was a smiling Tilin. There was Stanley, his hat pulled over one eye. And there was Tilin. There was Manila, as seen from the ship, lying low in the ocean. And there was Tilin.

Sidong had not left her sister behind.

Samkad grinned at me over Sidong's head, and I felt laughter bubbling up my throat. Tilin's spirit resided in the strokes of Sidong's pencil. The child had transported her sister home through the fierceness of her remembering.

At that moment a small black dog exploded out of nowhere, hurtling directly into Samkad's arms. 'Chuka!' Samkad cried. 'Chuka!'

And there above us, we heard screams of excitement. 'They've returned! They've returned!'

Tiny figures began to stream down the green mountain. The three of us turned and opened our arms like sunflowers worshipping the sun. Bodies pelted down towards us, the setting sun at their backs. They looked like they were on fire. 'Samkad!' 'Little Luki!' 'Sidong!' The mountains tossed their shouts back and forth as if they were playing an American ball game.

Samkad and Sidong ran up the mountain to meet them. But I hesitated, Mother, remembering how I had left the village filled with resentment. I was sorry and I was guilty and I was happy and I was sad and I was ashamed.

But Sidong suddenly stopped and turned.

For a moment, standing like that, with the sun in her hair, her back straight, one hand raised, I was reminded of Lieutenant Loving signalling his band. He only had to lower that hand for his men to explode into music.

And then I heard it. The deep humming of a thousand voices. A song unlike anything we had heard at the World's Fair. It was tree and earth and mountain. It was neighbour and elder and friend. It was unruly and ferocious and it was calm and loving. It was calling to me. It was home.

Later, the entire village milled around the Council House fire. We had danced to the beat of gangsas alerting our ancestors that there was a returning to celebrate. The ancients had ordered everyone to leave their paddies and join the celebration. We had feasted on boar and chicken, rice, vegetables and sweet potato. We had all sipped from the jar of ceremonial rice wine, sticky and thick and delicious. And now we sat, talking and remembering.

Sidong moved closer to the fire, her drawing things under one arm. She opened her book.

We watched as she began to draw. Suddenly the fire blazed higher and for an instant, she turned to gold. It looked as if all the light was coming from inside her. We all leaned closer to feel her warmth.

A Naming of Names

Antonio S. Buangan, who made it his quest to seek out the names of the Igorots who participated in the 1904 World's Fair, wrote: 'The naming of names [as well as their avoidance] . . . is deeply embedded in everyday and ritual life and they ultimately relate to what defines a community.'

And so here, dear reader, is my own naming of names. This is the community that kept me going on the long journey to writing this book and to whom I owe a deep debt.

Patricia Afable, Antonio Buangan, and Mary Talusan, whose heartfelt research I turned to again and again.

Joe Friedman, Cliff McNish, Helen Peters and Cristina Vinall, who were there at the beginning.

Marie Basting, Rosie Best, Peter Bunzl, Gail Doggett, Sara Grant, Tracey Mathias, Lou Minns and Kimberley Pauley, with whom I plant forests every day.

Cristina Juan, Jovi Juan, Carla Montemayor and Joy Watford, who share my fascination with Philippine colonial history.

My steadfast agents, Hilary Delamere and Jessica Hare.

My editor, Anthony Hinton, for somehow always finding the right thing to say and guiding me through a pandemic of doubt.

Linda Sargent, who mentored me to The End, day by day, word by word. So much love.

The team at DFB, who know how to give a book a good start.

And Richard for being my number one fan even when it was hard to see the light at the end of the tunnel.

Thank you too to: John Blanco, Julia Bruce, Myra Colis, Rochita Loenen-Cruz, Edwin Lozada, Averil Pooten, Mark Watan, the Filipino American National History Society (Oregon Chapter), Mio Debnam, Carolyn McGlone, Paula Zamorano Osorio, and Michael J. Truax.

What Happened Next

Dear Reader,

Wild Song may be fiction, but there really was a World's Fair in Saint Louis in 1904, officially known as the Louisiana Purchase Exposition, that showed off many technological wonders – the first X-ray machine, the first incubator, the first electric socket, and many more.

My story focuses on the Igorot experience, but there was a lot going on at the Fair. Every single one of the hundreds of Indian Nations who performed, sold goods, or were put on display, would have had a story to tell. So would the so-called 'Pygmies'; recruited from different African countries and unable to speak each other's languages, they created their own way of communicating with each other. And what about the trick-riding, steer-lassoing, target-shooting women who appeared in the Wild West Show – who outperformed the cowboys, despite having to wear corsets and ride side-saddle!

Many parts of my story were true – yes, Truman Hunt and Lieutenant Walter Loving were real people; yes, there were ugly brawls between Jefferson Guards and Filipino troops, and yes, shockingly, Igorot brains were 'harvested' at the World's Fair.

It's a fascinating story, but it's also tough history, not easy for anyone to hear, whether you relate to the indigenous people who endured the cruelties and prejudices of the time, or whether, for whatever reason, you feel somehow culpable for its historic wrongs.

Most of the accounts of the Igorot experience at the 1904 World's Fair portray them as dupes, victims, simple people who had been tricked into participating in a human zoo. In newspaper accounts of the time, they are represented as brutal, simple-minded, and clownish. Writing *Wild Song*, I wanted to explore the World's Fair through their own prisms – of belief, of relationships, of culture. And I wanted to show that they had agency. That every choice they made had a logic of its own.

The end of the World's Fair was not the end of the story. I thought you might be interested in what happened next.

The Igorots

Entrepreneurs – including Truman Hunt – began to recruit the Igorots to join travelling shows. The would-be impresarios plotted to sue the US Government with a court action that might have kept the Igorots in Saint Louis after the end of the Fair, so that they could exploit them.[1] To avoid this, Fair officials surreptitiously moved the Igorots out before the Fair closed and shipped them home to the Philippines.

But the impresarios were undeterred. Up to a decade later, the 1904 World's Fair in St Louis Igorots continued to be exhibited in fairs and sideshows across America and Europe. Village elders (who I refer to as 'ancients'), objected energetically to the travelling shows, but the US Government granted them permission. Other Igorots saw their travelling kin as lucky adventurers. They came to be known as *Nikimalika* – from '*niki*', meaning 'participated in' and '*Malika*', meaning America.[2] There were many Nikimalika who came to grief, however, such as Truman Hunt's troop (see below) and a group found starving and desperate in Ghent, Belgium in 1913, who only made it home after the US Government's intervention.[3]

The exhibitions worsened already discriminatory lowland attitudes towards Igorots. In 1943, eminent Filipino statesman Carlos P. Romulo declared: 'The fact remains that the Igorot is not Filipino and we are not related, and it hurts our

---

[1] Fermin, Jose D., *1904 World's Fair: The Filipino Experience* (Philadelphia: Infinity Publishing, 2004), 196.

[2] Afable, Patricia O., Journeys from Bontoc to the Western Fairs, 1904–1915: The "Nikimalika" and their Interpreters, *Philippine Studies*, Vol 52 No 4 (2004), 445–473.

[3] Prentice, Claire, *The Lost Tribe of Coney Island – Headhunters, Luna Park, and the Man Who Pulled Off the Spectacle of the Century* (Boston: New Harvest Houghton Mifflin Harcourt, 2014), 319–320.

feelings to see him pictured in American newspapers under such captions as "Typical Filipino Tribesman."' In 1958, an Igorot politician proposed that the word 'Igorot' be expunged and substituted with 'highlander', but his bill was defeated.[4]

Today, attitudes have changed, though one still hears many tales of low-grade acts of prejudice against highlanders. Many highlanders have embraced the identity, and a vast diaspora across the globe now defiantly call themselves Igorot, performing the dances and songs of their ancestors with pride.

Truman Hunt

Truman Hunt succeeded in recruiting fifty Igorots from Bontoc, and by 1905, he had set up an Igorot 'village' in Coney Island, while he took another group on tour of the sideshows of small-town carnivals and fairs. Despite intense competition from other showmen also exploiting Igorots, Hunt made a fortune.

In 1906, the Igorots took Truman Hunt to court for stealing thousands of dollars from them in wages. He had also seized money they had earned from selling handmade souvenirs, sometimes by force. Truman Hunt was only arraigned after a cat-and-mouse chase across several state lines. A sensational trial ensued, with his Igorot accusers appearing as witnesses. Hunt was found guilty and jailed. However, court shenanigans and a sympathetic judge soon overturned the decision and

[4] Scott, William Henry, *Of Igorots and Independence* (Baguio City: A-Seven Publishing, 1993), 41–70.

Hunt was freed. Hunt continued to dream of quick riches, investing in oil and peddling miracle cures, until he died in 1916, at the age of forty-nine.[5]

The Philippine Constabulary Band

The Philippine Constabulary Band, and its African American conductor Lieutenant Walter Loving, surprised audiences by their virtuosity and won two prestigious awards at the Fair. Their performances of classical composers such as Verdi, Tchaikowsky, Bizet and Wagner were so in demand, they were given special permission to perform in other American cities during the World's Fair. Five years later, they led the parade at the inauguration of President William Howard Taft and performed at the White House.[6]

Lieutenant Walter Loving

In 1904, the United States was a segregated society, and drinking fountains and toilets at the World's Fair were reserved for white people. Black people could not be served at any of the food establishments. To have a black man such as Loving, the son of formerly enslaved parents, conducting one of the Fair's most prestigious bands clashed with the racial narrative of the

[5] Prentice, Claire, *The Lost Tribe of Coney Island – Headhunters, Luna Park, and the Man Who Pulled Off the Spectacle of the Century* (Boston: New Harvest Houghton Mifflin Harcourt, 2014), 330–332.

[6] Talusan, Mary, *Instruments of Empire – Filipino Musicians, Black Soldiers, and Military Band Music during US Colonization of the Philippines* (Mississippi: The University Press of Mississippi, 2021).

era. It is striking how the many newspaper articles about the Philippine Constabulary chose to ignore or downplay the race of its conductor.[7]

Loving left the band in 1915 because of illness, but returned to Manila to resume its leadership from 1937 until his retirement in 1940, when he and his wife decided to remain in the Philippines. He was killed by Japanese soldiers while interned with other Americans in 1945.

The Dead

The 1904 World's Fair happened years before many breakthroughs in modern medicine, and authorities were prepared for inevitable death and disease in the large population of people on display.

One anthropologist, Aleš Hrdlička, felt this was an opportunity to increase the anatomy collections of the Smithsonian, now the largest museum, education and research complex in the world. Hrdlička was allowed to examine the bodies of native and foreign peoples who passed away in the course of the Fair. By July, 1904, he is reported to have collected over two hundred 'specimens'. We know from his letters that he kept the brains of at least two Igorots.[8]

---

[7] Talusan, Mary, *Instruments of Empire – Filipino Musicians, Black Soldiers, and Military Band Music during US Colonization of the Philippines* (Mississippi: The University Press of Mississippi, 2021), 84–85.

[8] Parezo, Nancy J and Fowler, Don D., Hrdliča: Collecting Skulls, Brains and Cadavers, *The 1904 Louisiana Purchase Exposition – Anthropology Goes to the Fair* (Nebraska: University of Nebraska Press, 2007), electronic edition.

Newspaper reports and records are inconsistent on the subject of deaths at the Philippine Reservation. There were reports of two Igorots freezing to death on the unheated train to Saint Louis, as well as the death of a teacher before the Model School opened, leaving Miss Zamora on her own. Another newspaper described the death of a Suyoc woman named Maura, of pneumonia, and how the Suyoc mourned her at the undertakers, Cullen and Kelly, though it did not say if her remains were returned to the Philippines.[9] There were other people at the Philippine Reservation who died – from beriberi, smallpox, pneumonia, suicide, a gunshot wound – but they are only mentioned in scattered reports and we don't know many of the individuals' names, who they left behind, and what became of their remains.[10]

The United States and the Philippines

The United States appropriated the Philippine Islands as part of a settlement with Spain after winning the Spanish–American War of 1898. From 1899 to 1902 Filipinos battled with American invaders in a war that Filipinos call the Philippine–American War, and that Americans call the Philippine Insurgency. The United States declared victory in 1902, even though major skirmishes continued for years.

---

[9] Buangan, Antonio S., The Suyoc People Who Went to St. Louis 100 Years Ago: The Search for My Ancestors, *Philippine Studies*, Vol 52 No 4 (2004), 474–498.

[10] Fermin, Jose D., *1904 World's Fair: The Filipino Experience* (Philadelphia: Infinity Publishing, 2004), 175–178.

When I first heard about the World's Fair, happening so soon after a terrible war, I wondered how Filipinos could agree to be exhibited like war trophies. Surely the war was still fresh in the minds of the more than twelve hundred Filipinos who went to America? Surely many of them had lost family and friends to the war? Would there not have been some acts of resistance or even vengeance? Indeed, I read that Filipino musicians managed to perform *Lupang Hinirang*,[11] now the Philippine national anthem, but at the time, associated with the Filipino resistance and banned by the US government. But if there were any other acts of resistance, they went unreported.

The Philippine Islands, along with Guam and Puerto Rico, became what the United States called 'unincorporated territories'– colonies by any other name. The Philippine Islands came to be known as 'the Philippines' under US rule, and later became the Republic of the Philippines when the US granted independence on 4 July 1946.

Candy Gourlay
London, 2022

---

[11] Talusan, Mary, *Instruments of Empire – Filipino Musicians, Black Soldiers, and Military Band Music during US Colonization of the Philippines* (Mississippi: The University Press of Mississippi, 2021), 197.

A Bibliography

Afable, Patricia O., Journeys from Bontoc to the Western Fairs, 1904–1915: The "Nikimalika" and their Interpreters, *Philippine Studies*, Vol 52 No 4 (2004), pp 445–473

Afable, Patricia O., The Exhibition of Cordillerans in the United States During the Early 1900s, *The Igorot Quarterly*, April to June ed. (1997)

Buangan, Antonio S., The Suyoc People Who Went to St. Louis 100 Years Ago: The Search for My Ancestors, *Philippine Studies*, Vol 52 No 4 (2004), pp 474–498

Clevenger, Martha R., ed., *"Indescribably Grand" Diaries and Letters from the 1904 World's Fair* (Saint Louis: Missouri Historical Society Press, 1996)

Fermin, Jose D., *1904 World's Fair: The Filipino Experience* (Philadelphia: Infinity Publishing, 2004)

Gilbert, James, *Whose Fair? Experience, Memory and the History of the Great St. Louis Exposition* (Chicago: The University of Chicago Press, 2009)

Fernandez, R. J., ed., *Tommy Halfalla – Ili* (London: Mapa Books, 2016)

Jackson, Robert, *Meet Me in St. Louis: The 1904 St. Louis World's Fair* (New York: HarperCollins, 2004)

Jenks, Albert Ernest, *The Bontoc Igorot* (Manila: Department of the Interior, The Ethnological Survey, 1905)

Jenks, Maude Huntley, *Death Stalks the Philippine Wilds: Letters of Maud Huntley Jenks*, ed. Carmen Nelson Richards (Minneapolis: The Lund Press, 1951)

Parezo, Nancy J. and Fowler, Don D., *The 1904 Louisiana Purchase Exposition – Anthropology Goes to the Fair* (Nebraska: University of Nebraska Press, 2007)

Quizon, Cherubim A. and Afable, Patricia O., Rethinking Displays of Filipinos at St Louis: Embracing Heartbreak and Irony, *Philippine Studies*, Vol 54 No 4 (2004), pp 439–444

Rice, Mark, *Dean Worcester's Fantasy Islands – Photography, Film, and the Colonial Philippines* (Ann Arbor: The University of Michigan Press, 2014)

Rydell, Robert W., *All the World's a Fair – Visions of Empire at American International Expositions, 1876–1916* (Chicago: The University of Chicago Press, 1984)

Scott, William Henry, The Apo-Diyos Concept in Northern Luzon, *Philippine Studies*, Vol 8 No 4 (1960), pp 772–788

Talusan, Mary, *Instruments of Empire – Filipino Musicians, Black Soldiers, and Military Band Music during US Colonization of the*

Philippines (Mississippi: The University Press of Mississippi, 2021)

Talusan, Mary, Music, Race, and Imperialism: The Philippine Constabulary Band at the 1904 St. Louis World's Fair, *Philippine Studies*, Vol 52, No 4 (2004), pp 499–526

Zimmerman, Jonathan, *Innocents Abroad – American Teachers in the American Century* (Massachusetts: Harvard University Press, 2006)

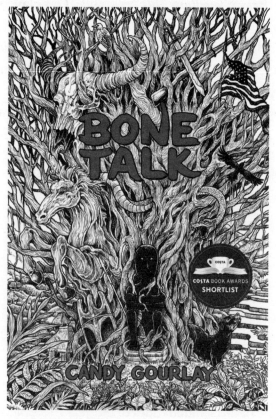

Praise for *Bone Talk* by Candy Gourlay

Shortlisted for the Costa Children's Book Award

Shortlisted for the Carnegie Medal

A United States Board on Books for Young People
Outstanding International Book

A *Washington Post* Best Children's Book

An *NBC News* Best Asian American
Children's/Young Adult Book

Endorsed by Amnesty International

'Shows us a moment of change, as two worlds meet,
and that it takes more than a ceremony to make a
man' *Sunday Times* Children's Book of the Week

'Very special' *The Times* Books of the Year

'One of the standout titles of the year' *Independent*

'Gourlay's evocative writing grips from the
outset' *Guardian* Books of the Month

'A master storyteller' *Scotsman*

'A mesmerising world of soulful ritual
and community' *Observer*